EELGRASS

"Times certainly don't die, they transform themselves like Chinese whispers."

JOE ASHBY PORTER

EELGRASS

A New Directions Book

Manufactured in the United States of America
First published as New Directions Paperbook 438 in 1977
Published simultaneously in Canada by McClelland & Stewart, Ltd.

Library of Congress Cataloging in Publication Data

Porter, Joe Ashby, 1942–
Eelgrass.
(A New Directions Book)
I. Title.
PZ4.P8462Ee3 [PS3566.0648] 813'.5'4 77–4996
ISBN 0–8112–0655–6 pbk.

New Directions Books are published for James Laughlin
by New Directions Publishing Corporation,
333 Sixth Avenue, New York 10014

CHAPTER ONE

This is the bottom of the island, this little point of tidal marsh. In mid-June the water is still chilly for swimming but you can stand in it and let the waves wash around your legs. Look down at the lazy eelgrass, how it catches bubbles, how they sparkle in the morning sunshine. Schools of small fish will come to the edge of the water and then veer away. On the bottom are starfish, sand crabs, and domed horseshoe crabs with tails like knitting needles you can lift them by. The rest of the island shoreline is more rugged and abrupt, but here the ground makes its way up from under the water very easily.

Across the choppy sunny waves out on the horizon the mainland lies like a mist. The water looks gray, it looks green and black and white. The air is fresh as can be.

The sand beach slopes up a short distance and then just beyond where grass and wild roses mark the beginning of the soil the farmhouse stands up three stories tall, the color of driftwood. Its many windows gleam. Wooden back steps lead up from the beach.

The farmhouse belongs to Daisy. She and four other young people are spending the summer here. Daisy is in the kitchen now cooking and preparing lunch for the others. She tastes the *pot-au-feu,* she stirs handfuls of marijuana into the rich dark batter for brownies. Daisy is plump and white like a dumpling, her dark hair is wound in a straggly bun, she sings to herself as she works in the quiet.

The large kitchen is Daisy's favorite room. It has a fireplace with a beanpot and a round table at which the young people usually eat. There are ferns in some of the windows. The cupboards are filled with pots and pans and dishes, china and earthenware, plates and bowls and cups, some chipped, some old and valuable, some made by Daisy herself, and provisions—canned soups and stews, nuts and grains, flours, herbs and spices in jars and tied in bunches—and two whole shelves of cookbooks that collect dust because Daisy seldom needs to use them. One of the cats is asleep in the rocking chair.

Daisy puts her brownies in the oven, moves the cat, and settles down in the rocking chair. She is placid but something disturbs her and she doesn't know what it is. Instinctively she reaches for her journal and opens it. Before she can look at it her attention is caught by the slow creaking of oars and she looks out the window to see old Jane, who is the oldest person on the island and who lived as a child here in the farmhouse, rowing her dory along the shore to gather driftwood to burn in her stove. Daisy watches absent-mindedly until Jane is out of sight and then looks down at the latest entry in her journal: "Annabel's cousin Jimbo arrived today. He says he's been traveling for a long time." Daisy looks at this entry for a while and then she writes, "We all seem to like him." She begins to sing again in her clear soprano,

> I'm a young spendthrift
> Would be an old miser
> If I could remember
> One day to the next.

Beyond the kitchen is the dining room where a guitar lies beside a cut-glass bowl of fruit on a gate-leg table. Beyond is the spacious living room at the front of the house. There are more cats here, dozing in window seats and on the brick hearth before the embers of last night's fire. A large red dog, Rufus, sprawls on the ragged sofa. Board games, books, and magazines are piled on low tables. There are ferns and petunias. Daisy's loom stands in a corner. On one wall is a poster showing twelve positions for sexual intercourse according to astrological sign. Prints of the Bronzino portraits of the Medici children hang above the sofa. There are braided rugs. More than one generation has come to terms with itself conversing and reading here.

Out on the wide front porch are chairs and a hanging swing where you can sit and look at the barn, the fenced pastures, and beyond them the woods.

CHAPTER TWO

The other young people were in the barn—Annabel and Thuggy perched on a low wall, Carter with his beautiful gold hair, beautiful face, beautiful body sitting on the steps that lead to the hayloft, Jimbo looking into one of the stalls at Big Boy the bull. Big Boy is coal black. He has a brass ring in his nose, his eyes are bloodshot, his neck and shoulders huge. He has short wicked horns. When he sees Jimbo looking at him he snorts and hooks his head this way and that.

"Mean-looking son of a bitch," says Thuggy. "And mean as he looks, at least." Short thickset Thuggy himself might look threatening without his ready smile.

"He stays locked up here all the time?" Jimbo wants to know.

"Not all but most," says Annabel. Her face is distinguished and not pretty. She wears a fringed suede skirt and a Levi jacket with the sleeves rolled to her elbows. Her earrings are gold hoops. She hasn't met her couisn Jimbo before this summer. Annabel more than the others seems at home in the barn. She offers Thuggy a stick of chewing gum.

Thuggy wears tennis shoes, baggy olive-colored Bermuda shorts, a purple silk undershirt, and a leather motorcyclist's jacket. He has an aluminum necklace of tabbed rings from snap-top beer cans. Jimbo today is wearing a blue work shirt, worn brown corduroy trousers, and sandals. He has wire-rimmed spectacles. Carter as always is dressed most simply. He has a white tee shirt and faded dungarees, nothing else—no footwear, no jewelry, no underwear. He says, "Big Boy mostly stays in his stall. But he has to be let out in the barnyard to be ridden. Hey Jimbo: you know you have to ride him?"

"Ride him?"

"Sure. All the rest of us have."

"Oh no," thinks Jimbo, "yikes!" The barn is large and cool. Jimbo looks from face to impassive face. "You *rode* him?"

"Yeah," chuckles Thuggy. "Even the women. Everybody did it once."

"What kind of a saddle . . . ?"

"No saddle, no bridle. You just hold on long as you can."

Jimbo looks again into the stall at the red eyes glaring from the black face, the lolling tongue, the steaming nostrils. "*Shit*. So when am I supposed to ride the fucker?"

Annabel says, "Fourth of July at the latest. But why don't you give it a try right now? Get it over with."

Jimbo edges toward the barn door, slips out into the barnyard, and climbs through the barbed-wire fence. Goose, a small black dog, runs to him wagging her tail, looking up doubtfully.

In the barn Carter stretches and says, "What are you two doing this afternoon?"

Thuggy says, "I think I'll go for a swim and then smoke some dope and sit on the beach, throw rocks at things."

Annabel says, "This is my housekeeping day. Sue Holcombe's cottage and then the millhouse if I have time."

"What are the people in the millhouse—what's their name?—like?"

"The Geaches," says Annabel. "I really don't know yet. He seems sort of pushy, she seems sort of pushed. I guess they're rich. So anyway, what are you up to this afternoon, Carter?"

"Don't know. Maybe I'll sleep, dig for treasure, sail out a ways and fish, write some letters, I don't know. I might do some chores around the house, maybe go exploring, get us another bucket of water. I can't make up my mind."

"You know man," Thuggy says, "you oughta be in the movies."

Annabel is braiding and unbraiding her hair. Several dusty chickens step with cautious aplomb into the barn. Daisy's cowbell rings summoning the young people to lunch.

CHAPTER THREE

After lunch when Annabel had made her way across the fields and by a maze of paths through the woods to the clearing around Sue Holcombe's cottage she shouted to announce her approach lest she be mistaken for a prowler and peppered with buckshot. She walked slowly picking her steps with care because rabbit holes concealed in the crumbly gray soil could turn an ankle. Annabel suspected Sue Holcombe of somehow contriving to attract the rabbits to make her land more dangerous.

Sue Holcombe is a small forty-six-year-old violinist with wrinkled brown skin and closely cropped coarse gray hair. She hates and fears intrusions on her privacy. Sometimes awakened by an unfamiliar sound at night she will stalk around the cottage in her nightgown, her shotgun cocked. Fall, winter, and spring Sue Holcombe teaches music theory and music appreciation at a women's college and plays her violin in a symphony orchestra. She spends all her summers here on the island. In return for the housework Annabel does Sue Holcombe is teaching her to play the violin. On many afternoons the quiet around the cottage is shattered by a horrible screeching.

Islanders wonder about Sue Holcombe. Some wonder why she is so interested in music, some whether she is a virgin, some simply what makes her tick. Some feel a pitying affection for her. She seems to have affection for no one. Annabel is the only one of the young people from the farmhouse who had been inside Sue Holcombe's cottage. As she reported to the others, what impressed her most was the large number of books, every one a biography of a musician or composer.

What impressed Annabel now as she approached the cottage was the cozy neatness of its white weatherboarding and dark green shutters. To avoid the rabbit holes Annabel was walking so carefully she seemed not to be making a sound. But when she was still fifteen yards from the door Sue Holcombe came running around from behind where she had been hanging out her wash, shouting, "Who's there!" Her hands were full of clothespins. "Oh, it's you. I expected you yesterday. What happened to you, you lazy girl."

Annabel merely said, "I'm sorry."

"Sorry never paid any debts. Come inside and get to work. I don't have time to listen to apologies." Sue Holcombe clapped her hands. "Nightfall won't wait for sluggards."

Except for the litter of cigarette ashes and butts the house wasn't untidy. Annabel fluffed pillows, straightened piles and shelves and books, dusted, took rugs out and shook them, and swept and mopped the floors. During the latter part of her work she was regaled by the sound of Sue Holcombe's practicing a short difficult passage over and over upstairs in the music room.

When Annabel was done Sue Holcombe gave her a violin lesson. It lasted only an hour but it seemed to Annabel to last much longer. Almost as soon as her bow touched the strings Sue Holcombe would stick her fingers in her ears and shriek, "Cacophony! You haven't practiced at all! You suppose you can absorb music like a sponge? Please try that again."

Much of the lesson concerned stance. Sue Holcombe said, "You must not slump and droop. The violin resents your slovenliness. Sometimes you make me wonder if you're simply too large. But the long fingers are good. Look: this is how to begin." Sue Holcombe clicked her heels and snapped to attention. Her expression was severe, proud, and defiant. She raised the violin into position. She paused. With a flourish she placed the bow onto the strings, pressing down firmly. She paused again. Then she swept off a beautiful chord.

"Theater is part of music. Of course," she said. "But only a small part nevertheless. You must practice your scales and you must listen far more carefully to what you play. Sometimes I wonder if you should have your ears examined."

When the lesson was done Sue Holcombe said, "Now make us tea. I want to have a talk with you." When the tea was poured Annabel waited for Sue Holcombe to open the conversation. But Sue Holcombe maintained a resolute silence, sipping and watching Annabel with her keen blue eyes.

"Do you enjoy teaching at your college?" Annabel said.

"I hate it. I can't abide the little sluts. Year after year I do all I can to shove some music into those brats, to no avail. What do they know? Have they ever suffered? Ha!"

Annabel was thinking. Finally she said, "I might feel the same way in your place."

Sue Holcombe said, "Tell me about your group at the farmhouse. Who's romancing whom? I'm curious."

"I don't know of any romances, Sue. We're all friends though."

"A likely story. Then tell me this: where does everybody sleep?" When Annabel had told her she said, "Aren't there any bedrooms on the third floor?"

"Yes, but none of us uses them."

"Did you ever go up there?"

"Yes. They're pleasant rooms. They do collect dust."

Sue Holcombe gripped Annabel by the wrist and stared at her. *"Is there a room with no windows?"*

Annabel shrugged and laughed. "Of course not!"

"Well then. That's all for today. Come back Tuesday. Not Wednesday, Tuesday. And be prompt if you're capable of it."

Watching Annabel vanish into the woods Sue Holcombe said, "Before the summer's over I'll have that farmhouse!"

CHAPTER FOUR

Full of Daisy's delicious lunch Thuggy stands a while on the front porch of the farmhouse and then ambles off past the barn to the shore. He jumps from the edge of marsh grass onto the sand. Thuggy smiles at the water. He walks up the beach to a cove where wild roses are in thick bloom. He takes off his tennis shoes and motorcycle jacket and sits. Thuggy enjoys seeing nothing but open ocean in front of him. "Right on," he says. The sun is hot, there is a cool breeze lifting small waves. There are puffy white clouds in the blue sky. Thuggy doffs his purple shirt, his Bermuda shorts and undershorts. He walks with his penis waggling cheerily down to the water. He puts one foot in but quickly removes it. "Fuckin' shit, that's cold." He squats at the margin.

A school of minnowlike fish which has been stationary shifts slightly. Thuggy scoops up a handful of sand and hurls it at them. They zip away from the waterline. "Little mothers," Thuggy says affectionately. He throws another handful of sand into the water and then lopes back up to his clothes. From the pocket of his jacket he takes a plastic bag of powdery gray-green marijuana, cigarette papers, and matches. He rolls a fat joint and lights it. Lying back with his ankles crossed, one hand behind his head, Thuggy smokes. Marijuana is his favorite drug and he has smoked many joints of it before. He finds it good to enjoy the drug naked in the open air here where there are no policemen to put him in jail for doing it.

Stoned Thuggy lies on the sand with his eyes closed. Millions of thoughts pass through his head and he lets them. Among them are many of Annabel, how tough and good-natured she is, how the muscles in her upper arms move, how sometimes she doesn't pay attention to what people say. In a while the dogs appear, big Rufus and small black Goose who have followed Thuggy's scent from the farmhouse. They try to coax the boy into playing. He lets them lick him. Since he doesn't move they chase each other over the beach and then lie near him on the sand.

An odd creaking comes from over the rise in the cove. The dogs and Thuggy leap to their feet to look. It is old Jane maneuvering her rowboat to shore to gather driftwood. "Why hello, Thuggy. Been swimming?"

"I, uh . . ."

"Gracious, do you suppose I've never seen a naked man? I was married for twenty-seven years. Maybe you should put your pants on though. If somebody else came along we'd both be in trouble."

"Far out," says Thuggy.

In his Bermuda shorts he gathers firewood along the shore and hands it into Jane's boat.

"How do you like our island, Thuggy?"

"Gee, Ms. . . ."

"Call me Jane. We all go by first names."

"I like it, Jane."

"Had good weather for you. I guess we'll have a storm or two pretty soon though. Generally do about this time."

"I don't mind," says Thuggy. "Shit, I've slept outside straight through storms before."

"Fishing's been good this week. Do you like to fish?"

"Jane, I never learned how. But I bet it's fun."

"Good way to waste a lot of time anyhow."

They work in silence until the boat holds as much wood as it can. Thuggy squats on the sand, smiling.

"You know, Thuggy," says Jane, "I was born and raised in Daisy's farmhouse."

"Oh yeah? Which was your room?"

"Above the back stoop."

"I think that's Daisy's."

As Jane pushes off with an oar she says, "Tell you what, Thuggy. If you want to waste some time one day, you ought to come out fishing with me."

"Far out," says Thuggy. He makes his way back toward the farmhouse, tossing sticks as he goes for the dogs to retrieve.

CHAPTER FIVE

A few days later Carter was in the hammock on the front porch of the farmhouse when Jimbo came around the corner and sat on the steps. Jimbo said, "What's happening?"

"I'm lying here doing nothing."

"Stoned?"

"Nope. You?"

"Nope. Hey Carter, what's over there?" pointing.

"Woods. And I think there's a house or two somewhere in there."

"Let's go exploring in there, man."

Through the gate, across the fields, and over the stone fence. The meadow becomes woods gradually—trees here and there, many of them apple trees, with little undergrowth other than thick green grass. Jimbo was nervous and happy. Carter walked with an easy stride.

"Look back," Jimbo said. "How small the farmhouse looks already. There's Daisy, tiny as can be, on the porch."

"Wow, how the fuck do you get in?" said Carter.

"There's a path."

The boys didn't say much at first as they penetrated the woods. They looked at the trees, the honeysuckle, the red-leaved sumac, and the occasional clumps of poison ivy. Keeping to the path, sometimes they bumped easily against each other. Eventually Jimbo asked, "You like music, Carter?"

"Off and on."

"I mean, what kind?"

"The regular stuff. You know, what you hear on the radio."

"I play classical guitar. You play any instruments?"

"I started learning guitar once. I wanted to sing but I found out I was tone deaf. So I quit the guitar. I really did want to sing though. Anyway, man, I'd like to hear you play sometime."

"But listen," Jimbo said, adjusting his glasses, "so is Daisy your woman?"

"No, man. Annabel either. They're not Thuggy's either. I don't have a woman. Sure I could dig one, but I sure don't want to be tied down."

"No," said Jimbo.

"Why? Daisy turn you on?"

"She certainly does—at least a little. But listen Carter, I don't understand why you don't make it with at least one of them."

"It just hasn't happened, right? Maybe it will, maybe not. Hard to say."

"You staying here all summer?"

"I guess. It's a good place, isn't it."

They followed paths until they came to a clearing with a big oak in the center. Carter said, "You want to sit a spell?" They lay on the ground, talked, and were silent. At length Carter sat up and saw that Jimbo was sound asleep. He shrugged. "I'd sing you a lullaby if I could sing." He wandered away.

Meanwhile Jimbo was dreaming. His father beckoned to him. When Jimbo didn't move he strode forward. His expression was solemn. He tried to speak but couldn't. He wiped his brow and kept trying. When he found his voice it was like a child's. By then Jimbo was waking up.

CHAPTER SIX

Outside the farmhouse Daisy, Annabel, and Thuggy are playing tag. Thuggy has been voted It. They have eaten some of Daisy's Alice B. Toklas hashish fudge. Thuggy looks this way and that, sprints, and falls on his face in the grass. Annabel dashes around corners laughing with her hands over her mouth. Daisy holds her skirt up to her plump white thighs and flees. "Eek! Eek!"

From different directions both girls rush into the barn. Daisy sighing falls onto a heap of straw. Annabel leans against a wall and slides down to the barn floor. Thuggy runs around and around the house with the dogs. "Am I warm? Am I cold?" In the barn the girls hold in their laughter. Thuggy gives up and falls asleep in the hammock.

"Do you suppose he's given up?" asks Daisy.

"I think so but I'm too exhausted to move."

"Me too."

They talk. Annabel tells Daisy of Sue Holcombe's inquiries about the farmhouse.

Daisy says, "Everyone says she's a touch crazy. Did you know she's some distant cousin of mine? I found it out when I inherited this place. I'd never even heard of her. After the will was read she told me she intended to dance on my grave."

"Accompanying herself on the violin surely. By the way, where are Carter and Jimbo?"

"I saw them going toward the woods."

Annabel whispers, "*I* know where they went."

Daisy scurries close. "Where?"

"They wanted to be alone together because they're *gay* and they went to the woods to *jerk off!*" Annabel and Daisy laugh holding their bellies, falling against one another. Annabel lies with her head in Daisy's lap. "Do you think Jimbo's going to ride Big Boy?"

Daisy's eyes twinkle. "This morning when I came for the eggs he was standing right over there. He was saying good morning to Big Boy and saying, 'Let's be friends.' He looked awfully scared, Annabel."

"Cowardice runs in my family, I think I've heard." She sighs. "Being a woman's not easy, is it, Daisy."

Daisy sighs. "No indeed. Being a man must be easy by comparison."

"I think so."

Daisy says, "I don't think I'd change though. Would you?"

"Take the easy way out? Not on your life."

There is silence and then Annabel exclaims, "Shit! I forgot, I was supposed to do the millhouse this morning because I forgot to do it yesterday." She leaps up. "I hope they don't yell at me. Well, bye, Daisy."

"Bye." Daisy lies in the straw dreaming.

CHAPTER SEVEN

In this part of the island the paths are so little used that grass has grown up in them, long but tender. The blades droop and lie in sworls that feel good to the soles of Carter's feet as he continues to explore. Branches of trees join high over his head. In most places thick underbrush alongside would make leaving the path difficult. There are more kinds of plants than Carter has ever seen together before. Softly as he walks, startled rabbits and other animals rush away from him, and a gull goes flap flap flap into the sky.

Carter enjoys his walk perhaps because it seems something of a luxury or waste of his time to be alone. It never occurs to him that he might be in any danger, for the air in which he can smell the ocean as well as the vegetation seems peaceful and sweet. As usual Carter is hardly thinking at all. When he comes to a forking of his path he stops, scratches his head, frowns and laughs and chooses one of the directions. Carter doesn't try to remember where he has been.

He hears female voices some distance away and goes in that direction until he comes to a clearing beside a brook where two women sit in the grass. They look alike and they make a pretty picture with the sunlight dappling over their long limbs and hair. They are older than Carter—he guesses they must be twenty-eight.

"Oh, hi. My name's Carter." He sits down with them. "What's yours?"

"Gail."

"Faye."

"Gail, Faye, hi. What's happening?"

"We were sitting here talking."

Carter thinks they are very pretty indeed. They make him feel a bit flirtatious. "Are you sisters?"

"No, we aren't." Their clothes are colorful and ragged.

Carter smiles. "Do you live here on the island?"

"Yes."

"So do I. In the farmhouse down at the point."

"We know. Daisy told us about everyone there. We just did some cocaine, Carter. Want some?"

"Sure. I never had it before. Expensive, isn't it?"

"Very," says Faye.

"You'll love it, Carter," says Gail.

Faye says, "We think it's the best drug because it's almost not like a drug at all."

"There are many ways to do it," says Gail. "You can ingest it or shoot it up . . ."

"Or you can put it on your penis, Carter, and make love . . ."

"But we prefer to sniff it."

"Often it's adulterated with speed, but ours isn't. Ours is very pure. Smooth."

They show him how to sniff a tiny mound of the white powder through a tube. "Let's have a game now. Okay Carter?"

"Sure." The drug has made tears start in his eyes.

Gail fans a deck of playing cards out on the grass. "Draw one. Whoever draws lowest has to tell something he wants to have."

Carter's card is lowest. The cocaine makes him think with extraordinary clarity and ease. "Fame. I want lots of people to know who I am. I'd like the whole world to know."

Faye says, "Fame is a bubble." The girls laugh and hold one another.

Carter says, "That may be true, if I understand what you mean. But look at it this way: the opposite of fame is a bummer. If nobody knew who you were, where would you be then?"

"You didn't know us and we were here in this dear glade."

"But if you didn't know each other?"

"That would be a bummer, as you say. But we do."

"There's no point in arguing with them," Carter thinks. "They don't understand arguments." He says, "How do you happen to know Daisy?"

"Goodness, we're her dealer. All that good dope and stuff? She buys it from us."

"We have quantities of it—marijuana, hashish, cocaine, speed, acid, Seconal—every kind of drug . . ."

". . . except one. They're hidden in these woods in birds' nests, holes in rotten trees, under flat stones, and buried where lilies of the valley grow."

"Hidden so well you could never find them, Carter."

He smiles and lies back on the grass. "I like this coke. Say, where do you guys live?"

"In these woods."

"I mean where's your house?"

"We don't have one. We live in the woods, eating nuts and berries, sleeping under trees in the moonlight . . ."

"There are caves . . ."

"Far out," says Carter.

Gail licks her lips and Faye brushes a leaf from her hair.

Carter says, "This one drug you don't have, what's that?"

"It's name is difficult so we call it Lethe Water. It's downer, tranquilizer, sleeping potion, and anesthetic all in one. It's *impossible* to get. We had one small bottle and we gave it away. To old Jane. You know her?"

"It's incredibly potent. We gave it to her for her rheumatic legs. She often can't sleep."

"Yet she's never used it! Summer after summer it sits on the ledge of her kitchen window where she puts pies to cool and she's never used any of it."

Carter sits up and shuffles the cards. "How about a game of strip poker."

"Sure, Carter." They smile and wink at one another.

Carter cannot decide which is prettier. He is beginning to have thoughts of making love with both together. It's something he's never done, he realizes. He plays poker well as he can but he loses the first hand. He strips off his tee shirt and throws it on the grass.

"Oooh, look at Carter."

"Isn't he beautiful."

Carter tosses back his golden hair and concentrates on the second hand. He loses again. "That puts me out." He unzips his Levis slowly, watching their faces.

"Heavens, you *are* beautiful."

"What makes it stand up that way, Carter?"

"I can't imagine," says Carter. He lies on his side to watch them play. Hand after hand is a draw now.

"Not again!"

"What funny luck!"

"Stop playing. Come and lie with me, one on each side. Rub coke on my cock, okay?" Carter smiles his dazzling smile.

Faye and Gail lean against one another laughing their tinkling laughs. They whisper and then leap up.

"We must go now."

"We've enjoyed meeting you, Carter."

They run through the trees. Carter calls after them, "You sure are pretty." He lies on his back and sleeps.

CHAPTER EIGHT

The millhouse is in the interior of the island beside a stream. Years have gone by since corn was last ground in the milling room. The house is large and made of stone. Inside it has been comfortably modernized. Jack and Priscilla Geach rented it for a summer's relief from the hurly-burly of city life. Jack, unable to take so long a vacation from his financial concerns, fitted out a room upstairs with what he needed for an office, including a kerosene-powered teletype machine. Priscilla agreed to act as secretary should the need arise. On the day Annabel finally came to do housecleaning, before she arrived there was turmoil in the millhouse.

Jack Geach was slumped over his desk, troubled by an unexpected financial crisis of enormous complexity. He hadn't slept for days as he struggled to unravel ramifications of the matter. It seemed almost certainly possible that he stood in danger of a setback that would leave him in the financial position he had held three years before. Yet there were moments, glimmerings of moments when it seemed at least conceivable that by dint of the correct elaborate manipulations he might come out of it all very much richer. He might even manage to be a millionaire before he was thirty-six. Then he would allow himself a vacation. But now with the strain and sleeplessness his vigilance was waning when he needed it most. Jack's face was haggard and his voice hoarse from shouting into the microphone of the ship-to-shore radio he used for the many telephone calls that had become necessary of late. The ordeal made him feel heroic but now he was a gloomy hero. He stamped his feet, beat his fists against his head, and moaned, "Damn it, damn it, damn it."

Downstairs sweetly anemic-looking Priscilla Geach had washed the breakfast dishes and was sitting at the kitchen table to plan the next day's menu. Her mind strayed from food to her daughters. During their first week on the island they had been hyperactive but they'd seemed peevish and listless since. When she took them swimming they said the water was chilly. They no longer talked of their "wishing tree" nor played in the woods because of a "freak monster." Priscilla wondered if it were their ages (nearly three, and five)—a difficult stage they were passing through. This reminded her of another problem: Edith's birthday was July first, and Priscilla hadn't yet chosen a gift. Little Edith said she wanted "a surprise, not another toy."

Priscilla was returning her attention to her menu when she heard Jack's loud moans borne in on the breeze at the window. She went up, massaged his temples, and urged him to take a nap. When he said he didn't dare she convinced him to come down for a cup of coffee at least. Priscilla apologized, "The place is starting to get out of my control," gesturing. "When is that Annabel going to show up?" she complained. "Have a muffin with your coffee, darling. How's it going?"

"Oh Priss, your concern is such a support to me," Jack said. "I certainly couldn't have advanced as far as I have without you, that's for sure. Just knowing you understand some small part of what I must be going through sustains me when the going gets rough, as it is now." Priscilla laid her hand over his. He went on, "People don't appreciate how difficult high finance is. Nothing's more difficult. I've been through hell, Priss, these past few days. Literally." Priscilla nodded her sympathy and squeezed his hand. He continued, "But it's so thrilling too. So rewarding. I wouldn't trade it for any other life. I'm thrilled by the challenge. And the responsibility!—knowing so much money and thereby so many lives depend on my decisions. It really is truly awesome to be so important. Imagine, Priss, I'm dealing with sums of over four million dollars in this one series of transactions alone." She nodded and Jack said, "I think I may see the light at the end of the tunnel. But it'll be at least two more days and nights of feverish work. Sometimes I wonder if I'll have the stamina, not to mention the vision and insight. But I think I'll pull through. I've never been a quitter, Priss." His eyes shone with refreshed vigor but he had to repeat his last sentence to make his hoarse voice audible over the screams that suddenly issued from the living room.

"Why must they fight!" Priscilla's face fell. Weary from lack of sleep and worry about Jack and the girls, she sometimes wondered if she were happy after all.

Jack and Priscilla stood in the doorway. Edith had climbed atop a bookcase and was hurling books and toys down at her older sister, Hester, who was trying to reach her. Both were shrieking.

"Girls, girls," said Jack, with no effect. Then he said, "Priss, *please* stop them. I'm going up to the office now and I *must* have quiet. You understand, dear." He took the stairs three at a stride.

Realizing Hester would eventually scale the bookcase, Edith had descended the opposite side, and now the girls were battling in the center of the room. Hester's weapon, a Teddy bear, was large but unwieldy and soft. Edith's tin rooster was more dangerous but so small she could land few blows.

Priscilla screamed, "Girls! Stop fighting, stop, stop!" When they paid her no heed she collapsed sobbing on the sofa.

At this juncture Annabel arrived and, taking in the situation at a glance, rushed into the fray to separate the girls. They immediately joined forces to attack her. Hester pummeled her in the face with the bear and Edith with the rooster gave vicious jabs to her legs. But Annabel's strength and size prevailed. She forced them to the floor and held them there with one hand on each belly. Whereupon, enthralled, they began to giggle. Priscilla dried her eyes and said, "I can't thank you enough, Annabel."

Released and dancing, Hester and Edith echoed, "I can't thank you enough, Annabel." They tugged at her sleeves and fingers.

Annabel said, "Don't try to be friends with me. You've made your mother cry. I'll play with you when you've been good. Now go outside."

Outside Hester said, "You were bad, Edith."

Edith said, "I was not. You were. I hate you, Hester." She marched into the woods. Here, skipping and looking back from time to time to make certain she was not followed, she came at last to what she and her sister had named the wishing tree. She said, "The only clothes I ever get are hand-me-downs, hand-me-downs, hand-me-downs. I'm tired of hand-me-downs! I wish a new pair of Mary Janes. I wish red Mary Janes like Hester's but brand new. For me, for my birthday." Then Edith skipped away unaware that she had awakened Jimbo from his dream of his father. He peered around the tree at her.

CHAPTER NINE

Pleased to be rid of her sister, Hester played by the millstream. She was barefoot and wore her everyday dress of blue-and-white checked gingham with flowers embroidered on the bodice and a full skirt. Her honey-blonde hair was braided into pigtails at the top of each of which was a barrette of light blue plastic. She had two pennies in her dress pocket. She was a pretty child but somewhat solemn. Already she was brown as an Indian from the sun.

Hester looked for fish in the stream. She waded and watched the water, more brilliant than glass, rush over her feet. A green frog leaped from a stone. Hester smiled. The bottom of the stream was sandy and pebbly.

When Hester came to the mill wheel she climbed its axle frame up to the second-story balcony. She tiptoed into the office where Jack bent over pages of computations. Hester set a hassock on a filing case, climbed atop, and leaped like a monkey onto her father's back. Jack was too weary to be startled by even this brusque interruption. "Oh, hello Hester." He gave her a vague kiss and said, "I'm busy now, dear."

"I want somebody to play with me," she explained.

"Play with Edith, dear. Daddy's doing something very, very important now. Out."

In the hallway Hester said, "All *he's* doing is making *money*." Hester's room was sunny and airy and decorated with her colorful paintings. In the open closet her several dresses hung neatly quite out of her reach. On a shelf beneath were her white sandals and glossy red patent-leather Mary Janes. Hester rummaged in a trunk of toys. Picture books, balls, hoops, games, and building blocks failed to interest her. She selected a doll and laid it in its bed. "I told you it was time for your nap. Go to sleep. No more talking. You've been bad and bad girls make me furious." She smoothed the sheet and blanket over the doll and sang a lullaby to it. Then she said, "You may wake up now. Go play outside with your sister." She tossed the doll into the toy chest and the bed after it.

Hester lay on the braided rug. A white butterfly alighted on her shoulder. "Everybody that's my friend," she said, "has to be Edith's friend too. I don't understand it." When Annabel appeared to clean the room Hester made a silent and haughty exit.

Hester helped her mother plan the next day's menu.

"Where's Edith?" Priscilla asked.

"In the woods."

"Why didn't you go along with her? It's a lovely day."

"Mother?"

"Yes, dear."

"I don't have any friends of my own, do I?"

"What do you mean?"

"Everybody that's my friend is also Edith's. Grownups say they like us the same. And if children play with me, why do they have to play with Edith too? We're not the same at all."

"Be patient. When you go to school next year you'll make lots of new friends. They'll all be your own special friends."

"Not Edith's?"

"No, because she won't go to school for another two years. She'll be lonely then, Hester, because she won't have you to play with."

"How many days is it till I go to school?"

"Don't think about it and the time will pass before you know it. Meantime you must be patient with people. Even if they did like you better than Edith it wouldn't be kind of them to say it, because it would hurt her feelings, wouldn't it."

"I suppose." Hester wandered out onto the lawn and sat in a swing suspended from a majestic elm. She swung in as large an arc as she could. On the forward stroke her pigtails stood straight out behind her head. She said, "I don't want to be patient because I wish I had a real friend of my own right now."

CHAPTER TEN

Night seems to fall very slowly on the island. Since there is no electricity people use the dusk light in the sky for a long time before they strike matches to ignite kerosene lamps and candles. The day birds grow silent, the night birds begin singing. In June there are fireflies among the trees. Because dogs sleep or stay close to home at night the rabbits venture out of their burrows then to nibble new grass and to dig vegetables out of unfenced gardens. In the quiet the breezes are more noticeable than by day and the sea and land seem to give more of their fragrances to the air, itself so transparent that even when it is fully night you can see easily by the moon and stars in the clearings around houses and along the shore.

But in the woods the darkness is intense, especially near the top of the island where there are no houses or paths, especially in the grove where the millstream begins, and most in the ragged cave in that grove where now Babe stirs from his day-long sleep. Few on the island know he exists.

Grunting and huffing he rises from a bed of twigs. Startled mice scamper deeper into the cave. Babe shakes himself and steps out into moonlight. He glares upward with an awesome mixture of hatred and delight.

Babe's face is terrifying. His matted red-gray hair stands out at every angle. Beneath the ridge brows droop from like moss, his eyes shine darkly. Sullen lips part over misshapen and broken teeth, and from their corners saliva dribbles down the nasty beard.

Babe's tunic is a patchwork of fur, leather and cloth, burlap, scraps of ladies' pink underclothing. He is short but heavy and powerful: he can slither through underbrush or scramble up a tree as easily as he walks on cleared ground. He does not know how old he is, cannot remember whether he came to the island long ago or was born here. He can remember no contact with human society.

This Babe would like to kill the other islanders whom he sometimes watches, hidden in the brush—to kill them as he does the rabbits and birds he catches, dismember them and gnaw the flesh off their bones. Obscurely he fears them and believes he must await the time for his attack. Yet now in the darkness he comes down the center of the island, avoiding paths, to the houses. Babe prowls by the millhouse and sees Priscilla Geach reading to Hester and Edith downstairs, and Jack in his office poring over the day's stock market returns. On the seaward side of the island he sees old Jane in her rocking chair by a window. Guided by the fragrance of marijuana he stalks about the glade where Gail and Faye recline in a circle of mushrooms and gaze into one another's eyes. At the farmhouse he sees Jimbo walk out to the barn, Daisy, Carter, and Thuggy talking in the kitchen, and Annabel in the living room filling the kerosene lamps. On his way back up the center of the island he stops to watch Sue Holcombe sitting in her parlor reading. He lurks far from her window, crouched and scarcely breathing. He sees Sue Holcombe start and raise her head. She frowns intently out into the darkness. Babe ceases to breathe until Sue Holcombe is reading her biography again. He inches backward into the cover of the trees to hunt his night's food.

Babe expects to see the destruction and end of everything, and he yearns for that time.

CHAPTER ELEVEN

Forest birds were raising their heads from beneath their wings, opening their bright eyes and looking about at blue hints of dawn in the sky—they were uttering tentative chirpings when old Jane, always the first person on the island to stir, rose from her bed.

Jane's boathouse is on a narrow inlet with good water at the extremest neap tides, an excellent natural harbor which once provided sole access to the island. Stone steps covered with barnacles that make footing safe lead down from the house to beneath low-water mark. Ancient iron mooring rings are set into the steps at intervals. On either bank strangely wind-pruned but plentiful evergreens shelter the cove.

Waked by fresh pain in her legs, Jane opened her bedroom window curtains and glanced over the dim horizon. She braided and pinned up her gray hair, donned a dress of printed cotton and, leaning on her cane, descended to her kitchen. She arranged kindling and split logs over the embers in her stove and when they were burning she prepared her breakfast of eggs and pan-fried toast and coffee. Though it was still dark in the boathouse Jane was not one to use the kerosene in her lamps needlessly.

Today was Jane's seventieth birthday. She smiled to think of it. She was eating her breakfast at a kitchen table beside a row of windows that looked out into the evergreens. Later in the day, if someone returned from the mainland with the island's mail, there would be letters and cards. Twenty, thirty years ago her birthday had brought flurries of them. Now there would only be a few. A card from her son-in-law (her daughter was dead) and from her granddaughter a polite brief note. Two of Jane's cats came to be fed. She filled their saucers with milk. One of them had brought a field mouse and Jane opened a window and tossed it out into the grass. The most enjoyable letter would be a long one from Charlotte, who had worked at the same shoe factory as Jane more than half a century before and who, like Jane, had been widowed for decades. Charlotte had married for money and now in her old age lived comfortably on a large estate. Her letter would contain a customary invitation to come and live with her. Jane would decline with warm thanks in the letter she would send for Charlotte's birthday in February. Which of them would die first? Jane wondered. There would also be a card from Jane's lawyer and one from her doctor. These were the certainties, and after them there might be mail from any of several old and new acquaintances. There might even be a surprise—that was always possible!

"Well . . ." said Jane. Her husband John had been a sailor. He had died after twenty-seven years of marriage when Jane was forty-eight. His boat had capsized in a terrible storm. The little cabin boy's body had washed ashore on the mainland to the north and more than a year later Jane had come upon a portion of the centerboard covered with other tidal debris near the top of the island, but John's body had been carried out toward mid-ocean. Of late birthdays made Jane think of dying and wonder how much longer she would survive John. Years ago she had supposed that when she finally died she would be able to rejoin him. Now she thought otherwise. Now it seemed that surely after death there was nothing, that all that remained of her husband were her occasional thoughts of him. "Well, I guess I'd best get that chore done," she said, glancing at the tide schedule.

Jane made her way back upstairs and removed from a closet a leather valise stiff, roughened, and reddish with age. It was what she had taken on her honeymoon and by now it was her only memento of that time. "Ratty old thing," she said. With it on her arm she came step by step downstairs, out her kitchen door. She walked around her house through dewy grass in the blue-and-gray dawn out to the point of land at the mouth of the inlet. The tide was beginning to ebb, moving a sluggish sea-ward current by the point. Tears came into Jane's eyes when she tossed the valise down into that current. She stood for several minutes watching it bob away from shore. A gull rode it for a while searching for food and then flapped away crying. Old Jane turned and walked toward her house.

CHAPTER TWELVE

While Jane was cooking her breakfast, down in the farmhouse Jimbo awoke. With him there was never any lingering sleepiness. Out of a sound sleep he came wide awake. Hence it was difficult for him to remember dreams, and he had trained himself to try immediately. This morning he was unsuccessful. He put on his wire-rimmed spectacles, his wristwatch, his underpants and trousers.

Jimbo's room was rather bare. Toilet articles lay beside the pitcher and washbasin atop a chest of drawers near the window, against which leaned his guitar in its case. There was a stack of recordings of classical guitar music on the shelf of his night table, kept here (not downstairs with the phonograph) lest someone else play and damage them. On the night table lay issues of *Scientific American*, a statistics text, and a volume of Chinese poems.

As Jimbo washed and shaved and combed his hair he regarded his torso in the mirror. Although the proportions and forms differed but slightly from Carter's, it seemed to Jimbo that those slight differences made all the difference in the world. Where along Carter's sides panels of muscle defined themselves, Jimbo's ribs were undeniably apparent, and below was a mild fullness which by no stretch of the imagination could be construed as muscle. Jimbo's shoulders weren't wide enough to satisfy him nor his biceps large enough. Indeed his arms from shoulder to wrist looked thin, making his hands look all the larger. His neck was longer and his Adam's apple more prominent than Carter's. And, while Jimbo's hair was darker, his skin was fairer so that he couldn't achieve Carter's golden tan. Yet Jimbo was not troubled or envious. He looked into his own lively blue eyes with one brow raised—a philosophical look that said, "Who has time for envy? Not Jimbo."

He pulled on a striped tee shirt and went down to the kitchen. Softly as he went he woke Thuggy whose sleep was a series of naps like the dogs'. As best they could the two made a clumsy and not delicious breakfast, soiling more utensils than was necessary and leaving them to be washed later. They took their coffees out onto the back porch. It was the middle of dawn. A brisk wind lifted whitecaps from the gray water.

"Kinda pretty," said Thuggy.

"Yeah. Hey, let's have a sail before the others get up."

"Sure, man," said Thuggy.

Each, assuming the other to be a good sailor, neglected to mention that his own experience was limited to having seen Daisy manage the boat. Daisy had made it look childishly simple.

They put the boat into the water, raised sail, and tacked out. Jimbo was at the helm. Thuggy lay on the bow and let his fingers drag in the water, but since the boat bouncing over the waves bounced him like a rag doll on the deck he soon retreated to a seat. The spray wetted both boys to the skin. "Far out!" said Thuggy. Jimbo sang, "Yo-ho, blow the man down!"

All seemed well until Jimbo observed that the wind was carrying them out toward open ocean faster than he had suspected. "Coming about!" he shouted. "Never heard of it," shouted Thuggy. The boat spun in circles. Thuggy tried to steer, with no more luck than Jimbo. The wind was rising. "Fucking shit," said Jimbo, "we've got to lower the sail." When the sail was down the boat was steadier. "We're still moving though. Toss out the anchor," said Jimbo. "Anchor?" said Thuggy. There was none to be found nor when they thought of paddles did they discover any of them.

Jimbo grabbed Thuggy by the shoulders. "I'm scared out of my skin. What can we do? There's nothing but water in front of us for thousands of miles. Thuggy, we could die!"

Thuggy was scared too but he couldn't help laughing. "Listen, if we don't come back the others'll figure what happened and send help, right? A rescue plane to tow us back, Coast Guard, shit like that."

"But if we get carried out far enough they might not find us even with planes. That's happened, Thuggy, I've read about it. We have to think of something quick!"

"Can you swim?"

"Sure. You?"

"Yeah. You think we could make it to the island from here?"

"I think so," Jimbo said. "We've got to. It's our only chance and there's not a second to lose."

"What about the boat?"

"Let it go—we have to."

They stripped to their underpants and prepared to leap into the water. Jimbo said, "We stay close together. And don't panic. We can always float if we get exhausted."

"Then we'll start drifting out again."

"Fuck! Well, anyway . . ."

"Right. Here goes."

At that moment the boat ground to a halt on a mussel shoal.

Old Jane meanwhile, kneading dough, had noticed the sailboat's antics. "Those silly boys." She watched them through a spyglass. Knowing that, given the wind, tide, and current, the boat would run aground, she had gone back to her bread. "Let them cool their heels a while. Teach them some respect for that ocean." One of their distress signals—quickly, slowly, quickly they stood and then sat—puzzled her until she realized they were sending S.O.S. in Morse. When her dough was ready she set out to rescue them.

Jane towed the boys to her landing. "I think you'd best send Daisy to sail her back," she said. "Your lips are blue. I wonder if you've caught colds. Well, come and dry out at my stove."

They had coffee and some of Jane's bread with butter and rose-hip jelly. The food and warmth made Thuggy drowsy but Jimbo was enlivened. "What do you think would've happened if you hadn't seen us?" he asked.

"You'd've got your noses sunburned anyhow."

"But I mean if nobody had seen us and we hadn't swum to shore."

"You couldn't swim in with the sea high as it is. The tide would have lifted you off and I expect you'd have been lost."

"Wow, wait till I tell the others!" Jimbo said, and then, "What are these books? May I look at them?"

"Of course. A bunch of old things that've stuck to me . . ."

"Hmm. *The Comedy of Errors*, maps, Longfellow, some kind of textbook. Oh, *sprechen Sie Deutsch*?"

"I taught it for five years."

"Oh. And what's this, Jane?" A thin folio bound in navy-blue suede.

"Architect's drawings for the farmhouse, isn't it?"

"Interesting. They must be awfully old. Oh, I nearly forgot—I'll be right back, Jane."

Jimbo ran down to the dock and returned with Jane's honeymoon valise. "It was out there on the shoal. We knew it was yours by the initials. So you see you have a reward for saving our lives." Her expression and her laugh surprised him.

"Why thank you, boys," Jane said. She would toss it out again on the evening tide.

"Wake up, Thuggy," said Jimbo. "We should split, the others'll worry. Thanks again, Jane."

Thuggy said, "Right, thanks a million, Jane."

CHAPTER THIRTEEN

Soon after the boys have left for their sail Annabel wakes. She listens and hears no sound in the house. Dear Annabel, how healthy and vigorous she is, how beautiful her firm legs and the sweep of her back and with what a rich brown like lacquered wood her hair lies in the streaming sunlight! Today, free of assigned tasks, she wakes early in a cheerful mood. When she has washed her face in well water and brushed her hair she stands at her window and gives tingling slaps to the front of her torso. She does several kinds of calisthenics, bending and stretching. The cool of the air makes her nipples stand up like elves' caps until she slips on a simple dress.

Then Annabel lifts the violin she has rented for the summer from Sue Holcombe and assumes arresting stances before her mirror. She won't touch the rosined white horsehair to the gut and wire lest she wake the others, but she can practice the fingering of scales. Up and down the strings her fingers descend like pistons and raise soft resonances that pass from the fingerboard and bridge into the amplifying body of the violin and thence into her jawbone so that she can know whether the pitch is correct. After the scales she practices the first tune she has learned,

"Oats and Beans." The more carefully she listens the more she forgets her posture until she notices herself in the mirror and stands proudly again. "*Voilà.*"

Down the hallway, dim even in day, Annabel walks softly supposing herself the first to arise. As she passes Carter's bedroom his door by a wonderful chance swings open. "Yes?" Annabel says, raising her eyebrows and preparing to smile until she stands transfixed by what she sees within. It is Carter asleep on his wide bed in the center of the room, in the center of a square of sunlight that falls over and around him gilding the sheet that covers him scarcely to the waist and also gilding Carter's skin and hair. His face is impassive, his full lips are slightly parted. Beneath the sheet his penis lies half erect. A mild breeze blows through the room and it seems as if this breeze has melted the flesh off Annabel's bones for the moment.

As her vision adjusts she is able to muse on the boy's strength and delicacy. She would never think of leaving her point of vantage so long as he slept but when at length he stirs she closes the door and descends to the kitchen.

She cannot help laughing. "Have I fallen in love?" she wonders. "I hardly know the child. I wonder, does he have a respectable mind? No, clearly I'm not in love with him. However I do think I might get a little something started, if only for the sake of the experience. Before summer's over. Should I? But why not. I will then, I'll give it a try." A chill of nervous excitement runs over her.

She finishes her tea, considers, and then swallows half a five-milligram tablet of Dexedrine to counteract her customary morning laziness and to make the day sparkle even more than it already does. As the drug takes effect Annabel is inspired. She drops several capsules of green Dexamil into the pocket of her dress.

Daisy wanders half asleep into the kitchen. "Good morning. Am I the last?"

"Carter's asleep—his door was open—but I think Jimbo and Thuggy are up. It's a pretty day, isn't it."

"Pretty," Daisy says vaguely.

Annabel gives Daisy a kiss on the shoulder. "I'm off to the millhouse, see you later."

"Later," Daisy says, smiling at a pot of boiling water.

Outside Annabel dances in the sun. If she had the violin with her, how she could flourish it now!

CHAPTER FOURTEEN

Daisy fed cats and dogs and chickens and Big Boy who glared at her and foolishly rammed his head against the barn wall. Then she took a pail and walked across the field into the edge of the woods to the community well. She had drawn her water and was returning when she heard Faye's and Gail's melodious voices approaching. Daisy squatted behind a clump of honeysuckle. Soon Faye and Gail entered the clearing. One perched on the side of the well, the other leaning against a fallen tree, they sang this round:

When children play
In the green elm shade
Hearts fail,
Fathers fall in the sun.

Cold dew shines
On the new-mown grass
All the noonday long

While eager boys
And careless girls
Dance and sing love songs—

But children weave
Garlands of leaves
And hearts fail,
Fathers fall in the sun.

Then Faye said, "Let's hide the hashish candy here under this stone in the well platform."

"Is it wrapped?"

"Yes."

"Good then."

When the package was hidden Gail said, "But what if someone should be spying, watching us this very minute?"

They peered at the vegetation around them. Faye said, "Even if someone were watching, he wouldn't steal from such as we poor creatures."

"You don't suppose? Daisy, for instance. She loves our dope and she loves candy, and this is delicious candy made with splendid hashish."

"But Daisy could buy it. And since we always deal fairly with her I can't believe she would steal our treasures."

"Surely not. Then let's hurry away."

"We have errands in other parts of the island."

When their talk and laughter had faded into the distance among the trees Daisy crept from behind the honeysuckle. Her heart pounded with excitement. It was easy to find the plastic wax-sealed package beneath the stone. When she opened it odors of maple sugar, walnuts, and vanilla filled the air. Overcome, Daisy gobbled down all six large squares. She replaced the wrapping beneath the stone and began to run home. Halfway there she remembered her pail and returned for it, walking now. The drug was taking effect. The honeysuckle seemed to await her, extending its blossoms, and when she bent to lift the pail the scent of the shrub pleased her so that she lost her balance, sat down suddenly, and spilled the water over the grass. "Heaven!" cooed Daisy. The beads of water slipped down blades of grass to nestle at the roots. Daisy's laughter seemed to raise echoes from the woods, time seemed to slow and move jerkily. At length she remembered the empty pail and came to the well to refill it. The well was not very deep but it fascinated Daisy as if it were when she looked down into it. It exhaled a delicious coolness. Daisy leaned farther and farther over the rim and then—did she feel a push from behind? did she hear silvery laughter or was it her own shriek?—she tumbled headlong down the well.

The hashish was so strongly in effect that the dark icy water seemed pleasant to Daisy when she bobbed to its surface. And when it occurred to her that she might drown there, even this seemed not unpleasant. "No one can live forever. But would I pollute the well? Maybe the reverse, the water would purify me." The stone walls were smooth and mossy. Far above was a circle of blue sky crossed by the wooden pulley frame. Daisy's skirt spread around her on the water. She was content merely to float and sing. So it was that Jimbo and Thuggy returning from their adventure with the sailboat heard her voice issuing from the well and contrived to hoist her out with the well rope. They filled the pail and the three walked back to the farmhouse for lunch.

CHAPTER FIFTEEN

Annabel and Carter had prepared lunch—tuna salad sandwiches, potato salad, and crème caramel—fortunately, for Daisy was in no condition to do it. Around the big table conversation was lively. Jimbo and Thuggy described their sail, Daisy's musical laughter moved above the talk, and sunlight sparkled on glasses of cold Rhine wine. Annabel said there was "a big ocean out there, seriously," and urged the boys not to be so reckless in the future. Carter wished he'd been with them. He said, "Being lost at sea and not getting found would be bad, but almost being lost must be outta sight."

Jimbo said, "It's fun afterward, but when it was happening we didn't really have time to enjoy it."

"Yes," said Daisy, "enjoyment's fine but you don't want to go overboard."

Jimbo nodded. "We had to keep ourselves under control. If we'd panicked even for a second, well . . ."

Annabel said, "What you discovered is that you have courage and self-control. Good. They'll come in handy, won't they Jimbo?, when you ride Big Boy. So you needn't wait any longer."

Jimbo turned this way and that, holding to the edge of the table. "I didn't feel seasick the whole time," he said.

The hashish made Daisy hallucinate. Boundaries between things seemed more substantial than the things themselves. Cheerfully she said, "Of course I was the one in real danger."

"Silly girl," said Annabel. "How did you manage to fall down the well?"

Daisy said, "What've you been up to, Annabel?"

"I took some speed over to Jack Geach. He's wheeling and dealing around the clock and can't stay awake. He didn't know about amphetamines. I think he was suspicious at first."

Thuggy said, "Not much of an adventure. You oughta have come sailing, kid."

Annabel said, "But Daisy, what's the well like from inside?"

"Rather sweet," said Daisy. Her dimples were twinkling.

Carter said, "Far out. So, I think I'll have me a swim. Anybody coming along?"

"Me," said Annabel.

"Me," said Jimbo.

"Me too," said Thuggy.

Daisy said, "I'll wash dishes to atone for being a delinquent *Hausfrau*."

When the others had gone Daisy forgot about dishwashing. She waded up the lee shore to a flat boulder covered with a thickness of gull droppings. She lay here and watched the waves with great attention and simultaneously she dreamed. She was a ship-boy in the crow's nest of a storm-tossed galleon and she was sound asleep and snug. Oblivious to the raging weather and cries of sailors below, she slept and dreamed she swam under the waves. She meandered over dim valleys, circled a sunken ship, and then rose to the surface where she floated and let the waves rock her to sleep. Carried along in the current she dreamed she was in the barnyard with a basket of cupcakes and Jimbo sat on the fence and played his guitar. But his drowsy music was broken by Hester Geach who had climbed onto the boulder with Daisy and said, "Hi. Who are you?"

Daisy was pleased to meet the child. Hester thought she had found a special island friend of her own. But when she saw that she had no control over Daisy's laughter—everything she did provoked it—she was offended and climbed down. "It's not polite to laugh at little girls," she said.

"I can't help it," said Daisy. "I'm sorry."

Not placated, Hester marched away. When she glanced back she saw Daisy's smiling face at the edge of the boulder.

CHAPTER SIXTEEN

"No more calls for five hours," says Jack Geach into the two-way radio. "Don't let anything happen. Postpone everything. I think I have an idea." "Yes Mr. Geach. Over and out," says the voice of one of the three secretaries who are working in shifts on the mainland. Jack shuffles the clutter on his desk but cannot locate the paper his idea is written on. "Am I losing control of my faculties?" he asks. "If only I could stop the clock and get a good night's sleep! If only there weren't all those other men out there trying to make money too, then I wouldn't be under such terrible strain, strain that would have broken a lesser man long ago for sure, no question about it!

"Jack Geach wouldn't have it any other way though. He relishes the keen competition of being pitted against the best business minds in the country. Ha, ha! It's the greatest fun in the world. There's nothing like it, I wouldn't trade it for a million dollars. Or rather I wouldn't trade it for the security of an average middle-class existence, not in a million years. I'm very thankful I was blessed with so much talent. The only other thing I would wish for is to be able to stop the clock from time to time. After all, I'm human."

Comforted or at least distracted by these reflections, Jack tilts back in his chair with his hands behind his head. He allows himself the luxury of closing his eyes for a moment and then several moments. He is awakened by the chair's toppling over backward.

"Jack?" calls Priscilla from downstairs.

"It's all right, dear," Jack mutters. When Priscilla appears at the door he waves her away. He returns to his desk grimly determined. As he searches once more through the data sheets and pages of computations and strategies his hand comes upon the green capsules given him by Annabel. Although earlier he was, as she guessed, suspicious of the gift, now he shrugs in scorn. "Probably placebos. Better double the dosage."

Since Jack's stomach contains only black coffee the capsules soon dissolve and take effect. Jack won't correctly attribute the effect until later. Now he believes that reserves of sheer will and inspiration have opened in him. Fatigue vanishes from body and mind, attention concentrates to a joyful intensity. The littered desk becomes a treasure trove, for wherever he looks hidden relations among figures and diagrams manifest themselves. Where earlier he had doodled idly now his pencil can scarcely move fast enough to record the illuminations that shower upon him—and yet his handwriting is more regular than since he was a schoolboy. He covers page after page, moving from deft clarifications of basic terms through stages of increasingly comprehensive summary and deduction to a plan, well articulated and elegant beyond anything he had approached before.

As he radios instructions to his secretary he realizes that hours have passed. The sun is low. Jack stands on his balcony to do arm-lift exercises, proudly surveying the landscape. "I'm only thirty-five and I feel and look younger."

"High finance," Jack continues, "is a science. No, it's really an art I'd say. It really is an art. Very creative." He says, "Being in a position as envied as mine is and having so many people look up to me and envy me, well, I must say it's reassuring and challenging. Life is good: I appreciate life."

Jack hurries downstairs and begins to hug Priscilla. Her gasps and blushes increase his ardor. "Heavens, not here! The girls will be home any minute!" she cries. "Time they learned a few things," says Jack. He has undressed himself and Priscilla. Now she feels the gentle breeze on her body and, looking at Jack's handsome and happy face, begins to enjoy the situation. She shakes her finger at him. "You men are all alike." She flees around and around the sofa. "Help, help!" Their bodies gleam with sweat. Jack captures Priscilla and on the sofa they make more energetic and uninhibited love than ever before in all the years of their marriage. "Oooh," says Priscilla, "I love it when . . . oooh, when they flop against me like that." "So do I," says Jack. When he and Priscilla have done he runs up the stairs intending to shower and go back to work. But as he crosses the bedroom the effect of the drug ends. And so when Priscilla has gathered the clothes and climbed the stairs she finds him on the bed asleep.

CHAPTER SEVENTEEN

The young people had brought two bottles of wine to the beach. Annabel and Carter wore brief European bathing suits, Jimbo's was a larger flowered one, and since Thuggy had none he wore faded Levis cut off at the knee. They had played football in the brisk water until a wind blew the ball away over the waves. Now they sat and lay on the sand. Small Goose and big red Rufus had come along. When there was swimming Rufus had swum out beyond the people as if to prevent their straying far from shore, while Goose who never swam ran back and forth and barked. Now that things were quieter the dogs were exploring underbrush above the beach.

Seawater dried on the skin, salt itched and sparkled. Thuggy lit a pipe of hashish. He nudged Annabel. She and Jimbo smoked some, Carter and Thuggy smoked a great deal. Thuggy said, "Mmm, taste the wine now."

Jimbo said, "Let's play hide-and-seek by closing our eyes. Everybody's It. No talking and nobody opens eyes till I say to, okay?" The others closed their eyes. Jimbo kept his open to watch their antics.

Each scooted a few feet from where he had been and waited, except that Thuggy kept having fits of giggles that revealed his position so that he would need to move again. Then wonderful things began to happen. Thuggy puckered his lips and made mischievous kissing motions. Carter was most stoned and most active. He walked unsteadily, went into a crouch waving his arms like a dancer, and then walked in a new direction. He was trying to find someone systematically by walking in a spiral but the center about which he traveled moved and he described a series of loops up the beach. When his path brought him into honeysuckle at the woods' edge he heard a rustling and followed it inland with his eyes still closed, out of Jimbo's sight. Annabel had done some exploratory crawling and now lay on her back. She let sand drift through her fingers onto her belly. Thuggy blew his kisses and he would shrug as if to say, "So what?" Watching these doings Jimbo hugged his knees in glee.

Jimbo moved to Annabel and laid his hand on her shoulder. She showed no acknowledgment. What was she thinking? he wondered. She was deciding that Carter had found her and she would do nothing to break the spell. Jimbo slid his hand lightly along her arm. The sun and the sand were hot, the cool breeze carried the strong fresh smell of the ocean. Jimbo was so delighted with his mischief that he trembled, and when he thought of more he was unable to control himself. He lifted the cheese and bottles of wine off Thuggy's jacket and sped away up the beach past where Carter had entered the woods.

Annabel wondered what had become of Carter. "Being so stoned he's probably lost me. That means he still has his eyes closed. Should I open mine and look for him? No, because for all I know Jimbo and Thuggy have opened theirs. I don't mind being teased later, but if I open my eyes now and they see me do it the jig'll be up and I'll have to join them in playing tricks on Carter till he opens *his*. So I won't open my eyes. I'll cough." Annabel coughed gently, frowning and rubbing her throat for spectators. Thuggy heard and crept toward her. When his hand came upon her thick hair he smiled.

Thuggy was a gentleman in his way—not one to take unfair advantage. How could he guess Annabel would treat a one-in-three chance as a sure thing? His hand moved over her ear, over her throat and clavicle, down under the top of her bathing suit. Annabel and Thuggy were blissful.

"Goodness gracious, what are you doing?" At once they sat up and opened their eyes, to see each other and a bewildered Hester Geach scratching her head.

All Annabel could say was, "Well!" She felt she was blushing.

Thuggy said, "Hi, little girl." He winked and then turned back to admire Annabel's glowing face. "Listen, kid," he began.

Annabel ignored him prettily by telling Hester, "Good children don't sneak up on people. I feel like another swim," she went on, "—by myself this time." Over the beach she marched swinging her arms and shaking out her hair. Nor when she entered the water did she slow much, but her proud thighs moved on through the waves. Thuggy and Hester watched.

"If Annabel was talking about me," said Hester, "she didn't know what she was talking about. Because I didn't sneak, I only walked. If Annabel always gets angry she probably doesn't have many friends. She should have told you my name because she knows me (she works for my mother). My name is Hester." But Thuggy still called her "little girl" and as they talked Hester concluded that, while he was affable and never seemed to laugh at her as Daisy had done, he was too silly to be a close friend of hers. She waved good-by and continued her progress along the shore. Thuggy put on his jacket and went to look for the dogs.

CHAPTER EIGHTEEN

Edith Geach, the youngest person on the island, has slipped into her sister's room and is staring at her sister's paintings. Compared to her own efforts they seem wonderfully verisimilar. Edith wishes that merely by examining them she could understand wherein lies the difference. She is annoyed that she cannot. She considers ripping the pictures from the walls and marking over them with crayons. She decides against it: her sister would make new ones and also the culprit would be identifiable.

Edith squats in the doorway of her sister's closet. In this light the red patent leather is vermillion. The shoes cast no shadow on the pine floorboards. Edith's hair, skin, and features resemble her sister's but Edith is smaller and more like a mouse. She puts on the shoes and clop-clops around the room. From downstairs come her mother's laughter and cries, "Heavens, not here! The girls will be home any minute!" Edith replaces the shoes. She dances down the back stairs, out onto the grass. Pausing to think and then running along when she hears a noise, she makes her way into the woods. The late afternoon noises frighten her. She would not brave the woods did she not think it worthwhile to make her position quite clear by another visit to the wishing tree. How bad it would be to wait for the shoes until her sister had outgrown them and then receive them with the gloss scratched and cracked!

Near her destination Edith hears voices. Seated under the wishing tree in the clearing are Faye and Gail, strangers to Edith, with a wicker basket. Their clothes are of rich colorful fabrics irregularly weathered. Gail has been strumming a mandolin. She says, "My dear, give me a Mary Jane." Edith's hair stands on end.

Faye takes from the basket only a peculiar cigarette, lights it, hands it to Gail, and says, "Hello, Edith. Come and join us in a game of Fish." Gail takes a deck of playing cards from the basket. The game is described. "If you win you can make a wish and it will come true," Faye explains. Edith is confident of victory.

Gail wins quickly. Edith watches her close her eyes to wish. Edith plays the next hand more cautiously. She lays four jacks out on the grass. But as the game continues it is Faye who lays down more and more cards, while Gail and Edith are told, "Go fish." Edith says, "I still think I'll win," until at last Faye has won. Edith is furious. She crumples some of the cards, shreds others, and finally throws the lot of them into the air. "I hate your stupid game," she screams, and stamps away.

Scarcely has she left the clearing when Carter enters from the other side. Leaves and sprigs of honeysuckle have stuck to his bathing suit and entangled themselves in his hair. With his eyes closed he moves slowly, arms outstretched. He smiles. He can hear and feel that he has come to an open space. Faye and Gail sigh and lean weakly against each other.

"Ah," whispers Gail, "his feet on the grass."

"How his arms move from the shoulder," Faye whispers.

"His face, his neck, torso . . ."

". . . pelvis, what assurance, . . ."

". . . what simplicity! Shall I summon him?"

"I shall swoon . . ."

Gail strokes her mandolin. Carter follows the sweet sound. When he is near the girls they whisper to him. "Don't open your eyes, Carter." "Lie down." "Smoke this." It seems to Carter that many hands feel of him and that he hears sighs and whispered laughter.

CHAPTER NINETEEN

Jimbo was scrambling up out of a gully where he had consumed the stolen wine and cheese and buried the bottles in the sand when he met Hester Geach.

"Who are you?"

"Hester. Who are you?"

"Jimbo. Hi."

"What were you doing?"

"Having a secret picnic. Are you exploring, Hester?"

"I live in the millhouse almost all the way to the other side of the island. But I'm tired now."

"Look," said Jimbo, "there's a path. It probably goes straight through."

Holding hands they walked in silence. An aged and nearly blind seagull, no longer able to fly, hobbled ahead of them and finally cowered in a clump of poison ivy to let them pass. "I've seen them before and I don't like them," said Hester.

"Interesting."

Hester looked up into Jimbo's eyes. "Those are nice glasses," she said. In fact she thought them odd.

"Would you like to try them on?" They made Hester so dizzy she sat down on the grass. Everything was blurred and swayed if she moved her head. The glasses seemed still odder. "Kind of funny—but nice. Thank you."

Jimbo sat beside her. "Why doesn't this island sink under the water?" she asked.

"It can't. It's not like a boat floating on the water. It's like the top of a mountain that sticks out of the water. Do you understand?"

"Yes." Hester buckled her sandal. High above, a wind went whish whish through the tops of the trees. "I know how to write my name . . ." Hester fell asleep leaning against Jimbo.

After half an hour he patted her cheek. "Wake up! Wake up, Hester."

"Did you take a nap?"

"No, I thought about things. All set to go again?"

"I'd like to pick some dandelions . . ." They grew in twos and threes alongside the path where direct sunlight fell. Hester hopped back and forth to gather them. "Want to be friends?" she asked, handing the bouquet to Jimbo.

He blushed. "Far out."

"?"

"Sure, Hester. It's a deal."

She turned cartwheels. "Yippee! Yippee! We can play lots of games, have secrets . . ."

Jimbo too turned cartwheels through the light and shade. ". . . have lots of secrets, play lots of tricks . . ."

When he returned to the farmhouse Annabel was hanging out her bathing suit to dry. "Where'd you get the dandelions?"
"It's a secret," said Jimbo.

CHAPTER TWENTY

In her music room Sue Holcombe lays her violin in the green plush lining its case. She inserts the bow in its crevice and clicks the case shut. From around her dry brown neck she unclasps an early Victorian necklace of gold and amethysts. She wears it whenever she gives a concert and whenever she rehearses one, as she has done today. The concert is scheduled for November when she will have returned to her college community on the mainland. This afternoon however she has fantasies of performing it here on the island in triumph on the porch of the farmhouse when she has taken that property from Daisy. A cigarette burns unnoticed in Sue Holcombe's hand as she envisions Daisy and the other young people huddled on the lawn weeping from anger and bitter disappointment, yet dazzled in spite of themselves until she ends and says, "Now go and never set foot on this property again! Shoo! I'd drown you if I could, and laugh to high heaven." Aloud she says, "They probably wouldn't appreciate the music anyway."

Sue Holcombe's hair is tied with black grosgrain. She wears black Oxfords and a shirtwaist dress of light green cotton. As she descends the narrow stairs of her cottage she lights a second cigarette from the first. Look, with what energy she stands in the twilight frowning. What is amiss? Her eyes dart here and there, she frowns more. Has she forgotten something? Impossible, she prides herself on the power of her memory. For years she can recall student impertinences or details from biographies of musicians. Yet she trusts her intuition—"It separates the musicians from the dolts"—and something seems wrong. She sniffs the air. No, unless a greater than usual salt tang. Are there unnoticed pains in her wiry little body? None. Grinding her teeth she stares over the banister at her living room. The good old furniture she has bought at auctions for next to nothing stands in place. On her writing desk the corner of an unfinished letter to a newspaper on the mainland trills in the breeze. The breeze as it passes through the screens has an odd regular pulse like breath. Sue Holcombe listens. She hears real breathing other than hers from the high-backed sofa. At the foot of the stair her shotgun leans against the newel post.

Jump, jump—Sue Holcombe with her weapon cocked and aimed runs to the center of the room. What she sees makes her thrust the gun aside contemptuously. It is Carter in his bathing suit with sea salt on him, stoned out of his mind and unutterably beautiful. His beauty is all but lost on Sue Holcombe.

"You must be one of Daisy's pieces of ordure. This isn't the farmhouse, young man. This is Sue Holcombe's cottage. Decamp immediately. You're intoxicated, I see. Disgusting, predictable. Now get off my sofa before I count to three or I'll kick you off it!" She stamps, snaps her fingers, and points toward the door. Carter looks there through the screenwire and sees a rabbit hop across the scruffy lawn. He looks at Sue Holcombe. Her grimace and rigid gestures seem charming to him. Even as her hard words ring in his ears he is inspired to interpret them to mean, "Fuck me! Fuck me, fuck me!" "Good idea," he breathes.

In an instant Carter has slipped off his sky blue bathing suit. Sue Holcombe's eyes widen, her frown darkens. "What is the meaning of this? I have never been so affronted!"

"Sue Holcombe," Carter murmurs. He stands before her and smiles gravely down at her. He reaches out to unbutton her dress. "Ruffian!" she screams.

How Sue fights now! kicking and pummeling, as Carter has his way with her here on her braided rug. She is not strong enough to hurt or resist him. Hot tears spurt from her angry face and she makes a horrible music with her shrieks. Carter has removed her dress, her ugly brassière and her prim cotton panties, and her Oxfords. In its rage her body reminds him of a child's. He pinions her arms against the rug and wedges one, two knees between hers. "Vile!" shouts Sue Holcombe as Carter's cock works gently into her vagina. She tries to bite his chin but he dodges. She spits in his face. "How dare you!" she says. She tries to foil him by thrashing this way and that but he follows her every move. Sue Holcombe grits her teeth, shudders, shakes her head. "This is appalling," she says.

Exhausted, she ceases to fight—what is the point?—and lies limp with eyes closed. Carter fucks beautifully with great concentration, lowering himself so that they touch and rub the length of their torsos, arching above her so that the island breeze passes between them, now thrusting like a machine, now slower and uncertainly, changing his tempo abruptly or gradually until he says, "Oooh, oooh, I'm coming." She feels his ejaculation. He kisses her on the shoulder and in a few minutes rolls onto his back. By this time it is almost dark here at the cottage.

It occurs to Sue Holcombe that since she has been raped she may now freely kill Carter with her shotgun. Two things restrain her. There would be a scandal, and also Carter has begun to talk and to say things that interest her. He lies with his hands behind his head and tells of life in the farmhouse and his adventures on the island. Sue Holcombe dons her clothes, lights a cigarette, sits in a Quaker rocker. He has much to say about Faye and Gail, their playing cards and Lethe Water, but Sue Holcombe is impatient for information about the farmhouse. With what subtlety she can muster she inquires about its construction.

"I don't know, it's an old place," Carter says. "You should ask Jimbo, he's seen the architect's drawings."

"*Where?*" Sue Holcombe gasps.

"I don't remember." Carter's thoughts wander. "Sue Holcombe," he says, "that lovemaking was far out, wasn't it?"

She hisses, "Out of my sight, out of my house, whatever your name is. Perhaps I won't have you prosecuted for the indignity you forced on me. But if you breathe a word of this monstrosity you'll be locked up before you can say Jack Robinson."

She sits alone in the dark. "*Jimbo*, is it? The creatures are playing right into my hands!"

Carter hears rustlings in the brush as of something accompanying him until he reaches the pasture at the farmhouse.

CHAPTER TWENTY-ONE

"Hi Jane." Jimbo waves to the dory riding far out on the gray water under an overcast sky. He has emptied trash and garbage into the tide that moves across the bottom of the island. Beer bottles and bright orange peels fan slowly toward open ocean, attracting gulls. Jimbo skips up the back porch stair. "Not especially clement, but especially beautiful," he says to the company lingering over breakfast. A second pot of coffee perks. Everyone is pleased to sit and talk while the wind rises outdoors. Each drinks coffee in his own way. Annabel suddenly as by a reflex lifts, sips, as her eyes move from face to face or are distant or thoughtful. Daisy cups her cup in both white hands. Thuggy, Carter, and Jimbo have their own distinctive manners. Thuggy has forgotten to comb his hair and Jimbo says it looks like monkey fur. "I had a dream last night about my father, but I can't remember it," Jimbo says.

"Want some dope?"

"Nope."

"I thought it would be warm here at all hours but after dark sometimes it's damn cold," Jimbo has once said. Now Daisy is knitting him a sweater with reindeer and snowflakes. Her needles click and flash.

"The stove feels good."

Thuggy says, "If I write a pornographic story, will you all read it?"

"Mmm, sure."

"I've never read any pornography," muses Annabel. "I suppose I should have." She hands a tray of bacon to Carter.

Carter winds the phonograph and lays on a thick old record. Bessie Smith sings, "You'll be my man or I'll have no man at all—there'll be a hot time in old town tonight."

"So . . ." Carter says, "I'd be delighted to read Thuggy's smut."

Jimbo says, "I was thinking about islands and shores. What you forget is that inside and outside depend on size. If this island were big enough we'd say it surrounded the ocean, rather than vice versa."

"Thuggy, I think you should put Rufus and Goose in your story," says Annabel.

"Them and Big Boy," says Carter, running his beautiful fingers through his beautiful hair.

Jimbo leaps up at this. He is by the window. "That reminds

me." He turns to regard them. "While you were playing hide-and-seek on the beach I came back and rode Big Boy."

The young people are still and then Thuggy says, "Congratulations."

"Of course you have a witness," says Annabel. "Otherwise it doesn't count. Not that we don't trust you, Jimbo."

"I do have a witness, and here she is now." He opens the door for Hester Geach.

"Goodness!" says Daisy.

"Who's that?" Hester wants to know, pointing at Carter.

"That's Carter," says Annabel. "This is Hester Geach, Carter. Isn't she pretty? Isn't Carter pretty, Hester?"

"Men aren't pretty. May I have a glass of milk?"

Jimbo says, "Sit beside me and tell these people about me and the bull."

Hester smooths her skirt, sips her milk, and begins. "Jimbo and I are friends. We walked in the woods and I picked a bouquet of dandelions for him. We went to sleep together and we played, too. We had fun, didn't we, Jimbo?"

"We certainly did. But tell about the bull."

"The bull's name was Big Boy. He frightened me but not Jimbo. Jimbo sat on the bull's back and rode on him like you ride on a horse."

"Where?" asks Carter.

Hester stares at him. It occurs to her that perhaps men can be pretty after all.

"Where, Hester?"

". . . in front of your barn." She glances up at Jimbo who nods in confirmation. She drinks some milk and continues, "The bull jumped around. Then Jimbo fell off on his head, but it didn't bleed." Everyone listens carefully, Daisy has dropped her knitting in her lap. Hester is pleased. Jimbo beams.

Annabel says, "What did you think of the bull's white face and his red body?"

"It was very nice—for a bull," Hester says. "Especially his white face. May I have some more milk?"

"But, but . . ." says Jimbo, wondering that this could happen so quickly. Annabel lifts her coffee cup with great precision. "You've made a real friend, Jimbo." Daisy, then everyone else begins to laugh. Hester is covered with shame that grows with the laughter. "Good-by," she says.

The laughter subsides. Jimbo says, "If the trick had worked, who would it have hurt?" When they all have wandered out of the room he says, "Besides, it hardly seems fair. *I* didn't see *them* ride that mother-fucker."

CHAPTER TWENTY-TWO

Toward twilight Sue Holcombe had an accident where a clump of poison ivy grew up more than ten feet beside a poplar in the woods not far from her cottage. She wore workman's gloves and carried scissors and an aluminum stepladder which she erected and mounted. She began snipping off the topmost sprigs of poison ivy. Her intention was to plant them irregularly about her cottage as a nuisance for visitors. She lost her footing, dropped her scissors, kicked over the ladder, and found herself suspended from a branch of the tree by the cross-straps of her jumper.

Meanwhile Hester Geach had taken a walk to mull over Jimbo's betrayal of her. Her lips moved as she turned the problem this way and that in her mind. She wondered whether Jimbo and his friends had conspired to make a fool of her or whether it had happened spontaneously. Nor could she understand why her mention of the bull's white face had prompted the hilarity. Hester's own face now turned red at the memory. She wondered whether her sister would have been treated so badly. And what did the prettiness of the one named Carter signify?

As she considered these matters Hester was, all unawares, in great danger. Babe, foraging down through the woods, had caught the smell of her tender flesh and followed it until now he lurked close alongside grinding his teeth, drooling, so excited he dug his ragged nails into his wrists. When Hester rounded the stand of ivy and came upon Sue Holcombe dangling from the tree, Babe's eyes narrowed with suspicion and hatred. He held still in the brush.

"What are you doing up there?" asked Hester.

"Come here, child," said Sue Holcombe.

"My name is Hester," said Hester without moving.

There was a pause.

Sue Holcombe restrained herself and said, "I'm pleased to meet you, Hester. My own name is Sue. Goodness, you've come along at an opportune time! I was standing on my ladder and it fell, you see, and my dress caught on this branch. Would you hand me the scissors, please? I've dropped them."

Hester came forward doubtfully. "Why were you standing on the ladder?"

"I was cutting sprigs of poison ivy. You see . . . you see, dear, it's poison and if it grew too tall it might make the little birdies' stomachs itch. Thank you, hold them just a bit higher, good."

Babe growls as the scissors pass from the child's hand into the woman's. He starts, his hackles rise when Sue Holcombe places the instrument behind her back and suddenly leaps down from the tree.

Hester smiles but Sue Holcombe is brushing herself off and starting to walk away. Hester says, "I'll bet you're glad I helped you."

"No, not in the least, child."

"My name is Hester!"

"I don't care what your nasty name is. You should be in bed at this hour and not wandering around like a tramp. I hate children. Sometimes I cut off their noses!" The scissors snap and swish in the moonlight. Babe from his hiding place and Hester from the clearing watch with awe. Babe panting, tongue lolling out, slips back and speeds away. Hester runs to the millhouse as fast as her legs can carry her. "Hmph," says Sue Holcombe.

Annabel was waiting on the cottage porch. "Wasn't I supposed to come at seven-thirty?"

"I doubt that you've been waiting long. If you have, let it be a lesson to you."

The music lesson began with Annabel's playing "Oats and Beans" from memory.

"Yes. Now tell me what you thought about as you played."

"My posture I guess. Keeping in tune . . ."

"Yes, you must always remember those things. But if you

want to approach being a musician you must use more of your mind, because what you're thinking about shows in the music. You might for instance have thought about an ear of oats and a bean. Or better a harvest festival with people clapping hands and doing rustic jigs. Even that would be rudimentary. I don't mind telling you these things because I know so much more about music than you that I couldn't transmit a tenth of it if I talked from now till doomsday. Anyway, you must try playing the song as you think about various sorts of things. The song will be different then though you may not notice the difference, insensitive as you are. Try it again now. And think about, oh, let me see—being chased by an old fat man."

The pitch was falser and a phrase was omitted but Sue Holcombe said, "You surprise me. So. Before your next lesson play 'Oats and Beans' fifteen times thinking of fifteen different things. Now scurry downstairs and brew us some tea."

In the parlor Sue Holcombe said, "Tell me, Annabel: who else lives in the farmhouse with you and Daisy?"

"Thuggy and Jimbo and . . ."

"Jimbo," interrupted Sue Holcombe. "That's an interesting name. Tell me about Jimbo. Whose beau is Jimbo?"

"Daisy's maybe? He's not mine. He's my cousin but I'd never met him before. You'd have enjoyed seeing him try to con us this morning." Sue Holcombe listened intently to the story and laughed when it seemed appropriate. "We decided he'd have to ride Big Boy in our presence since he's not quite trustworthy. The Fourth of July's the deadline. I wonder what he'll do. Sue?"

"I was thinking. Now, Annabel dear, you must be off. Let me say you are progressing. Modest as it sounds, it's nothing to be sneezed at: few of my students manage so much. Walk slowly as you leave. My yard is full of rabbit holes and you'll break your legs if you're not careful." She felt momentarily benign toward Annabel because the girl had provided information that ought to enable her, Sue Holcombe, to snatch the farmhouse from under the young people's feet, as it were.

CHAPTER TWENTY-THREE

At four o'clock in the morning Priscilla Geach rises from bed. She smooths her pale orange hair in the dark room. She walks down the hallway barefoot, wearing her short nightgown of fine silk. Still sound asleep she passes her children's rooms and the study where Jack is working. She descends the stairs and slips out into the night. Dear Priscilla is very beautiful now—her slender body moves with unwonted ease and grace. Though she is asleep her eyes are open. She walks away from the millhouse and its clearing, into the woods. The air is mild and the grass Priscilla walks on is wet with dew. Softly as she walks, her presence is known to creatures of the woods in a large circle around her. Many tiny ears perk up and many bright eyes regard her as she passes.

Down in a thicket with a grisly meal, scowling to recall Sue Holcombe's scissors, Babe hears and smells Priscilla coming. He drops the remainder of the carcass and begins to stalk her. In the moonlight the blood on his hands and face is black. Copious flows of saliva mingle with grease and scraps of flesh in his whiskers. After he has trailed her for a while and seen her between branches, he hurries ahead to a place of ambush where her path will turn. Here Babe crouches and waits. The small creatures who had quietened at Priscilla's approach are utterly silent and motionless around Babe.

When Priscilla rounds the turning of the path Babe leaps up before her, his broken teeth bared in a hideous snarl. Because he does not know whether his prey will rush into the undergrowth or back down the path or, knowing flight vain, try to attack, he waits with muscles tightened for whatever form her terror might take, not two yards away. Yet Babe finds no fear in Priscilla's wide-eyed direct gaze.

Priscilla doesn't see Babe at all. What she is seeing is a dream. She dreams that as she sleeps in her bed beside Jack someone taps on the window. When she opens it an old friend invites her to a "two-hundred-person party." The friend says, "You'd be a breath of fresh air, Priscilla." After a brief hesitation she decides to go. "How long has it been since I've been to a party that big?" She doesn't wake Jack or her children, both of whom, she notices, have worn red shoes to bed. "Come," her friend urges, "hurry, out the window."

Never in Babe's memory has confrontation with him so failed to produce any reaction. Mystified and awed, he backs out of the way to let Priscilla pass, which she does, leaving him to growl and wonder until hunger drives him to hunt other animals.

Sometimes dreaming, sometimes not, Priscilla continues her walk. She meets with no further adventure. Toward dawn she makes her way back to the millhouse, to the bed where she lies down and awakes. The night is turning into day. Priscilla thinks of her family—Hester who yesterday ran home with tales of a woman's cutting off her nose, little Edith who has developed a fretful longing to understand the card game Fish, and Jack who was still at work in his office.

CHAPTER TWENTY-FOUR

Lanterns and candles were lighted in the farmhouse living room. There the dogs were asleep and Jimbo and Daisy sat talking and sipping hashish from a gaudy water pipe. Daisy asked about Jimbo's travels. He conjured up any number of cities, towns, and countrysides and told of people he had met. Though Daisy found his tales disappointingly silly she enjoyed his excitement and eloquence. As the effect of the hashish increased, both minds wandered. There were long silences that might have been disconcerting without the drug. Neither Jimbo nor Daisy would have objected much if by some miracle they found themselves naked in a warm bed together. Jimbo wondered, "What would happen if I stood up nonchalantly, humming maybe, walked over and kissed her on the cheek?" and "Does she like to fuck?" and "Could I possibly figure out how—what—she thinks merely by watching her and listening to her?" Daisy unraveled a mistake in the reindeer sweater. Jimbo didn't yet know it was for him.

"Goose is chasing rabbits in her sleep." Goose made a soft "woof." Rufus's ears lifted.

"Good doggies," Daisy said. It seemed to Jimbo almost as if she meant herself and him. He laughed. Daisy gave a bright quizzical look.

"Good doggies." It was Carter in the doorway, brilliant and fresh from a night swim. ". . . I have some too?" Toke after deep toke and Carter seemed stoned as Daisy and Jimbo. "Ah . . ." Carter felt pleasant tinglings run over him. "What?" thought Jimbo.

"Hey man," said Carter, "why don't you . . . I mean why don't you play some guitar for us?"

Daisy nodded eagerly. Jimbo returned with the instrument and a record. "So you can hear a different interpretation of the same work." First Jimbo. He played well, he thought, surprising himself, and the drug made his audience follow the changes and reverses of the music closely. Then the record and without a performer to watch the music grew more vivid, especially the fingers sliding over the strings.

Daisy wanted to make a comment but forgot each that occurred to her before she could utter it. Carter looked at the photograph of the guitarist on the record cover. "Wonder how many copies of this there are in the world. He must have made other records too. And people who don't buy them have still heard of the guy, more all the time. Turn me on!" Carter luxuriated in the idea of the musician's fame.

Daisy said, "Some day the same thing might happen to Jimbo." Her expression said, "Why not?"

Jimbo blinked. "I doubt it. I never thought about it. If I were good enough I wouldn't mind. I'm really bad in some ways though."

"What ways?"

"For instance my slow tempi are mechanical. His aren't," pointing to the record.

"Copy his?"

"Mmm . . . And that way get to understand the underlying principles. Except I think it might not be very efficient or something."

"Efficient," purred Daisy. Here in the wavering golden light Jimbo's use of the word amused her.

Jimbo nodded. "Anyway I figure the whole point of music is that the underlying principles are devilishly obscure. If they were obvious, well, why bother?"

"Doesn't seem fair," said Carter.

"Sometimes I've thought there aren't any underlying principles. But I don't quite see what that would mean."

"Me neither." Carter moved so that his bare back rested against Jimbo's legs. "Get famous, Jimbo."

"Daisy? Look, Daisy's asleep."

"Oooh, Jimbo, doesn't she look good, good. Let's undress her without waking her up."

"Good idea."

"Think of balling with little Daisy, man!"

The boys watched the rise and fall of Daisy's splendid breasts. Jimbo didn't know what to make of the situation. "I'll put away my guitar and the record." When he was gone Carter stood, walked over to Daisy, and gave her a kiss on the cheek. "Too pretty to wake," he said. "So . . . so, how's about old Jimbo?"

When Carter had left the room Daisy's eyes opened. "I wasn't asleep at all," she said.

Upstairs Jimbo was undressing when Carter knocked on his door. "I come in, man?"

Surprised and pleased that Carter was being so friendly, Jimbo in his boxer shorts sat on the bed. Carter in his sky-blue bathing trunks leaned against the window sill. He said, "This farmhouse is a fucking big old house."

"You're okay, Carter." The window was open and a light warm breeze stirred in the room. Carter and Jimbo, stoned, smiled at each other.

"You like to play tricks," Carter said.

"Oh sure." Jimbo felt tongue-tied. He wondered what Carter was thinking.

"So anyway, man, let's you and me take our clothes off and get into bed together."

"Wow, Carter." A pause. "Are you sure?"

Carter shrugged. "I guess."

"Far out," said Jimbo. He was laughing.

Because Carter was very tired from swimming he fell asleep

soon as he lay down. Jimbo was a little relieved and a little disappointed. He extinguished the lantern and sat looking out at the waves until he too was sleepy.

CHAPTER TWENTY-FIVE

Old Jane and Thuggy went fishing before dawn. Feeling his way downstairs Thuggy had noticed light from the living room, peeped in, and seen Daisy there asleep on the sofa. The dogs woke and followed him to the kitchen where he fed them and himself. He and they trudged along the shore up to the boathouse. It was dark and foggy. Waves rushed loudly and mysteriously against the stone in Jane's harbor. She waited in her dory. Since with Thuggy rowing they made no progress, Jane took the oars. They dropped anchor near a mussel shoal. Jane had brought a flashlight. They baited their hooks with seaworms Jane had dug out of the mudflats at low tide yesterday. It was dark all around them.

Thuggy said, "I used to play with flashlights when I was a kid. I had to learn Morse Code in the Boy Scouts, so my buddy and I would go out at night and send messages. He'd be on one hill and me on the other."

Jane bent forward baiting the hooks. Her freckled hands were deft. Her shoes and Thuggy's scraped against the bottom of the boat when they dropped their lines over, hers to port, his to starboard.

Gray, blue, and yellow, dawn came and presently much of the fog lifted. "Hey," said Thuggy, "is this the shoal Jimbo and I ran aground on?"

"Same one. You were a mile or so farther down."

"When will the fish start biting?"

"There's no very good way to tell, Thuggy. We mightn't catch anything. Are you bored already?"

"Not me, Jane."

Today the waves were low and easy with no whitecapping. In the huge mild wash of air and sea water the boy and the old woman sat rocking in the little boat.

"Want a sandwich?" Thuggy withdrew a paper bag from the pocket of his jacket.

"Why, thank you. I see you're a born fisherman. Oh, peanut butter and jelly."

They ate the sandwiches and talked for a while. "You've got a bite, Thuggy," Jane said. It was a large mackerel.

Thuggy was delighted. "Should I hit him on the head?"

"No—he won't last long anyway out of the water. And you know they hardly feel any pain . . ."

Then Jane caught a fish. "Just my luck," she said, about to throw it back.

"Wait," Thuggy said, "he's big!"

"Why, it's only an old cod."

"Give it to me then—"

"Well. I don't know why anybody'd want an old cod in the summer though."

"I guess you're right." Thuggy tossed the fish overboard.

"Thuggy, why'd you take it into your head to come here this summer, anyhow?"

"No place else looked better."

"Daisy's not expecting to stay over winter, is she? Nobody's done that in years."

"No . . ."

"You know how to swim, don't you Thuggy?"

He kept a straight face. "I never tried it. If I fell in you'd have to rescue me."

"Don't hang over the edge that way then."

"I was looking for fish and . . . Yikes, Jane, what's that?" Gliding low through the grass, through the boat's shadow.

"Sand shark."

"But . . ."

"A biggish one. They don't much bother with people though." She pursed her lips and watched Thuggy watch the fish.

An hour later Jane said, "They're just not biting. Let's pull in our lines. No, no, I'll row. Teach you about that another time."

Nearing the dock Thuggy stood to wave to the dogs waiting there. Immediately Jane turned the dory so that he careened overboard. She quickly drew out of his reach.

"Help!" he laughed. "I . . . I can't swim."

"Time you learned," Jane called, rowing away toward shore.

Thuggy floated a few minutes and then struck out after her. Rufus leapt off the dock, swam out, and the two of them swam methodically back. "Rufus my friend, that's one foxy broad."

CHAPTER TWENTY-SIX

Through most of a sweet dappled morning Sue Holcombe works in a truck garden designed to attract rabbits. She wears sneakers, khaki trousers, a sleeveless blouse and canvas gloves, and a sunbonnet of starched cotton. Hoeing and mulching, she listens to the songs of a catbird in a tulip poplar. Later when she has put the hoe, rake, trowels, and bonnet and gloves in the shed, she brings her violin out onto the front stoop of her cottage and plays what the catbird sang, loudly and with great fidelity. When she has the bird's attention she improvises short passages which it tries to imitate, not always with complete success. Sue Holcombe is struck by the soullessness of its voice. She concludes the experiment by playing a not too difficult and musically absurd sequence several times, to fix it in the bird's repertoire.

Inside with a refreshing margarita and a cigarette she prepares herself a light lunch. According to her pedometer she has already today done movements equivalent to a nine-mile walk. As she eats she leafs through a mail-order catalogue and draws red circles around photographs of models wearing garments suitable for her fall wardrobe. Some of the models speak into telephone receivers, some glance at their wristwatches, many wave to friends not included in the photographs. They all smile inanely and eagerly. Sue Holcombe gazes at the page. She lights a cigarette slowly, and then she understands. Looking down at these animated faces is in fact like looking out at the younger but otherwise indistinguishable faces of the students who come to her lectures to learn about music at the college on the mainland.

Sue Holcombe is not yet ready for her daily violin practice. There are chores to do here in the long low kitchen. The knives haven't been sharpened this summer nor the collection of brass school bells polished. Such domestic work is tolerable, even pleasant, on occasion. Sue Holcombe could cite corroborative instances from lives of many great musicians. The brass polish is in the same drawer as the whetstone, along with twine, glue, screwdrivers, a hammer, and assorted nails. Outside the catbird sings the incongruous song Sue Holcombe has taught it. The violinist's bright eyes narrow, her narrow lips purse. Other catbirds will learn the song from this one, still others from those.

Knives are keen, bells shine. In the music room today Sue Holcombe will begin mastering a composition new to her. She studies it in the window seat. "A good piece of music," she thinks, "is a trap laid for the listener, and the wariest can be taken by any performer worth his salt." Poring over the music, making bowing and fingering notations between staves, she forgets herself and her surroundings. Time passes.

Rabbits thud over the ground outside, birds fly noisily past the window. No trespasser to be seen. "Must have been those damned curs of Daisy's. They ought to be poisoned." She lights a cigarette. "This is the last summer they'll set foot on this island."

Sue Holcombe thinks. Suddenly she hops down and runs across the hallway to her bedroom. "Of course! Of course!" When she has located a mirror in her vanity table she kicks off her sneakers, sheds trousers and underpants, and sits on her bed to examine herself in the clear light. It has occurred to her that the young rapist Carter may have given her a disease. "They all must be crawling with things, the way they live!" Fortunately a minute inspection reveals no symptoms. "So." Sue puts her clothes back on. "Nevertheless I'll fumigate the house when I've sent them packing. Excrement breeds vermin."

Sue Holcombe places sheets of music on a stand and opens her violin case. She dips a cotton swab in sweet oil to clean her ears before beginning to play.

CHAPTER TWENTY-SEVEN

Hester Geach couldn't sleep. There were no matches (they were forbidden) to light the lantern with. She dressed and slipped out into the still dimly lighted hallway. She knew her mother would have collapsed in bed or would be irritably sipping coffee down in the kitchen and that her father would be busy in his office. The ceilings of the hallway were high. Hester crept into her sister's bedroom.

As it happened Edith too was insomniac. She was thinking about the ladies she'd met by the wishing tree, and their game of Fish. Remembering the incident made Edith snivel angrily and toss and turn so that her bedclothes grew lumpy. She had been on the verge of a tantrum.

The sisters sneaked outside. They followed the millstream through meadows and woods to the shore. The tide was low. The girls jumped along boulders down the beach. At the bottom of the island they looked up at the high farmhouse with bright and dim yellow lamplight in many windows. They continued around the point and up the other side of the island until they came to the inlet where the boathouse is situated. They had never been here.

Jane was playing solitaire. Her hearing wasn't as keen as once but she had seen her cats perk up their ears and stare toward the windows. Unobtrusively she removed a flashlight from beneath the table and suddenly shined it out on the surprised and almost terrified children. She laughed and beckoned for them to come in.

"My, my, you must be the Geach girls. Would you like some hot cocoa? My name is Jane. Sit down and tell me your names. Isn't it past your bedtimes?"

Edith explained that since her birthday was imminent their mother had allowed them to be up later than usual. Hester hung back. The outcomes of her attempts to find an island friend had made her wary. But little Edith was aggressive. She wanted to know what Jane had been doing with the cards. The old woman dealt Crazy Eights hands. Edith's was best but the rules of the game mystified her and her strategies resulted in Hester's victory. Edith loured as Jane and Hester explained her errors. Jane dealt a second hand. "Arrange them according to suit, girls."

Edith looked at her cards for a moment and then threw them onto the worn-thin linoleum, snarling. "Cards are silly."

"Naughty!" said Jane. Edith wept. Jane said, "You must be

tired. Curl up in that easy chair and look at this picture book. Maybe you'll sleep." Intimidated, Edith obeyed. But she harbored a grudge. She peeked over the top of the book and imagined revenges like dousing the gray head with ink or muddy water. After her birthday she would wear new shoes and be treated with more respect. She fell asleep.

Hester was pleased by her sister's misbehavior and Jane's recognition of it. She was further pleased by Jane's continuing to talk and play card games with her for almost an hour. Then she was enchanted when Jane rowed her and Edith around the island in the moonlight to the mouth of the millstream. "Good night, girls. Come visit me again."

Safe on the shore Edith said, "I don't want to!"

"Well, maybe you'll come, Hester."

"Yes. I had a nice time. The cocoa was delicious. Good-by."

As they waded up the millstream Edith said, "She's not nice, Hester." Bemused by having at last apparently found an island friend of her own and wondering how she deserved such luck, Hester didn't reply.

Hours later old Jane had a nightmare. Her household goods had turned into newspapers and magazines. The light was dim. Uniformed men spoke of "contingency plans." Noticing Jane, one of them frowned and came to attack her with a broom. She woke amazed and trembling.

CHAPTER TWENTY-EIGHT

Storm clouds are blowing up from the horizon. The young people at the farmhouse play volleyball until it is too dark to see. Inside after their evening meal they settle down before the fire in the living room. Doors and windows are shut against a strong cold wind.

"Listen to it," says Jimbo. "Reminds me of winter before last." He tells of being lost at night in snowy streets among warehouses and vast discount drugstores. "I tried to relax to stop shaking." Daisy brings Scotch for everyone. Thuggy says, "Get some speed too, Daisy. It's a good combination for talking." People, dogs, and cats bask in the warmth. Annabel leafs through a magazine dated 1903. On its cover is a scroll with the words "A Journal of Civilization." An engraving of a musical instrument makes Annabel think of Sue Holcombe. "On my way from the well I almost tripped over her. She was on the ground looking at this house with binoculars. She said she was bird-watching." "Out of her head," muses Carter. "In some respects, certainly," says Annabel. She is beside him on the sofa and when she speaks she smiles at him as if to say, "There's no harm in my disagreeing with you, is there?"

Daisy pats Thuggy on the head. "By the way, you promised to write us some pornography."

Thuggy waits.

Daisy says, "I think you need incentive. A deadline, say. Say the Fourth of July." For various reasons the phrase lingers in people's minds.

Thuggy says, "As a matter of fact, I wrote some today."

"We want proof. Let's hear."

"It's not finished . . ." Thuggy takes a folded manuscript from his pocket.

Carter says, "Will it embarrass us?"

"Not me," says Daisy. Everyone finds comfortable listening positions and Thuggy reads the following:

> Mr. and Ms. Drake from America with their children Betsy and Ernie arrived one morning at a secluded château in the south of France. The Drakes were a handsome if middle-aged couple, both vigorous and athletic. The tall husband had dark wavy hair. Ms. Drake's pampered locks were ash-blonde. Their attractive children were approaching puberty. The family and their playful dog Rufus gleefully sprang from their Land Rover and ascended the broad steps to the château. In the entrance hall they were greeted by Madame Encore, who lisped in fluent English, "You must be my guests the Drakes. Come in the salon." The portly Madame summoned her swarthily leering servant Lelouch to remove the Drakes' luggage.
>
> Mme. Encore was an expert hypnotist. With a snap of her fingers she mesmerized the Drake family as they entered her lavishly appointed salon, making them believe

they had become statues temporarily. Even the dog Rufus fell under her spell. "Now Lelouch," she laughed, "bring me a *vin ordinaire* and then make an inventory of their possessions. Meanwhile I shall deal with them."

The pale buxom Frenchwoman quickly undressed Ms. Drake, murmuring "Mon Dieu" as she released the shapely breasts from the imprisonment of their brassière, and as she slipped down Ms. Drake's expensive panties and ran her fingers over the exuberant pelt. "Very interesting," murmured the Madame, sipping her wine. "And now for the handsome Monsieur," she smirked as she removed his three-piece suit and other clothing. "*Formidable!*" she gasped, kneeling before him to examine his virile crank. In a trice she had taken it in her mouth and given him a passionate fellatio. Patting her lips with a lace *mouchoir*, she turned to the immobile siblings and purred, "Your turns will come, my sweets." With these words she waddled from the room.

Everyone begins to applaud but Thuggy says, "Wait, there's more." He pulls another scrap of paper from his pocket and reads:

That evening the hostess herself was the victim of a trick. As she bent over her stove Lelouch lifted her skirt and began to caress her surprisingly bare buttocks. "Wicked servant," she teased, alternately pursing and shaking the fleshy cheeks and bending further to expose her moistly sophisticated labia majora. "What do you await?" she yelped. Whereupon the impudent Lelouch snatched a highly seasoned *chorizo* from a nearby table and plunged it into the Madame's eager orifice, twirling and vibrating it. "Excellent!" screamed Madame Encore. But after her climax her spirits were dashed when Lelouch, chuckling uproariously, explained, "You have been fucked by a sausage!"

"Are my ears red?" asks Daisy.

"You know, man," says Carter, "you could probably get that published."

"It's fun to write. I was in the hammock, writing it word by word, taking my time. That's the secret of it. I took my time." Cross-legged on the rug, Thuggy smiles like a clever Buddha.

Daisy is thinking. "He couldn't publish it without our consent. He wrote it for us, so it belongs to us all."

It is after midnight. Very loud music from the phonograph fills the room so that everyone can be in sight and near and yet quite private conversations can take place. There is laughter, dancing, clapping of hands. The dogs wake and retreat. Sometimes the music is beautifully precise, at other times it is hardly noticed. When anyone leaves the room others feel a pang of loss. When Daisy says, "I have to wash my hair," and prances away, Jimbo wonders if there is an implied criticism, and whether he should follow.

Alone in the shower Daisy washes her hair and then her whole plump body, often bursting into fits of tittering—watching her toes wiggle like a family of animals at play in the rain, or as she thinks of Jimbo abashed to be caught out in a lie. When she returns to the living room aglow and still damp she is eating chocolate cake.

Annabel hardly knows what to do next. She is beside Carter on the sofa and her heart pounds when she considers trying to seduce him. "You're a coward if you don't, now that you've thought of it," she tells herself. She turns to him and says, "Do you think I'm a coward?"

"Not a chance."

"I am, anyway." Her mind is racing but to Carter she looks so still and thoughtful he laughs aloud. Annabel thinks, "He merely looks like a god, he can't help it." He shrugs as if he has read her thoughts. She whispers in his ear, "Listen, I feel extremely fine. I'm going to get a glass of apple juice."

CHAPTER TWENTY-NINE

Having effected step two of phase three of his plan in spite of unforeseen complications, Jack Geach walks in the woods for relief. Overhead the bright moon breaks irregularly through clouds. Thundering from the open sea. Jack would not mind if the storm moved in over the island and drenched him. His most recent dose of Dexedrine makes the sharp cold pleasant. Jack knows it is well past midnight. Perhaps, he thinks, the rising sun will find him outdoors. How wholesome and varied he finds his life! "One day when somebody is writing my biography I'll have to be sure to remember to tell him about tonight. People would be grateful to know what zestful pleasure I took in simply walking. It would show how confident I was, like a noted general on the eve of a great battle, really, I guess." Jack felt at ease even though the fatigue and amphetamine made him so jittery he flinched when his passage started rabbits in the underbrush. When he stumbled over a dark body in the path he trembled and laughed for a moment and then angrily he said, "Jesus! What the hell's going on here?" Then, bending and peering, "Oh, it's you, Annabel. Can I help you up or anything? Are you all right?"

Annabel had heard Jack's approach and trembled herself, expecting Carter. "Hello, Jack. I was walking and I sat down to think."

"Oh! I see. Well, I'll leave you to your ruminations . . ." The bright moonlight falls on them. On Annabel's strong cheekbones Jack sees tears sparkle and in her hand he sees an odd cigarette. He sits beside her and says, "My goodness, Annabel, that's not a joint is it?" frowning authoritatively.

"Yes, it is."

"Are you an addict?"

She smiles, brushing away her tears. "This isn't addictive."

"Oh, I thought it was." They are in darkness. "Are you going to smoke it?"

"Yes, I was going to. It's . . . soothing."

Jack peers at Annabel's face when she ignites her cigarette lighter. If someone else came walking would he be implicated in Annabel's illicit activity? Would his career be endangered? Such considerations make him smile and shrug. Fascinated, he sits so still that Annabel forgets his presence until the next space of moonlight. "Would you like to smoke some, Jack?"

"Why not?"

The marijuana makes Jack loquacious. "Sometimes, Annabel, I don't know what to think about the way things are going nowadays. There seems to be so much immorality around! Things aren't at all the way they were when I was your age. With young people, I mean, and sometimes I'm deeply troubled about Hester and Edith. I make a great deal of money, and of course I'll make more and more—I'm not bragging, at least not without good reason. I don't mind saying that I have good reason to be proud. Where was I?"

"Hester and Edith?"

"Yes. Sometimes, Annabel, I'm gravely disturbed by the rampant immorality and lack of ambition in young people today. I make a great deal of money. I can afford to protect Hester and Edith, I can give them the best protection money can buy, but still sometimes in spite of myself I grow grumpy. Still, they're children, aren't they? Sometimes I think I'm happiest when I'm playing with them. I wish they were here now."

"To see you smoking pot?"

"Of course not!"

"How do you feel?"

"I'm not sure . . ."

"The first time it's usually hard to recognize the effect. You've smoked a lot though and it's strong, so you should be fairly high. Does my voice sound strange, does time seem to be moving oddly?"

". . . yes . . . and, and the . . . snow . . ." Jack feels as if he is younger than his own children. Where there is grass, stone, earth, he sees snow. He sees snow lying in high drifts beside the path and half covering Annabel's extended legs. "It's beautiful, with the moonlight. I think there's been a blizzard."

Annabel half closes her eyes. "The well is frozen of course, the millstream. The rabbits are eating snow and red berries. And yet you know, Jack, I don't feel the least bit chilly. It must be the marijuana."

"She's amusing herself at my expense," Jack thinks. The snow has disappeared. Jack and Annabel feel small in the blustery darkness under the rushing clouds.

CHAPTER THIRTY

Although through the night Sue Holcombe had been in her parlor smoking and drinking coffee, her eyes were bright as ever. With wonderful economy and inventiveness she had selected first one and then another piece from the waste of information given her by Carter and Annabel, to construct a sort of malign sonata of schemes. She had worked backward from the desired end, her possession of Daisy's farmhouse. "But how to begin it, how, how?" She ground her small teeth. Then, as if she were being rewarded for protracted thought, she saw Edith Geach run into the clearing. The child wore a yellow mackintosh and a red fireman's hat. Under the clouded sky her colors were intense against the green grass and foliage. Sue Holcombe nodded, frowning and smiling at the same time.

In her doorway Sue Holcombe called, "Come here, Hester dear!" Edith ran forward. Sue Holcombe said, "Don't worry, I won't cut your nose off. Come inside and have a nice cup of tea."

"I'm not Hester, I'm Edith. Hester's only my sister."

"So much the better. Come in out of that wind."

Edith removed her coat but not her hat. Sue Holcombe said, "I want you to help me play a trick on somebody. It will be loads of fun."

Sue Holcombe knew very well that a child's judgment is imperfect, yet she supposed no mishap would occur. It turned out to be easy to persuade Edith, to whom the plan seemed a chance for good revenge. Skipping through the woods Edith was maliciously happy. Her eyes shone beneath the brim of her hat. The fine rain made the grass slip under her tiny feet.

In the boathouse kitchen window she saw Hester and old Jane playing cards. Edith was angry and jealous! She ran through wet underbrush and began to crawl toward the house—small though she was, had she approached upright she would surely have been noticed, so brightly costumed. At last, flattened against the wall she stood on tiptoe, snatched the bottle of Lethe Water off the window sill, and tucked it into the pocket of her mackintosh. Her heart pounded.

Again in the woods and safe (as she supposed) Edith paused

to examine the pretty bottle with its faintly violet liquid, a teaspoonful of which would have given her a quick and painless death. Sue Holcombe's design would have been marred, but no evidence would link the tragedy to the violinist. Indeed the main responsibility would devolve on old Jane for her not having better safeguarded the dangerous drug. Luckily Edith returned the bottle unopened to her pocket and scampered on toward Sue Holcombe's cottage through the rain, hooting to provide a siren for the fire truck she seemed to be riding. Sarcastic laughter came from glistening crows along her path.

Sue Holcombe pretended to be displeased. "This isn't the right bottle. I wanted the other one."

"There was only one!"

"Ah," thought Sue Holcombe. She said, "Yes there was another. You've made a terrible mistake. Everyone will be angry if they find out. Your mother and daddy will spank you within an inch of your life. I suppose I won't tattle. But you mustn't say a word about this, not even to your sister. Oh, it frightens me to think what people would do to you if they knew. Now run away, fast as you can!"

Edith sped across the grass, her siren wailing.

Sue Holcombe felt as if the farmhouse were already hers. Even the fact that her plan would necessitate giving unexpected aid to someone, even this failed to dampen her spirits.

CHAPTER THIRTY-ONE

In the parlor at the farmhouse this June evening Daisy, Thuggy, and Carter are playing Chinese checkers before the fire. Jimbo chews a pencil and then writes in a notebook,

1. Islands & shorelines. Boundaries, relativity of being surrounded or contained, etc.
2. Dictionaries and the game of Telephone.
3. Taste—"good taste," etc.

He scratches his head and thinks, watching the flames, how they respond slightly to violent changes in the wind above. Goose's black muzzle peeks from under the sofa.

Daisy's belly has begun to shake. "Carter's headed toward the wrong triangle! You smoked too much dope, Carter."

Impassive, Carter says, "I did it on purpose."

Footsteps on the porch. Annabel sweeps in with rain on her brown hair.

"Whatcha been up to, kid," says Thuggy.

"Don't ask. I went for a walk and who should I run into but Jack Geach. What with one thing and another I gave him a joint (he'd never had any)." As she talks Annabel hardly notices anyone but Carter whose skin in the firelight seems a richer honey color. "He couldn't recognize the effect so he got stoned without realizing it. Then what do you suppose?" All wait. "He started to get *fresh*. He looked down, he looked up, he chuckled to himself. He shrugged, he sighed, he leered, and then he looked me in the eye and said, 'How about a roll in the hay?' I couldn't believe my ears. With him? I jumped up and ran here. I think he was chasing me. Imagine!" When she laughs she forgets even Carter. Everyone laughs. "But I left another joint there in the grass and if he smokes it too he might pass out and catch cold or something and then they won't let me do their housecleaning any more. Oh, I forgot, he offered to pay! In fact I think I still . . ." From the pocket of her shirt she pulls what proves to be a twenty-dollar bill. She tosses it onto the low table beside the Chinese checker board. "He shoved it in there and I didn't have a chance to return it."

Daisy looks grave. "What will you say when you see him?"

Thuggy stretches his legs. "You shoulda balled him, kid."

"Are you a virgin, kid?" asks Carter. Thuggy's ears perk up though he looks absent-mindedly into a bouquet of wild roses. As for Annabel, after a pause she says quietly, "I don't feel like answering silly questions just now, please." When Carter blushes she leans down and kisses him on the cheek. Everyone is bemused until Daisy gasps, "Thuggy!" for he is lighting a joint with Jack Geach's twenty-dollar bill. Annabel says, "Oh dear, now I suppose I'll have to come across."

Rain splatters against windowpanes. Rufus wanders in and flops down near Goose. He glances at her, at the people, back at her. Daisy feels content. She says, "Jimbo? What did you do tonight? Speed?"

Jimbo adjusts his spectacles. "Some coke. There were things I wanted to think about."

"?"

"I haven't finished. But dictionaries for instance."

". . . ?"

"Their drawbacks. For instance, because of them people don't need to ask each other what words mean." In the large old farmhouse the young people listen to Jimbo. "Then there's the fact that they're awfully nationalistic. Dual-language ones are better but I think the best might be to have lexical entries in one language like English and definitions in all languages at random.

"Another thing I don't like is that they're automatically conservative, the ones that try not to be more so than those that don't. And then there's this: why should I assent to the massive and innumerable assumptions about the nature of language embodied in dictionaries? They might all be correct but when you stop to think about it the chances are pretty overwhelmingly against it."

Annabel has been considering. "If we only found out definitions by word of mouth it would be like that game of Telephone or Chinese Whispers. Each time the meaning would change a little until finally it would be completely different. Well?"

Jimbo nods. "Exactly. Or at least maybe. Because passing along a message isn't the same as passing along a definition. There are no constraints beyond intelligibility on messages, but the meaning of a word has to jibe with the meaning of all words. All other words in all languages, really. But suppose it did happen like in Telephone. That might not be so bad. Nobody knows what words mean anyway. Did you ever read a newspaper?"

Daisy is munching a chocolate bar. "That reminds me of the last time those rough boys from the mainland sailed out and broke people's windows. I was playing Chinese Whispers then. Goodness, I hope they don't come this summer."

"Thuggy'd defend us," says Annabel. Thuggy only half hears. Stoned, he is dreaming of his dirty story. In his mind's eye he sees Mme. Encore on a steep hillside above a lake remove her last article of black-lace underclothing and lie back on the French grass. Lelouch leaps from behind a tree and mounts her.

But as he is about to enter her the crafty Madame executes a backward somersault and Lelouch tumbles down the hill and into the lake. "In this way," Thuggy thinks, "Mme. Encore had her revenge for the trick Lelouch played on her with the sausage."

CHAPTER THIRTY-TWO

All afternoon old Jane had been in some perplexity. The Geaches had returned from shopping on the mainland and brought the island mail, including a letter for Jane. It was from Jane's old friend Charlotte and announced that she had the unprecedented intention of arriving on the island for a visit. The news had displeased Jane and her displeasure had troubled her. Finally she had decided that instead of worrying about the matter she would bake a pie.

Near Jane's boathouse are three mulberry trees. She had spent the overcast dusk there filling a wicker basket, taking care not to let the fruit stain her dress with its indelible carmine. She had constructed the pie with extraordinary slowness. Now it was in the oven baking. Jane had lighted a lamp. She sat in a Morris chair beside her kitchen table. The boathouse is too near the shore for fireflies to frequent it, but Jane could see some of them among the branches of the mulberry trees. Jane's hands lay on the old oak. The diamond of her engagement ring twinkled. Even as a child Jane had disliked diamonds, finding them unfriendly and not quite in good taste, but when John had presented her with the ring she had simulated delight. Years later she had revealed her true feelings about the gem to him and yet, in spite of his occasional protests, she had worn the ring until his death and ever since.

Jane thought: the reason I don't want Charlotte to come is that I'm happy as a clam to have a life behind me. I know by now, thank heavens, what I want to remember and think about. If Charlotte comes she's sure to start talking about people I forgot twenty years ago. Yes but Janie (she thought), you *have* invited her and if she has no more sense than to accept after all this time you're going to have to ride it out. Might do you good. "In a pig's eye," she said.

Jane's hands were still lovely, she thought. Rowing had calloused her palms and her strength was perfectly evident, but the long fingers were graceful and the nails like those of a girl.

"Gracious!" Jane hurried to the oven as best she could. Only the edges of the crust were burned. "Well, then." She placed the pie on the window sill to cool and was turning away when with a start she noticed the absence of the bottle of Lethe Water. Could she have knocked it to the floor? Apparently not. Outside below the window? In a cold raw wind she held a lantern and poked among the seagrass with her cane. Nor here. One hand on her cane, the other holding the lantern, Jane stood beside her house before a high moonstruck sea frowning darkly.

She had never used the anodyne but tonight in her bed, gasping from pain in her old legs, she wanted it.

CHAPTER THIRTY-THREE

Around the shore and high overhead the night wind is blustery but the air is calmer in the interior of the island in places like this secluded valley where Faye and Gail have a cheerful campfire. Look, how their dark eyes gleam. Listen, how their voices interlace sweetly:

> Froggie went a courtin' and he did ride,
> Mmm hmm,
> Sword and pistol by his side,
> Mmm hmm. . . .

Gail sits with her chin on her knees, a bottle-green silk shawl around her, her feet peeking out. Faye reclines against a fallen tree with honeysuckle on her yellow dress and in her hair. Near the fire are a clay bowl of strawberries, a willow branch, and a chased silver pipe. "My dear . . ." Gail says.

Jack Geach comes stumbling down the hill into the circle of firelight. "Oh, I thought this was a house. Well! Are you girls camping out? Say, whose property is this, anyway? I seem to have lost my way." Jack sits jauntily on the grass. "You must be friends of Annabel's, no doubt. Sweet girl. Works for me." Jack is about to introduce himself and explain that he is spending the summer managing huge financial transactions from the mill-house but, as sometimes happens because of strong marijuana, he finds himself unable to articulate anything. He thinks, "There are so many . . . choices." He feels not at all frightened but rather a bit puzzled, looking from one girl to the other, smiling at them as if they understood his difficulty. He isn't frightened and yet for a moment the actuality of other people strikes him like a new discovery. He wonders whether he might have fallen in love with these girls, they seem so beautiful. Have they been talking together or to him?

From beneath her shawl Gail holds out three playing cards, deuces of spades, clubs, and hearts. "Two black, one red." She exhibits them to Faye and Jack. "Keep your eye on the red card." She lays them face down in a row on the grass and then shifts them back and forth, one over the other. "Who knows where the old red card is? Who'll lay five on the old red card?"

"I will!" Faye slaps a five-dollar bill on one of the cards. "No!" thinks Jack, "it's the middle one!" He proves right. Gail takes the money under her shawl and begins shifting the cards again. "Where's the old red card? Watch him dance . . ."

"There!" says Faye, halting the movement with a ten-dollar bill. This time she wins. Though Jack finds it suspiciously easy, he now stops the play with a ten-dollar bill. "Wait!" says Gail, "thirty says it's this one. Match or out." Jack complies—how can he lose? But as it happens neither he nor Gail has won. Faye sweeps the money under her shawl. "Where's the old red card, where's he hiding?" Jack searches his wallet. "I thought I had another twenty."

The cards disappear under the green silk. "Better luck next time," says Faye, "and don't forget: it's only money." Her voice is so light and kind that Jack smiles and nods in agreement. "Nice meeting you."

Alone and lost again in the dark woods, dear Jack is of two minds. One perplexes itself more each second, thinking, "There's no need to be the least tiny bit disturbed by the loss of a mere thirty dollars! Why, compared to the extremely vast sums I enjoy managing every day, why, it's laughable and silly, really. Ha, ha: it makes me laugh. If *I* can't afford to laugh at such things, I'd like to know who can! A sense of perspective is an essential ingredient of success in high finance, for sure. And perspective is certainly a two-edged sword. For instance, even if I amass a million dollars before I'm thirty-six, there will still be men who have more than I do! Wait, how can I have overlooked this? There must be an answer that great financiers down through history have known. But what is it? I wish I had talked with those girls about the matter, to clarify my ideas. I'll have to remember to discuss it with Priscilla."

Jack's other mind merely records with an impassive happiness. In the darkness, how much peripheral vision takes in. How skin responds to noises. Heavy cold air falling into lungs. How the path rises and falls.

CHAPTER THIRTY-FOUR

It is wonderful and agreeable that as Jack Geach has these adventures and many others in the night he should have been in mortal danger from the terrifying Babe who has lurked near and a hundred times been on the verge of attack—and, had he attacked, there would have been no hope for Jack. But now Babe veers down toward the bottom of the island, out of the woods, half leaping, half crawling across the pasture to the farmhouse. A fine rain has darkened his mane and his yellow eyes gleam. He is near the farmhouse. The wind carries his rank scent away from the lighted house to the dark barn. A gray cat awakes and flees to the hayloft. Big Boy looks up, paws the ground and rams his head against his stall door. The noise and Babe's stench go together away from the island and join other sounds and odors over the wide sea. Babe glares up at the farmhouse windows.

Inside the young people and the dogs are together before a lively fire. Thuggy has read aloud a new segment of his obscene story, lying on the sofa. Carter sits on the floor nearby. In one old chair is Jimbo. Annabel and Daisy are near the fire. Annabel is combing Daisy's long hair to help it dry. Daisy's hair is so beautiful that Annabel will now drape it fondly over her wrist, now give it a tug that makes Daisy wince.

Carter is thinking of Thuggy's story. He has laughed at it less than the others. Yawning and twisting, stretching his arms over his head, he notices that Thuggy has an erection under his baggy trousers. "Far out," thinks Carter. His hand falls as if by accident on Thuggy's penis and then moves away. Thuggy chuckles, rumples Carter's golden hair.

Jimbo with his bright eyes behind flashing spectacles has observed this with some astonishment and much curiosity. When Carter's eyes meet his, Jimbo can think of nothing to do but return Carter's friendly smile. Daisy sings a pretty song and everyone is pleased, especially Jimbo.

"I have to pee," says Carter. The wind outside is chilly and the moon is bright. Carter stands at the edge of the porch to pee. He gazes over the fields at the dark woods, still thinking of Mme. Encore. His penis grows in his hand and then shrinks. If Carter looked down his hair would stand on end. He would see Babe crouched in the grass with saliva cascading down his beard. Carter's pee curves and sparkles over the railing.

"Hey Carter, come in!" calls Daisy, and Carter re-enters the house. "I want to play Chinese Whispers," Daisy explains. "Go there between Annabel and Jimbo, good. That's right. Everybody has to whisper what he hears to the next in line, and immediately. No waiting, no asking for a repetition. Ready?" Rufus is sleeping but black Goose with her muzzle on her forepaws looks up at the young people's faces.

"Ready, Thuggy?"

Between cupped hands Daisy whispers "I like funny boys" into Thuggy's ear. He whispers "Light and thundery" to Annabel, who in turn whispers "Hi, me puppy" to Carter. Carter whispers "I'm impulsive" into Jimbo's ear. Jimbo shouts, "What? I can't hear you." His eyes are closed.

"Too bad, you'll have to guess," says Daisy. But Jimbo doesn't hear her for he has fallen asleep. He shouts again, "Speak up!" Everyone watches Jimbo. What Jimbo watches in his sleep is his kindly father struggling to make himself heard. Jimbo puts his ear near the old lips and at last hears his father urge, "*Ride that bull, son!*" Jimbo opens his eyes, sees his friends' faces and remembers the dream. "Okay then," he thinks, "so I have to. I will then." "I was dreaming," he explains foggily, "and I remember it. I need to think," wandering toward the stairs.

"How funny!" exclaims Daisy.
Thuggy nods thoughtfully.

CHAPTER THIRTY-FIVE

At dawn it was still blustery. The sky was red between dark cloud banks. "But will he bite?" Sue Holcombe asked herself. "If he had a brain in his head he would. But I can't depend on that with these creatures! The bait is perfect, but how to present it? *How?*" All night she had worried the question, pacing in every room of her cottage, and then through the woods, and finally here on the thin beach near the boathouse harbor, below high-tide line in damp sand and sharp blue mussel shells, frowning and smoking.

When old Jane's dory bobbing at anchor caught Sue Holcombe's eye she threw her cigarette onto the sand and thought, "Hmm . . . I wonder. When I've evicted those pests from the farmhouse I must try to do something about the boathouse. Even if it isn't quite mine by rights, I should be able to use the farmhouse as collateral to evict Jane. It would be for her own good. She's much too old to live out here alone. Better a home on the mainland! Well, one step at a time. The farmhouse first. *Will this Jimbo bite?*"

Jane also had been awake all night. She had tried to sleep and finally she too had come out to walk on the beach. Movement relieved the pain somewhat. She walked with two canes. It hardly seemed fair that now, when she would have used the Lethe Water, it had disappeared. She wondered whether Faye and Gail had known she wasn't using it and had retrieved it to give to someone who might need it more.

The paths of old Jane and Sue Holcombe crossed here in the lurid dawn. Each was surprised to see the other.

"I was just thinking about you, Jane," said Sue Holcombe. "How do you feel?"

"Not too bad. How are you, Sue?" Jane sat down slowly on a large rock.

Why was it, Sue Holcombe wondered, that she felt so strong an inclination to perch on the same rock with the old woman and chat? in spite of the habitual bridling standoffishness she also felt. "A musician who disregards his whims is only a music box," she sometimes explained to her students. Now she thought, "In fact, I must remember this moment as a scenic and emotional analogue for bars ten through eighteen of the second movement, the passage no one has done well" (she was thinking of the concerto she was scheduled to perform in the fall). She said, "How's the fishing, Jane? I haven't been out." Shrewd bright eyes looked into shrewd bright eyes.

"Better than last year, when they're biting," said Jane. "The cowyard still seems the best place. Don't want the trouble, though, you can get something now and then off the steps here."

"Thank you. I might well."

"Yes indeed," said Jane.

After a few minutes Sue Holcombe lit a cigarette and said, "We certainly have our quota of strangers this summer! The people in the millhouse and then that horde of ragamuffins with Daisy." She clucked and shook her head as though perturbed. "The girl Annabel has some redeeming qualities. She's been studying violin with me. Of course she's been late for every lesson. But she does apply herself, and that's more than I can say for nine tenths of my spoiled students on the mainland."

"I'd imagine. Well, I haven't met Mr. and Mrs. Geach but their children come to see me. I like them both, even that naughty Edith." Jane smiled. Sue Holcombe said nothing. Jane went on, "I don't know all the youngsters at the farmhouse. Yes, I guess they must be more shiftless than you or I were at that age. Some of them aren't the best sailors in the world." She described her rescue of Thuggy and Jimbo. "But they did seem nice enough, especially young Thuggy. He's been out fishing with me. I don't know Annabel. And there's one more besides Daisy, isn't there? A nice-looking blond boy. Well, I guess there's room for them and more too in the farmhouse."

Sue Holcombe shivered, staring at old Jane in the dim light.

Jane said, "We mustn't lose our heads, Sue."

CHAPTER THIRTY-SIX

Carter sleeps, his hands loosely opened, his knees apart, dreaming a lascivious and musical dream as if outside time. A gull alights on the window sill. It regards Carter with its fierce eye, screams, waking him, and flaps away. Gradually Carter is aware of his surroundings. "Mmm," stretching, resting weight on various muscles.

In the kitchen Daisy, Annabel, and Jimbo are finishing breakfast. Carter eats eggs with gravy and drinks hot cocoa.

"Where're you going, Carter?"

"Walking. See you later, sweethearts."

Their smiles are so radiant that, once out of the house, Carter considers returning to flirt with them. But the hot soothing sun entices him into the woods to a clearing where he lies on the grass and falls asleep again. When he wakes shadows are long, the air is milder, and Hester Geach is watching him.

"You were talking in your sleep!" She giggles.

Carter approves of her sudden movements, her small hands. "What did I say?"

"I don't remember."

Carter admires her mischief. "Tell me."

"If you can remember my name."

"Hester."

"That's right. Well, what you said was silly. You said, 'Hand me the towel.' "

Carter is enchanted with the little girl. He thinks she will grow into a beautiful woman yet he finds her perfect now. For the first time in his life he is understanding how urgent a child's innocence can be. The long dark grass cushions Carter's naked back and Hester's naked legs. "Our skin's the same," he thinks. He says, "Hand me the towel, Hester." She gives him a clump of grass, he gives it back. "Dry me off," he says, "I just took a shower."

Solemn and dazed, Hester Geach kneels and bends to rub the grass over Carter's torso which unlike her father's is hairless except for the line running from his navel down into his dungarees. She dries the light fine hair in his armpits. The crumpled grass has begun to stain Carter. Hester rubs it on her own arms to stain and perfume them. "I took a shower too," she mutters.

"I might catch cold if you don't dry my feet." She brushes back her pigtails to concentrate. The grass towel works between toes, over ankle bones, up onto the soft worn denim. "He's silly to wear his blue jeans in the shower," Hester thinks. Carter watches merely waiting, his face like an angel's. The grass is on his knees, it is on his thighs.

Then Hester says, "What's that?"

"Don't you know?"

Now Carter thinks he may have let things go too far. In the back of his mind he seems to hear, "You'll be locked up before you can say Jack Robinson." But now such a spiteful hissing interests Carter not at all. A familiar daredevil mood comes over him. He thinks, "Anyway she's only a child and anyway I *like* her, little pretty Hester, she's the prettiest child I ever saw, goddamit."

Hester says, "No, I don't. What is it?"

"Hester, it's my dick, sweetheart. Haven't you ever seen a boy naked?"

"Does 'dick' mean 'penis'?"

"That's right, 'penis.' "

"I saw a little boy's once, but . . ." She tilts her head and taps with her forefinger against her temple.

"Dry it off too, and I'll explain."

"Why did you wear your pants in the shower, I wonder."

When Carter has removed his jeans Hester, patting and rubbing grass obediently, listens to his explanation. Accurate as it is, it contains many incomprehensible terms and Hester hesitates to ask their significance. All of this is agreeable and interesting to her. But when Carter's breathing alters, when his large hand massages her buttocks, when his penis begins to jerk, Hester is appalled and tongue-tied.

"Baby," says Carter, "oh baby," and this raises Hester's confusion to such a pitch that she sprinkles the bruised grass blades over him and hurries home.

CHAPTER THIRTY-SEVEN

Thuggy and Faye and Gail had not met, but he had heard of them and they of him so that introductions were brief when he chanced upon them one afternoon in the woods. He had spied them through an opening in the foliage and joined them where they sat in a mossy place near a stone fence. On a mat of woven straw rested a glass-and-silver serving tray holding three tulip-shaped dishes of pineapple sherbet. The sherbet was delicious, especially for Thuggy who had smoked a fat reefer not long before. "Outta sight," he said, "better than anything I ever tasted. Twice as good."

"What was next best?"

"A chile relleno once. I didn't think it would ever be topped. Hey, is that poison ivy?"

"It is." Rich deep masses spilled over the wall.

Thuggy wondered whether his being somewhat younger than the girls might be a mark in his favor. "We'll see," he thought. They were certainly lovely and desirable. There were rings on their long fingers. Despite the heaviness of the air they looked dewy and fresh.

Faye's hair was caught up in a white fillet from which some tendrils had escaped. She wore an embroidered muslin smock gathered loosely at her waist, falling to midthigh. The laces of her sandals were wrapped and knotted over the foot and up around ankle, shin, and calf. On her wrist was a bracelet of acorn caps with a pendant gold doubloon. She opened and closed a carved ivory fan. Gail's bare feet showed under the deep hem of a gray-and-plum striped satin skirt at the waist of which hung a silver cocaine spoon. Above, she wore what seemed to Thuggy a beaded bib. It lay wonderfully over her breasts and moved when she moved. Her bright hair fell over her shoulders. The play of her liquid glances and Faye's took the boy's breath away. A corncob pipe lay on the moss.

A blue lizard ran along the wall. Blackbirds on a thin branch were hopping sideways, preening and casting sharp skeptical looks everywhere, as if without their vigilance something might get out of hand.

Thuggy asked Gail and Faye if they wanted to see a one-eared elephant.

"What do you mean?" Gail asked.

Thuggy shrugged.

Faye said, "I don't believe it's ever occurred to me."

"Nor to me," said Gail. "Is it something you, Thuggy, would enjoy seeing?"

Thuggy laughed. "Just say yes or nod," he said and when they had complied, "Watch." His left hand went into his left pants pocket and turned it inside out so that it flapped at his side for the one ear, and his right hand unzipped his fly and fished out what represented the elephant's trunk. The girls applauded. Thuggy grinned and blushed. The trick had been in questionable taste but it seemed to have succeeded.

"Are you enjoying our island, Thuggy?"

"I like it," said Thuggy.

"No minor hitches or blemishes then?"

Thuggy considered. "Would unrequited love count?"

"Might it be requited?"

"Search me," said Thuggy. "No hassle either way though, to be honest. I mean I'd sure like to get into old Annabel's pants—but then I may not be able to, you know."

"Annabel does seem an attractive girl."

"Splendid in her way. And, as you say, enjoyment of her company . . ."

". . . the company of the others at the farmhouse, the island, the summer . . ."

". . . need not quite depend on her pants' . . . hospitality."

"Yeah," said Thuggy. "Except I do hope it's in the cards."

The girls laughed. "Everything's in the cards!" They laughed bending their long necks. The blackbirds on the branch cawed.

In a gap in the stone fence an old grape vine made a sort of *étagère* onto a low shelf of which Gail slid the tray with the dishes Faye had wiped clean with leaves. They bade Thuggy good day, leaving him to regret not having contrived to touch either or both.

CHAPTER THIRTY-EIGHT

The moonlight is bright and soft. Ground fog gathers in flimsy sumac, rhubarb, and weedy raspberries in the upper third of the island. This is Babe's domain, perilous territory if only Jack Geach knew. Here the "paths" result from natural process and accident and there is no human rhyme nor reason in their branchings and conclusions. When Jack takes a sharp turn to the right and finds his way blocked he may sit on the cold ground and giggle or he may frown, set his jaw and retrace some of his steps, but he is unperturbed.

There are voices around this bend: ". . . who you are, what you happen to be up for. That's all it depends on, I guess. But then . . ." Pushing through, Jack shouts a friendly "Hello there!" He finds two boys, Thuggy and Carter, in a glade in the hollow of a hill. The air is mild. "I'm Jack Geach. I live in the millhouse."

"Good evening, man," they say. "Sit down. We're talking about sex and friendliness, shit like that."

"Oh." In his eagerness Jack had supposed they were discussing financial transactions. "Telling dirty jokes?" Jack frowns in mock disapproval. "Say, did you hear about the two woodpeckers on vacation? . . . and he says to his friend, 'You know, it's amazing how hard your pecker gets when you're away from home for a few days!' Had you heard that one?"

"I never did. You, Carter?"

"Nope."

"My pleasure," says Jack. "Well, I must be on my way now. I have a great many very important things to mull over. Perhaps I'll run into you fellows another time. So long."

Jack leaves with the joint the boys have been passing and as he walks he smokes it as he has seen them do—whoosh, hold, hold, exhale. "Head full of pine needles," he says. "What did I say?" The thought of the innocence of his wife and daughters brings tears. Everything looks wet, even the sky, even the stars, even his penny loafers. "I should include all this in my biography," thinks Jack, "be frank and manly. Show my openness to every experience, how happy I've always been, even in my darkest hours. Jack Geach has always been bold when he had to be, and he has always admired himself. He's the kind of man who finds life very challenging and adorable, to tell the truth. After all, life is as rewarding as high finance, in a way. This island, for instance, is so beautiful," thinks Jack magisterially, "that it ought to be developed, anyway. I owe it to myself to put somebody to work on it right away. Huge returns, of course, and also a wonderful tribute to the world of business, very wonderful and glamorous. And, come to think of it, I could have all the suites bugged. All's fair in high finance, that's why it's so thrilling. We'll need electricity, of course. Money can do anything. I must make a mental note, I must remember to tell Priscilla to remind me. I'm truly fortunate to have a wife as beautiful and well educated as Priscilla. She's one in a million, at least. What? What did I just think?"

Has Jack been wandering for hours? He doesn't know. At length he comes upon Carter and Thuggy again. Have they moved or has he walked in some kind of circle? He cannot decide. The boys look rare and valuable. Thuggy has lustrous brown curls and merry dimples. He drinks from a can of beer. Carter is like a child so sleepy he can only make movements that are slow and graceful. "I could get them jobs as messenger boys," Jack thinks.

"Ask Mr. Geach," says Carter.

Jack sits and leans forward, all attention.

"In general," says Thuggy, "does it make you feel pretty good or pretty bad to know that other people turn each other on? For instance, suppose two people are happily and seriously fucking and you're there in the bed with them, stoned, say. How does it make you feel—good or bad?"

Jack frowns. "You mean . . ."

"Whatever you like. It's an interesting question, isn't it."

Jack wonders, "Are the two people married to each other?" He shakes his head, assumes a distant thoughtful expression, and hopes Carter or Thuggy will speak. There is a long silence in which each of the three, the two boys and the young man, thinks his own thoughts in his own way.

Then Thuggy says, "Well, suppose that instead of fucking they were hacking each other to pieces with butcher knives."

CHAPTER THIRTY-NINE

Chilly dawn, low tide. Far out on the mudflats a blue heron walks in the shallows. When he sees something that interests him he picks it up between the points of his beak, then lifts and shakes his head. He is in no hurry. He stretches a wing to preen a feather or two. With one eye he looks down at his tiny knees. His claws pierce the sweet gray mud. Now he casts a long regard far down the beach where two other large creatures, Daisy and Jimbo, are also gathering food.

"I saw him in the morning like this last summer too."

"Gosh. I'd like to know where he migrates to and from."

"Me too."

Jimbo and Daisy wade barefoot gathering mussels, shy and excited to be alone together this morning. Jimbo carries a pail into which the mussels fall, clatter, click. When the pail is full he carries it up above the high-tide line and pours the mussels into a bushel basket. It is nearly five-thirty a.m. The basket is half full of blue-gray mussels. Jimbo runs over the sharp stones and shells to Daisy in the water. She has tucked the hem of her skirt into the waistband. Jimbo admires her dirty white feet. He touches one of them with one of his long thin feet. "What if I had little feet like yours, Daisy?" he asks. Dear Jimbo, dear Daisy, how she peers into the water. The ocean seems remarkable.

"Wait, what's that?"

"?"

"Look—it looks sort of . . ."

"Yes . . . an arrowhead, isn't it?"

"Yes."

"They're rare but they do turn up sometimes. Indians used to live here."

"How did they get here?"

"Canoes? They must've been very content."

"They must."

"The island was covered with forest. Then white people cleared the bottom part and built houses. They raised cows and also a special kind of turnip that was famous."

"Look. There goes the heron." Flapping methodically, he

bends and raises dangling legs against his breast feathers. He is gone into the sky.

"Charismatic, isn't he?"

"Yes. Here's Annabel."

She leaves her violin case beside the basket of mussels. Rufus zigzags ahead of her out to Daisy and Jimbo. Annabel yawns, her hair falls over her puffy eyes.

"Hi."

"Hi, kiddos."

"Hi, Annabel."

"Annabel," says Daisy, "do you intend to practice 'Oats and Beans' here on the beach?"

"In the first place, I'm well past 'Oats and Beans.' I'm almost through 'Au Clair de la Lune' and I'm beginning 'Humoresque.' In the second place, I don't feel like practicing anything now because I've just come from a lesson."

"So early? Is she punishing you?"

" 'The violin is not a machine like the piano. With the violin you must go beyond mechanical skills. You must appreciate its moods and feelings. For instance, you should get out of your lazy bed and come to it at dawn or before. Surprise it.' So we had a lesson at four-thirty. She was wide awake."

"Gosh," says Jimbo, "wow, I'd like to see this Sue Holcombe."

Annabel frowns, purses her lips, considers. "As a matter of fact, Jimbo, that reminds me. *She* wants to see *you*. Wants to talk to you about something."

"What?" wonders Daisy.

As the young people talk big Rufus splashes across the mudflats toward a group of terns. He doesn't even notice that the water he runs through is full of small fish.

CHAPTER FORTY

"Rufus! Doggie boy! I've got something to read you!" All Rufus can do now is throw a cursory "Woof!" toward the terns before he runs up to where Thuggy sits in the sand near the basket of mussels and Annabel's violin. "You hungry, man?" Rufus snuffles Thuggy's face, glances into the boy's eyes. "You'll love this." One of Daisy's delicious biscuits, still warm. Rufus swallows it whole. There's also one for Goose who has followed Thuggy from the farmhouse. Goose's black eyes shine out of her dull black fur. Her small paws have long black nails, the bare gray nipple at the end of each of her hanging breasts wobbles when she moves. Goose is older and shier than Rufus. She places the biscuit on her forepaws to keep sand off it, and bites it in two. Her tail wags a little. "I want you to hear this too, Goosie. I love you, girl."

Daisy's, Jimbo's, and Annabel's curiosity has drawn them up to Thuggy and the dogs. They sit and lie on the sand and enjoy the sun's early light warmth. Their feet are drying. Thuggy welcomes them. Annabel uses her violin case as a pillow. Jimbo puts his spectacles in his shirt pocket and hides his eyes in the crook of his arm. Daisy scratches Goose's head. All listen as Thuggy reads from a wrinkled leaf of paper.

> One day Mr. and Ms. Drake—Harry and Pamela—drove from Mme. Encore's ill-famed villa to Monte Carlo, intending to spice their Riviera vacation with an evening of baccarat among the millionaires and roués who frequent that city's gay casinos.
>
> Immediately the sly long-limbed daughter Betsy scampered from the stately house into the gardens, whistling a merry tune. Betsy removed the perfumed top of her black leather bikini and exposed her primly budding knockers. Then she slipped the bottom of the suit down over her legs, tossing it away, whereupon she began to finger-fuck herself.
>
> Her brother Ernie, who was asleep nearby, leaped up and spied on his sister's antics. Ernie grinned to himself, "I shall tattle when Mommy and Daddy return. And in the meantime I can get my little rocks off." He yanked his broad tool out of his *Lederhosen* and began to stroke it.
>
> But Ernie's boyish gasps alerted Betsy to his presence. The siblings pranced about each other like young goats in almost incestuous admiration, coyly manipulating their privates, until Ernie announced, "Jeepers, I think I'm about to come, Sis."

> "Me too," cried Betsy. "Look, Ernie. There's Rufus's dish. I have an idea. I'll put the dish between my legs and then you can squirt your dong into it."
>
> "Oui, oui," nodded Ernie. "We can pretend we're Mommy and Daddy balling."
>
> Hysterically gnashing their teeth as though maddened by pleasure, the nubile adolescents achieved orgasm at the same moment whereupon they tittered deliriously. A few minutes later their sport was to have an unforeseen consequence.

Thuggy pauses, so transparently hoping for someone to urge him to continue that no one does, and then he reads on:

> Who should arrive on the scene but the dog Rufus himself. Observing that his dish contained what he took to be a type of French liquid dogfood, he promptly lapped it up, only to be rudely surprised and confronted with Betsy's and Ernie's mocking merriment, whereupon he overturned the dish and slouched away scowling over his shoulder at them.

Thuggy chuckles, Rufus, head angled, brow wrinkled, regards him. Does he want to play? Rufus's tail sweeps fine sand back and forth.

"Goose feels slighted. Look at her," says Annabel. She rests her muzzle on one paw and she too wags her tail.

Daisy sighs. "These dogs."

Jimbo and Thuggy lift the basket of mussels. Daisy has the pail, Annabel the violin. Young people and dogs troop up the beach toward the farmhouse.

CHAPTER FORTY-ONE

Shortly before coming to the island, Priscilla Geach had had a plastic coil inserted into her womb as a substitute for contraceptive pills. Those pills had begun to freckle her body lightly and on her face there was an almost invisible darkening of the

skin into a "mask" caused by the drug. Priscilla was glad to b
rid of these mimickings of pregnancy, but the new device ha
its own drawbacks.

It was midmorning and humid. Priscilla had dreamed of
shouting man. Her pale orange hair lay limp as silk on the pin
pillowslip, limp as her pink nightie. "Ouch!" she said when sh
opened her eyes, for her womb had cramped sharply. In a mo
ment she recognized the old unalleviated menstrual pain. "It'
ridiculous." Priscilla inserted a tampon into her vagina to absor
blood and then washed her hands in an ironstone bowl, an
then shook a drop of perfume made from lilies of the valley ont
her wrist.

The bedroom door opened. Priscilla turned, smiling. Edit
rushed into the room closely pursued by the larger Heste
The children's faces were scarlet, their demure nightdresse
splotched, streaked black, green, purple. "Help!" shrieked Edit
Hester shrieked, "Wait!" They raced about the room now ove
the bed, now under. "Girls!" Priscilla shouted. Her womb ache
viciously. "Girls, please!" Priscilla raised her hand to her fore
head and was inspired. "Girls, let me give you each a drop o
my perfume."

"Edith knocked over my tempera set," explained Hester. Sh
and her mother had retired to the wide rumpled bed and Edit
was putting her feet into her mother's shoes. Priscilla's wom
hurt and hurt and hurt, and she wondered whether in the futur
a famous and admirable research anesthesiologist might create
drug free of undesirable side effects to save Edith and Heste
these wretched pains. How did Annabel and the other girl at th
farmhouse manage?

Edith was pretending her mother's mules were red Mar
Janes. "When is my birthday?"

"Soon, dear."

"Your birthday is when you were born," remarked Hester an
then, turning to Priscilla, "How are babies born?"

"Well dear, you know what Daddy has instead of a vagina–
his penis?—well . . ." Priscilla described conception (Edit
giggled, Hester smiled uncertainly, remembering Carter's penis
and pregnancy and birth (the girls listened with glazed eyes)
"And some day you girls too . . ."

The notion made Edith grimace. Hester said, "I'll go to visit Jane today. She's my friend." Priscilla thought, "You're lucky, Hester. Your mother's never had a friend of her own. And Jane's lucky too, to be past the curse, not to have ridiculous pain like this." Edith said, "This perfume smells very good." She was blowing soap bubbles which wobbled prettily over the bed. "All right, Hester, but don't stay long. You mustn't tire Jane or she won't be so pleased to see you again, will she?"

"No . . ."

"Edith, I think you should go outside for a while too. Why don't you play in the millstream? One of your dolls might like to go swimming there."

Outside Edith had undressed a doll and was dipping its toes into the cold water when Hester called, "I'm going to play Crazy Eights with my friend," and skipped away. Edith hurled Lisa Tirt, the doll, into the stream and sat puzzled and frowning. Quickly she decided that she too could pay a visit, to Sue Holcombe for whom she had stolen Jane's Lethe Water (Edith didn't now recall Sue Holcombe's claim that the wrong bottle had been procured) in the rain, wearing her red fireman's hat and yellow mackintosh. Now as she picks her way across Sue Holcombe's difficult lawn Edith wears white sandals, blue shorts, and a white sailor's blouse with anchors embroidered on the collar. She seems the prettiest child in the world. Radiant in the doorway of the cottage, she explains, "I'm visiting you." Sue Holcombe is not honored. She says, "Go away and never come back. I have too many important things on my mind to think about children. I can't be bothered." There are tears then.

CHAPTER FORTY-TWO

Almost immediately new footsteps sounded on the boards of the porch of the cottage. This porch, too small for chairs or a swing, had been painted a year before but already sea air was lifting the green off the bony wood. In earlier times island children had passed rainy mornings here or lovers gazed into each other's eyes at dusk. Therefore to Sue Holcombe the porch was an annoying monument to squandered time and she planned to have it removed one day, even though it could announce intruders usefully. Thump, scrape, thump. "Hello . . . hello? Ms. Holcombe?" Jimbo rattled the screen door.

No one could have seemed less formidable than Jimbo here this late June morning as he shuffled and blinked his sleepy eyes behind his amusing spectacles. Yet Sue's heart quailed and seemed to her to echo the rattling of the door. She recalled the most distinguished violinists she had seen perform in order to assume now some of their cunning or courage. The thousand minute lines in her brown face sharpened. She said loudly, "Jimbo, is it? None too soon. Tall, aren't you. Wipe your feet and come in, young man." Behind rapidly, weakly exhaled puffs of cigarette smoke Jimbo saw Sue Holcombe's shrewd eyes and wondered, "Do I like them or not?" It didn't occur to him to wonder how old she was or whether she still menstruated. He wondered, "But listen. When I was little, didn't I go to a maiden aunt's house or something that made me feel the way this one does?" They were in the parlor. It seemed cool during the noon hour because no sunbeam came directly in any windows. "Who cares?" thought Jimbo. He said, "Uh, . . . you're a musician."

Sue Holcombe smiled.

"No flies on her," Jimbo thought. He asked, "Is that a harpsichord?"

"Spinet." She closed the instrument.

Jimbo frowned. He asked, "What do you think about Chinese music?"

"Whose boyfriend are you, young man? Annabel's or Daisy's? And why should you ask ridiculous questions? Chinese music? Naturally I've never given it a second thought. What do you take me for? Emphatically, I'm no dilettante. Chinese music indeed—I abhor such notions. As far as I am concerned there is no such thing. You might as well ask me about architecture. Indeed far better. But we'll come to that in good time. For the moment let me say merely that I have never been one to discuss subjects that have nothing to do with anything that matters to me. The sooner you understand that, the better. Chinese music is ludicrous and childish."

"How dare you . . . ?" Jimbo's voice was soft and friendly.

"You smell as if you've been on the mudflats this morning."
"Gathering mussels . . ."
"They're said to be very nourishing. I eat them sometimes ıyself, here. On the mainland I prefer a good rib-eye steak."
Jimbo asked, "Did you ever play the guitar—classical, I ıean?"
Sue Holcombe said, "Hmph."
So the talk went for an hour. Each participant was mildly ıocked by pleasure in the interchange. Why not? Sue Holombe in fact quite forgot the occasion of Jimbo's visit until at ngth he said, "I really should get back to the farmhouse. I ope we have another chance . . ."
Sue Holcombe tucked her grizzled hair behind her ears. She elt almost confused. "Just a moment." Now to his consternaon Jimbo saw an expression of the worst kinds of greed and ıiftiness on Sue Holcombe's small face. "Me?" wondered mbo. ". . . it happens," Sue Holcombe continued, "that a olleague of mine is preparing a monograph on the early archiecture of this region. She is particularly avid for information bout buildings here on the island. Of course I have co-operated ılly by telling her everything I know—and I know a great deal— bout my cottage. Now: several days ago one of the . . . one of our . . . your fellow lodgers mentioned in passing that there ere extant architect's drawings of the farmhouse. I've not been ble to sleep for thinking of how valuable these drawings will be my colleague. Perhaps you could tell me where they are?" ince Jimbo didn't reply immediately she hurried on. "I simply ish to copy them, nothing more."
Her horrid eagerness ended by making Jimbo lie. "Uh . . . ell, it seems to me I've heard of some drawings but I don't emember where. Why don't you ask Daisy?"
Sue Holcombe glowered. "Then tell me this: is there a room ithout windows?"
"Closets?"
"No! An actual room!"
"I don't understand."
"Think nothing of it." She lit a cigarette, exhaled a gray puff hrough pursed lips, watching Jimbo. In a moment she said, I've enjoyed our little chat. As a professor I am necessarily

adept at evaluating young people. I find that you are not foolis
I could give you good advice about numerous things, mora
practical, aesthetic, if I chose."

"I'm sure you could . . ."

"Quiet!"

Jimbo thought, "That maiden aunt of mine or whatever sh
was always had flowers in her house."

Sue Holcombe said, "Listen carefully. I can be of considerab
assistance to you. Specifically, I can make it possible for you t
ride Daisy's bull well before Independence Day. Don't ask que
tions yet, please. If your memory of those architect's drawin
were better I in my turn would doubtless remember how to sol
your bull problem, so that you can gain the respect of yo
peers. Though why you seek it is beyond me."

Jimbo was embarrassed.

Sue Holcombe said, "Tell me before I change my mind."

Jimbo shook his head.

"Then I'll allow you precisely four days, not a second more, t
consider. Don't let a golden opportunity slip through yo
grasp."

"It wouldn't be unprecedented!" Poor Jimbo certainly fe
hopeless and lonesome just now. He thought, "It's true I'
never quite unacceptable to anyone. But I'm afraid I'll alwa
be a little unworthy too." Then he thought, "We'll see, won
we."

Sue Holcombe patted him on the head. "Don't be a child,
she said.

Jimbo wanted to change the subject. "By the way, Ms. Ho
combe. When I came here a little girl was moping away fro
your cottage."

"Belongs to the offensive young pair in the millhouse,
believe."

"I saw her once before." Jimbo told the story of waking und
the oak to hear Edith say, "I wish a pair of new red Mary Jane
for my birthday."

Sue Holcombe seemed hardly to listen. "Good-by," she sai
Now there were bright triangles and trapezoids on the old floo
and rugs and the dust looked clean as sand on a beach.

Jimbo could not help himself. When he waved he let ıow some spontaneous affection. Sue Holcombe understood it erfectly.

CHAPTER FORTY-THREE

Daisy is cooking deftly and thoughtlessly. Her clothes are olorful. She sighs when she spills sugar and her skin is the oftest in the world. When she looks out her windows at the ea and licks her fingers anyone would want to marry her. Beside ıe windows stands an old vase full of the flowers that bear her ame.

"Right. And the pile of books and the cigar." Flash. "Anna-el's violin and this." Thuggy hands Carter a shirt of almost ansparent white cotton with white silk embroidery. "And the ern." Flash. "Naked in the doorway. Don't look, Daisy." Flash, ash. "Levis, and winking?" Flash. Thuggy finishes photograph-ıg Carter. Later in the cellar Jimbo will develop the film.

The boys help Daisy pour the mussels she and Jimbo gathered ıto a tub of boiling water, then drain them and remove the ıorsels of flesh from the opened shells. Thuggy uses one of the ıells as a toy mustache. Meanwhile Daisy has prepared green arlic flavored mayonnaise for these mussels.

Now Daisy dips both hands well coated with butter into a ırge bowl. She shapes a mound of dough into a patty and then ıto a ring which she enlarges by twirling it in the air. Still turn-ıg, the ring is lowered into a kettle of hot oil where it will be-ome one of five doughnuts large as dinner plates for tomorrow's reakfast, golden brown and puffed. "Make one for us to eat ow," says Thuggy.

At the table everyone is shelling crisp peas. "What are the ictures for?"

Carter shrugs. "To look at."

Conversation turns to the subject of fame. "I'll be glad when m famous," says Carter.

" 'When'?"

"Or if. But I really want to."

The peapods perfume the air beautifully. Thuggy is rubbin his belly. "Criminals get famous. You up for something illega Carter?"

"You kidding? But I want to enjoy it. And if you're alway hiding, what's the point?"

"What's the point anyway?" muses Daisy.

Carter is about to speak but Thuggy interrupts. "Partie People wanting to touch you."

"Carter doesn't need to be famous for that!" exclaims Daisy

"But it would be different," says Carter. "Anyway that's no the reason. I'm afraid the only reason is, the idea turns me or that's all. It fucking turns me on."

Thuggy says, "I could dig it if it wasn't too much of a hassle.

"Why it would be lovely, of course!" says Daisy. "But Carter if you really want to become famous, what in the world are yo doing here of all places?"

"I'm in no hurry," says Carter. Everyone is smiling.

"Look," says Daisy, "I'll split this doughnut three ways. A quarter for each of you helpful boys," and she eats the res herself.

"Gosh Daisy," says Thuggy, "you better stop being so pretty I'm about to get big pants."

"Me too," says Carter.

Daisy raises her eyebrows as if to say, "I don't mind a bit. "Where is Jimbo," she wonders, "and Annabel?"

CHAPTER FORTY-FOUR

By the water's edge Sue Holcombe is writing music. The shor is stone here. Small boulders and crags stand among millions o pale hot pebbles. Today under a high blue marbled sky the hea is shocking. Very few gulls wheel between the sky and the brigh ocean. Jack Geach has brought stage one of phase four of hi master plan to its conclusion, adjusting tactics to meet exi gencies that have arisen, some by chance and some from th moves of his unknown but increasingly predictable antagonist and rivals. "I'll reward myself with a swim," Jack has mutterec into his microphone before signing off. Modestly clad in hi cordovan penny loafers, maroon-and-black plaid boxer trunks, and white tee shirt, Jack marches over the pebbles with hardly a thought in his head toward a group of larger rocks and finds Sue Holcombe under a beach umbrella of blue canvas with CAMPARI in white on its crenelated border.

She sits on an inflated navy blue and dull orange plastic life raft a few inches from the water. "I've no idea who you are, young man, but don't speak yet, please. I'm thinking." Beside the life raft is a pitcher of martinis and a carton of cigarettes. Also a lighter in whose transparent base a fly-tied fishhook floats in benzine. Numerous butts are decomposing into paper, ash, and shredded tobacco in the shallows. Sue Holcombe wears khaki trousers rolled to midcalf and bunched and belted at the waist. Her halter top is white with a pattern of apricot cornstalks. On her feet are black espadrilles and on her head is a sailor's hat, the brim turned down to shade her eyes. Barnacles and other small tenacious creatures make the standing rocks look as if they had been wallpapered long ago. A few feet out is a dark rock which at the moment rises barely above the water. When a wave crosses this rock there is a little crown of droplets in the air, and the sound "plip."

Jack feels faint. Sweat trickles behind his ears, down over his ribs, down his ankles into his shoes. Sue Holcombe says, "I'm writing music. Shh." Jack sights along the beach envisioning moored yachts and an air-conditioned hotel with palm trees on its roof. He resents Sue Holcombe's presence and thinks, "Nobody wants to see people writing music on a beach! If people have to write music they ought to do it in the privacy of their . . ."

Smoke from Sue Holcombe's cigarette mounts painfully into her umbrella. Sweat makes Jack Geach's eyes burn.

CHAPTER FORTY-FIVE

"*Writing* music? You can't really write it, can you? I mean, what do you mean? I ask because I'm not quite sure I understand." So, having received permission to speak, having introduced himself, seated on the life raft under the blue umbrella,

Jack attempts to converse with Sue Holcombe. She displays a mechanical pencil, a draftsman's fountain pen, and a sheet of paper. In the upper margin of the paper is written "The German Shepherd." On groups of horizontal lines printed at regular intervals is what seems to be music. "Drawing, if you prefer—specifying. The word you use doesn't matter. Conventionally we speak of 'writing' music."

"You must meet my wife, Priscilla. She's very interested in music too. We have season tickets to the symphony. When I have vital work to do we give our tickets to someone less fortunate. What you're writing *is* classical, isn't it? That's the only kind . . ."

"Perhaps you were thinking what I have written is merely a sort of script and not the music itself? Stuff and nonsense! Don't make me laugh."

Jack eyes the cold glass pitcher. "You and Priscilla really . . ."

Sue Holcombe laughs. "If your wife wants to discuss music with me she can enroll in one of my two introductory courses on the mainland." How merrily her little brown face wrinkles!

"I write a good deal of music," she says, "and it is almost always very fine. Writing music adds immeasurably to my performances. You see, I am primarily a musician, not a composer. I am a musician to the tips of my well-insured fingers. I am not interested in composition for its own sake. In the first place we don't need any more music: there's already more than any violinist can master. And in the second place, everything written today is dung anyway. No, don't ask me to take composition seriously. I haven't the time to spare."

"Very interesting and stimulating, Sue. Honestly, I really mean that."

"I'm not surprised."

In the motionless brilliant heat these two people appraise each other. "May I?" says Jack, lifting the pitcher. He swallows, swallows, and swallows a third time before realizing that what he drinks is not water—an unpleasant discovery. "Jesus!" Jack would certainly like to break this pitcher on Sue Holcombe's head. After a moment he says, "I guess there's not much money in music any more though."

Sue Holcombe yawns. She says, "I would be pleased to have a great deal of money. Any amount."

"Get out of teaching then. I'd advise you to get out of music altogether, except that with as large an investment in it as you must have by now it wouldn't make sense, at least not unless you had a sure thing ready to go into, in my opinion. I don't happen to have had close personal contact with musical finance myself, but I do feel extremely sure you can make yourself a tidy little bundle if you play your cards right."

What will Sue Holcombe say now? With an awkward gesture she tosses her cigarette into the water.

"You see," says Jack, "Priscilla is very wonderful. But I think she feels the need to do more chatting here on the island. Now supposing you and she became friends. I myself would have all the more incentive to give you some sound and detailed financial advice. If not, well, after all, my time is highly valuable even when I'm on vacation. In fact, I don't imagine anybody has ever set foot on this island before me whose time is nearly so valuable as mine is, and I'm not bragging either."

"Well, go away now," Sue Holcombe says and then, as Jack steps out into the sunlight, "and by the way, young man: my own time is priceless."

Trudging down the beach Jack shakes his head sadly. "Pathetic. Just pathetic. Probably not even married."

CHAPTER FORTY-SIX

Gail and Faye spent most of the hot day in shady parts of the woods and when they performed chores like tending their herb garden they were slow, wan, and faint. From evergreens at the boathouse harbor they looked across the inlet at Jane, who lay in a hammock fanning herself with a newspaper. Faye and Gail elected not to visit the old woman. Perhaps it was the stillness of the air, they were silent as they walked among the trees. Descending a hillside covered with day-lilies they wept. Later they searched for Carter. Today he too might be in the woods and it seemed that meeting him might raise flagging spirits. But after stopping by likely places and not finding the boy they forgot him.

This is the lowest land on the island, a rocky open space below sea level with thin soil between rocks, thistles, rambling shrubs bearing thorns and burrs. The blackberries have let fall their petals. Their reticulated once green berries are a full red that will soon be brilliant black and sweet. Rabbits come for the fallen ones already.

This protected clearing would be a good place for a house were the ground not so low that flooding is always possible, and so rocky. The surfaces of the rocks are hot. Grasshoppers are here, many on stalks and twigs, wide awake. One whizzes across the air—bands of strong color show.

A grove of dead elms stands there, each shaggy halfway up with climbing plants. Yonder beyond a wall of firs, ivy, and flowering lilac lies a pool fed by a brook where Gail and Faye are sewing and washing clothes and talking. Listen to them.

"How much longer does Jane have to live?"

"How much longer do you suppose she wants?"

"They can't have been pleasant, can they?—the years of being alone after the years of not."

"Could you hand me a smaller needle, dear?"

"Isn't Daisy lucky to have Carter and her other funny friends at the farmhouse!"

"Daisy wouldn't be somewhere hereabouts now, peeking at us and eavesdropping, would she?"

"About Jane, though. Whatever must it be like to be so old and so bereft?"

"I shouldn't give it a second thought, my dear."

CHAPTER FORTY-SEVEN

One afternoon Jimbo rolled a twenty-dollar bill into a cylinder. Onto his desk he spooned a mound half the size of a chocolate kiss of white cocaine powder. Holding one nostril closed with a thumb he inhaled the powder through the tube into his other nostril. It stung, his eyes watered. But soon the nasal passage was anesthetized and Jimbo began to recognize more subtle and desirable side effects of the drug: so complete an absence of fatigue or pain that his body seemed to dissolve into his mind, with such freshening and clarity that thought itself grew extraordinarily pleasurable. Jimbo was naked, and with certain other drugs he would have been inclined to play with his testicles and penis. This afternoon however he donned a pair of overalls and walked downstairs, outside across the grass, and into the barn.

Everything inside scented the cool dim air. Bales and piles of hay, chickens' nests, manure, a wicker basket of apples gathered last fall and left to shrivel and rot through winter and spring, unfinished wood, earthen floor, all even here sweetened and mellowed by the sea. Jimbo stood in the center blinking as his vision adjusted.

"Hi, Big Boy. Remember me?" said Jimbo. He peered into a stall at a black breathing shape. "How're they hanging, pal? Haven't seen you in a while. Hey, you hungry?" The bull snuffed. "I see your crib is full. I had something different in mind though. What've you got to lose? Give it a try." Gingerly over the stall door Jimbo proffered a cube of sugar on his palm. Big Boy trotted forward and accepted it gracelessly.

"That's all I brought, sorry. Listen, how's about if I stay a while so you can get used to me? I did some coke and I sort of feel like talking. Let me know if you want me to split."

Whenever flies bit Big Boy he whisked them with his tail or tried to shoo them away by turning an ear. Otherwise he stood motionless and listened. At first he glared but gradually the lids descended over his red eyes.

"I was thinking about how uppers and downers suggest a continuum, right? A spectrum. I'm talking about consciousness, not anything physiological like heartbeat. So we all know about how consciousness modulates into sleep, i.e., into *un*consciousness at the low end of the spectrum. But what does it modulate into at the upper end as you become more and more awake?

"Well, if you O. D. with uppers you're finally going to lose consciousness, so it looks as if the continuum is bounded by unconsciousness at both ends. And though it might seem that the upper unconsciousness ought to differ from the lower, if we do strictly mean *un*consciousness I don't see how we can qualify it. Consciousness is all we can experience.

"Right, but in a manner of speaking what happens at the upper end is that you wake up more and more until finally you're asleep. That's got to be bullshit . . . ah, nonsense.

"You might want to say that the halfway point of the spectrum is the zenith and that either direction tends toward unconsciousness, toward 'sleep.' But that won't work either, because within the spectrum we do perceive a progression that makes us term a state near one end 'sleepy' and one near the other 'wide awake.'

"As I see it, the dilemma is that our continuum seems circular, going from unconsciousness through stages of wakefulness back around to unconsciousness, yet it also seems rectilinear, from low to high. And I was thinking that this situation seems fairly much like our perception of color. I've been using the word spectrum anyway—let's ride that out a little.

"We perceive colors in a circle. The well-known color wheel—yellow shades into green, green into blue, blue into violet, and so on around, perfectly seamless. At the same time we know this circle is really rectilinear—the visible segment of the electromagnetic spectrum. Now the way I figure it is this: if we can only perceive part of the straight line we *have* to perceive it as a circle. Let me explain.

"The middle's irrelevant—whether you conceive blue as part of a circle or a straight line, it shades on one side into violet and on the other into green. No, it's the ends of the continuum that concern us. So let's move along from green to yellow to orange to red . . . relax, I'm merely hypothesizing. Okay, now we're at one end of the visible spectrum. We know red 'really' shades into infrared and so on. But we can't see the fucking infrared.

"So what can red shade into on the side opposite orange? Not green, green's taken care of. In fact everything's taken care of except violet, at the other end, in a predicament like red's. So that means red *has* to shade into violet. Because everything we see has to have a color. That's part of what 'see' and 'color' mean.

"This has an interesting consequence. The point on the

wheel where the lower end shades into the upper—i.e. red-violet, where red shades into violet—that point is an unreal color which our eyes and minds create.

"You'll see what I mean if you think of a creature for whom the visible part of the total spectrum isn't the same as ours. There are such creatures—flies I think and maybe you yourself, I'm not sure.

"Take a creature who can only see yellow, green, and blue. Everything else would be invisible infrayellow or ultrablue. Now for him, same as for us, the ends of the visible spectrum would have to blend into each other—he has his own color wheel. So let's go around his wheel. We start with green and go either way, it doesn't matter. Green shades into yellow and then yellow, the end of the line, shades into blue, the other end. Then blue back into green and so around.

"But do you see what's happened? Let yellow and blue be twelve and six o'clock on his wheel. Green's at three. But at nine is a different color which results from blue's shading into yellow. When *we* shade blue into yellow we can only get green. This dude can get green but he can also get a completely different color, one we can't see at all. It exists only for him and his kind. It's determined by the boundaries of his visible spectrum. We see most of the colors he can plus lots more, but he sees that nine o'clock color we can't. So call that his *boundary color*. Well, similarly red-violet is our boundary color, the one that exists only for creatures whose range of visible color has the same upper and lower boundaries as ours.

"Maybe then the sleepiness-wakefulness scale is like a color wheel—a circular-seeming perceivable portion of a rectilinear continuum. If so, what we call unconsciousness would be like red-violet: the unreal boundary color of our consciousness wheel.

"Of course there's a more obvious analogy to the downer upper continuum in musical pitch—audible rather than visible frequency. A tone can descend or ascend out of hearing, and the auditory scale doesn't have the disadvantage of seeming circular. So why bring in color at all? Well, in the first place the pitch analogue is so obvious it's hardly worth the trouble. And in the second place why *does* pitch seem serially ordered and color not? Why the difference?

"Even if we look at the wakefulness continuum without analogues there are puzzles. We do seem to be able to form an idea of the lower end of the spectrum—sleep or absolute unconsciousness. But I don't think we have even a very clear idea of the real or putative upper end. I mean what can it mean to be *absolutely* awake?

"Anyway, the upper-downer is only one dope continuum. Hallucinogens suggest another, and here it's the top that's clear: total hallucination or some such. But, my friend, tell me if you can what the lower end of this spectrum is. No hallucination at all? Whatever might that be like? And why hasn't somebody found a drug to put us in that state?"

Jimbo spoke lightly, rapidly. Shadows were gathering in the great barn. Jimbo's voice was inoffensive and melodious.

CHAPTER FORTY-EIGHT

After talking to Big Boy about drugs Jimbo left a note at the farmhouse explaining that he wouldn't dine there because he had things to think about. All night he marched back and forth from one side of the island to the other along the fence that separates Daisy's pastureland from the woods. He thought about many things, most of all about Sue Holcombe's offer to enable him to ride the bull in return for the privilege of copying the architect's drawings of the farmhouse. "It's fishy," he thought. Remembering his father's words, "Ride that bull, son," in the dream, and his discomfiture at Hester Geach's having failed to delude anyone with her story, Jimbo found Sue Holcombe's proposal tempting. But the more it tempted him the less inclined he was to accept it. "I don't know what she has up her sleeve but I don't like it," he thought. He snorted more cocaine and turned the problem this way and that. Yet by dawn no resolution was in sight.

Everyone in the farmhouse was asleep. Jimbo crept up to his bedroom and tried to sleep too but the cocaine or something it had been cut with was so strongly in effect that even after swallowing a downer he remained awake. His mind wandered. "Plans

. . . drawings . . . 'without windows' . . . what the fuck, what the fuck . . ."

Jimbo rose and ran downstairs on tiptoe. He located a flashlight and ran out the front door. It was gray dawn. At the side of the house steps overgrown with wet grass led down to a cellar door. Jimbo pushed back curious Goose and sleepy Rufus who had followed, and closed the door behind him. Perfect darkness. "Ah!" thought Jimbo, "*no windows!* Well, well, well. Very interesting." He switched on the flashlight.

He shivered. More steps led farther down. The floor was hard dirt, the walls stone. Occasionally he heard what he took to be mice, moles, or harmless snakes. He was thrilled. Seeming to lose consciousness at moments he wandered from chamber to chamber. "The dogs know where I am, just in case," he thought. He felt brave and prudent, young Jimbo, and very pleased with himself. He felt lucky. The air was cold but not damp.

In the first chamber were shelves and a sturdy table. "Perfect for a darkroom," said Jimbo. "I can run a hose out the kitchen window. But what's this?" The cellar proved fairly empty. There was some hand-sawn lumber, a roll of fencewire, broken furniture. Once Jimbo found a number of Mason jars whose contents and labels had long since ceased to be intelligible. But there was evidently not a single cask of jewels or coins. "Piss on it," thought Jimbo.

A little drowsy now, he sat in an empty chamber. The flashlight beside him moved. "Yikes!" Jimbo leapt up and danced, stamping to frighten any animal. As it happened the flashlight had merely rolled into a depression which when Jimbo examined it proved surprisingly regular—quite square in fact. "A trap door!" It opened onto steps leading down into a small subcellar in one wall of which Jimbo discovered the entrance to a narrow, low-ceilinged but apparently negotiable tunnel. "Far out."

Slowly and cautiously as he advanced, it was noon before he reached the other end of the tunnel and, struggling through shrubbery, came out on the bank of a pond in the woods. At first he simply stood there. The light was almost black to him and the world seemed wide—"like a sandwich," he whispered.

"Hi, Jimbo. Come in, it's perfect." It was Carter calling from the middle of the pond.

Jimbo was stepping out of his moccasins when he said, "I didn't bring a bathing suit!"

"No problem," said Carter. "Nobody else knows about this place."

Shouting "Whee," Jimbo flew naked into the water.

CHAPTER FORTY-NINE

The two boys lie on the grass to let the sun dry them. "No, man, it really didn't hurt luckily." Coming up through the water and seeing feet paddling above, Jimbo had thought it would be a good trick to steal Carter's bathing suit for himself. Imagine his surprise at discovering that Carter too was naked. Imagine Carter's surprise when he felt Jimbo's mischievous hands between his legs. "I thought you might have interpreted it as an attack or something." It is easy to talk slowly this way on the warm grass.

"How did you find this place, Jimbo?"

"Oh, I . . . I can't exactly remember. Carter, you know Sue Holcombe?"

"Mmm-hmm," stretching, silkily virile.

"What do you think of her?"

"Nothing," says Carter. Since Jimbo has left his spectacles on a flat rock he isn't able to gauge Carter's expression.

"You know," Jimbo says, "if this was the mainland somebody'd come along and tell us to move."

"Tell us to put clothes on too."

Jimbo frowns sternly. "I resent orders."

"You know," Carter says, "you know, I was thinking maybe you and me ought to do some traveling together after the summer."

Jimbo is awestruck. "Why me?" he wonders. He says, "Far out."

Carter himself doesn't know what has led him to make the suggestion. A pleasant feeling of surprise stirs in him. Jimbo lies on his stomach, white, bony legs akimbo, his eyes closed. He chews a fingernail. "I'd like to look like him for one day," Carter muses.

"I'm kind of hungry," Jimbo says. "I was up all night and, come to think of it, I haven't eaten a thing."

From nearby comes a tinkle of bells and a cry, "The brownies!" Carter and Jimbo stare at each other. They hear, "They must be headed for the pond. Bad luck, Gail dear." As the tinkling goes sweetly away out of earshot Jimbo and Carter hear something descend through much underbrush toward them, until over the grass rolls a crumpled silver sphere and comes to rest before their noses. They smell chocolate.

"Brownies!" exclaims Jimbo, opening the foil—moist and delicious ones, the boys find. Brownies warm the stomach, sun warms the skin. The boys doze. A bright-eyed robin hops by, disregarding them.

Waking a bit, each boy feels somewhat amorously aware of the other and somewhat bashful. It is Carter who in time breaks the spell of silence. "Hey man, I mean, maybe I could . . ." laying the back of his hand against Jimbo's ribs.

"Gosh," says Jimbo.

Now there is a quite different silence as each from moment to moment thinks, "Far out" and "What's going to happen next?" Jimbo lies very still. Carter touches him here and there with hand or mouth. The penises stand jauntily. Jimbo's rests on Carter's tongue.

The boys are sleepy but since the afternoon is drawing to its close they decide to return to the farmhouse.

"But how do we get out, Carter?"

"Through here." A narrow path which always seems about to end but does not. "You must've come this way."

Jimbo shrugs. Along the path flowers open and close. The boys hear birds chirping and perhaps away among the trees once more a tinkle of bells.

CHAPTER FIFTY

"Gail, Faye?" Jane made her way with two canes through the dark woods calling "Faye, Gail?" At length she found the girls sitting on a low branch of a tree. She explained that the Lethe Water had disappeared. They were astonished. They hadn't retrieved the flagon and they regretted that they couldn't lay their hands on any more of the precious liquid. As far as they knew, no more existed. Poor Jane was disheartened. Her rheumatism wasn't painful just then but she feared the respite would be brief. It's your own fault though (she thought), for leaving it on the sill like that. Shame on you, Jane.

By the boathouse she met Jimbo and invited him to have mulberry pie and tea with her. They sat in her parlor. Through the screens in the door and windows, beyond the shaggy moving grass they saw the vast ocean.

"As a matter of fact Jane, I walked over here specifically to see you, to ask about something." On a low shelf under the window lay the plan of Daisy's farmhouse. Jane had lighted only two lanterns, one beside her rocking chair and one over a table on which lay a sheaf of stationery and an unfinished letter.

"What's that, Jane?" Over the mantelpiece, a blue felt pennant with a grinning fox's head in yellow.

"That? I bought it at the teachers' college I went to when I was a girl." Clearly Jimbo wasn't quite ready to talk about what was on his mind. "I met my husband John there. His sister and I roomed in the same boardinghouse. It was cold as could be that winter. After seven o'clock at night there'd be no heat in the radiators! I'd read in bed, with all my blankets and coats wrapped around me, and eat apples. I remember I'd eat four or five apples in an evening. John was a sailor. He came to see his sister once and we all went ice-skating. I met him that way and he was always a good husband to me."

Eyes lowered, Jimbo scraped the last bite of pie off his plate.

"We loved each other for twenty-seven years. He bought this house for us and after he had his own three-master this was his port of call. He'd come back from the Indies or China and sail right in here. My goodness . . ."

Waves crashed in the little harbor. Jane sipped her tea. "What do we have to talk about, Jimbo?"

Jimbo laughed. "I wanted to know what you thought about a proposal Sue Holcombe made me." He recounted his interview with the musician. "I thought you might see what she's up to if she is up to something, and I'm pretty sure she is."

"You could knock me over with a feather," Jane said. "Well!

Yes, it does sound as though she's up to something I'd be inclined to say. But you can't be sure with an odd one like Sue. Might be a touch of harmless craziness."

"Nothing occurs to you that might explain it?"

"Not a thing, Jimbo. It makes me curious, that's for sure. The silly old drawings can't be valuable. Don't know why I've never thrown them away myself. Why, you're welcome to them, Jimbo."

"But what should I do, Jane? I mean, should I give them to her or not?"

"Whatever you want."

"Oh . . ." The room was peaceful and still. "Oh," Jimbo said, "I guess I don't really feel at all like making this deal with her. Not at all. And I even sort of like her, you know." He shook his head, puzzled by the suddenness and assurance of his decision.

Jane watched with interest. In a few minutes he bade her good night and withdrew. "Hmm!" Jane thought. She rather admired the boy. Smoothing her dress over her knees, she sat looking at the letter on the table. It was to her wealthy friend Charlotte on the mainland, and advised that lady not to appear on the island because . . . But Jane hadn't yet contrived an excuse. "Oh . . ." Jane said. At the table she began a different letter: "Dear Miss Holcombe, I have decided . . ." She was humming a sweet air she had learned from her grandmother.

CHAPTER FIFTY-ONE

In the most gold and reddish water Annabel swims like a champion. A shoulder rises, the whole arm rises and arcs. The side of her head rests on the water as on a cushion. The water is like varnish beading and snaking, and when Annabel's arm breaks it the shadow is green. She curls to right herself and lowers her feet to the weedy floor. She strides through surf and over the warm beach, breathing deeply as she can. Gleaming water falls from her elbows into the sand.

Annabel skins off her bathing cap and sits on a blanket beside Thuggy. There are bottles of beer and a silent radio. "Have a beer, kid," Thuggy suggests. He watches her tilt the bottle up.

"What are you reading, Thug?"

"*The Conquest of New Spain* by Bernard Díaz, one of the Spaniards who first came to Central America."

"Is it good?"

"It's far out. You know the Mexican civilization was so impressive, and the Spaniards had only expected to find like monkey people living in trees—well, when they came into this city they couldn't believe it was real. They talked it over and decided they must all be asleep and having a communal dream. Pretty good, huh? for a bunch of soldiers."

"Annabel is beautiful," Thuggy thinks. She is large and beautiful.

She says, "I suppose when they were fighting, when they were killing they must have been disappointed to think it was only a dream."

Annabel lies on her back. Thuggy is sitting cross-legged beside her. "But it's always like that when you're fighting, really fighting. It's like a dream."

"You've been in fights?"

"Right. It's the adrenaline. You hit somebody, he hits you, and you make a mental note that it's happening, but it doesn't hurt. I was a good fighter."

"Often?"

"Had to be. But the fights I got into were mostly for friends. Like this kid Denny. He was a pretty good fighter himself, but small. This other guy took it into his head to make Denny's life miserable, for no good reason I ever found out. This dude, name of Carlos I think, would hang around and every time he saw Denny he'd beat the shit out of him. Denny fought like a man every time but he didn't have a chance, Carlos was such a big fucker.

"I got tired of seeing old Denny with black eyes and busted lips so I told Carlos I was going to fight him unless he laid off Denny."

"What did Denny say?"

"He didn't know about it. So Carlos kept on leaning on Denny and I had to fight him. I didn't want to. Even then I liked it better if things could be settled peaceably. Fighting's strenuous. I'd rather drink some wine and talk."

"So you fought this bully Carlos?"

"Yes, and afterward he let Denny be."

"What was it like, the fight?"

"Pretty equal. More so than Carlos expected. It was in a vacant lot after midnight."

"You had seconds?"

"And thirds, fourths, enough to make sure neither of us got mobbed. They made a ring and we fought till Carlos couldn't stand up any more. Denny heard about it but I don't think he ever knew why I'd fought the guy."

"Carlos didn't tell him? No, I guess he wouldn't. So then Denny . . . could whistle a happy tune."

"Yes."

"Where is he now?"

"In prison, I heard. He became a soldier and then he shot somebody he wasn't supposed to."

"Anyway," thinks Annabel, "Thuggy's a real gentleman." He is throwing empty beer bottles far out into the flashing water. Annabel shakes sand off the blanket.

As Thuggy follows her to the farmhouse he decides he will try to seduce her now. But his desire is thwarted.

"What's this?" Annabel asks. Scattered over the desk in Thuggy's bedroom, they are photographs of Carter.

"I took them and Jimbo developed them. Carter's a good model."

"They're not bad. Gosh, Thuggy, look at the ocean!" Harsh gold and red, ever more blinding. Annabel snatches one of the photographs and secretes it under her towel. "I have to take a shower," she says. "See you later, Thug." Thuggy can only pat her bottom as she runs out the doorway.

In the photograph Carter is playing chess. He looks up as if surprised by the camera.

CHAPTER FIFTY-TWO

"Ninety-nine, one hundred." Priscilla Geach finishes brushing her pale orange hair, the many colorless strands of which give it a delicate translucency. Dressed for dinner, she wears a long dress of ivory-colored linen and gold sandals. Her simple necklace and bracelets are coral. Rose enamel shines on her toenails and fingernails, and her perfume is costly.

Jack is busy in his office, Hester in her room has fallen asleep beside a jigsaw puzzle. Downstairs Priscilla finds Edith with paper and crayons at the kitchen table. After checking the evening's dishes—meatloaf, stewed tomatoes, and ice-cream sandwiches for the girls, Senegalese soup, leg of lamb and onions, watercress salad, and *babas au rhum* for Jack and herself—she stands with her hand on the back of her daughter's chair to admire and praise. "That's nice, Edith."

"It's a kitty sitting on a tricycle."

"Yes, I see. It's very nice."

Edith's expression does not change. Her mother, touching another picture, says, "This house is nice too."

"It's not a house. It's my dolly Lisa." Edith stares at the picture.

"Of course it's Lisa. I hadn't looked carefully. Yes, Lisa's very pretty there." Edith does not move. Her eyes slip sideways toward her mother.

The woman smooths the child's hair. "Hungry?" Edith nods thoughtfully.

"Are you looking forward to your birthday?"

Edith nods.

"Have you thought about what you'd like Mommy and Daddy to give you for a birthday present?"

The child nods.

"What would you like?"

"I'll show you." On a clean sheet of paper a brown crayon goes down, across, up for the shoebox. Edith draws the Mary Janes in bright clear red. Finally white marks over each shoe represent candles. "You see?"

Priscilla wrongly assumes that the colors Edith has chosen are arbitrary. But even were she not so handicapped it wouldn't be easy for her to interpret the picture. A duck? smiling, with large eyes? A jump rope? It could be almost anything, Priscilla thinks. Edith's stillness weights the quandary. "You see?" again in the tiny obstinate voice.

"Yes," says Priscilla bravely.

"Promise?"

"Yes, Edith." There is no going back. "Now run upstairs and call your sister. It's time for your supper." Priscilla cannot but smile as she places the picture on a high shelf in the cupboard where it will be safe for later fathomings.

CHAPTER FIFTY-THREE

The dinner was delicious but Priscilla didn't want dessert so that when Annabel came for housecleaning the next morning she was rewarded with a *baba au rhum*. Priscilla explained that she and her daughters were going swimming. Annabel wondered if Jack would use the occasion to apologize for the advances he had made in the woods, or to make further advances, or to demand the twenty-dollar bill which he had pushed into her shirt and which Thuggy had burned. Her anxiety was allayed when Priscilla added that since Jack had gone for a walk to sort out his ideas Annabel might tidy his office.

Annabel began with this task. There was much to do. Pictures were awry, furniture overturned, and the floor was littered not only with shredded paper but also with broken cups and saucers and feathers from a burst pillow. Having dealt with this disorder Annabel proceeded to the clutter on Jack's desk. Here her attention was caught by the salutation "Dear Annabel" on a sheet of paper protruding from a folder marked "TOP SECRET." After a moment of genuine hesitation she slipped the letter out and read it. After all, it was addressed to her. With much ridiculous periphrasis it apologized for the episode in the stormy woods, urging or warning Annabel to speak to no one of it, not even to Jack himself. He seemed to have forgotten the money. Annabel chewed the end of a pen. She wrote "Dear Mr.

Geach, I beg you not to give the matter a second thought" in the margin and replaced the letter. Cleaning the rest of the house was uneventful.

Her violin case under her arm, Annabel waded in the mill-stream some distance from the house and then sat on the bank with her feet in the water. She wore a cowgirl's shirt and shorts made by cutting off the legs of blue jeans. Crayfish ventured from among stones and walked over her toes. When she rose to leave they fled backward into hiding.

Sue Holcomb's cottage also had to be cleaned and water brought there from the well. At last it was time for a violin lesson. Sue Holcombe seemed less irritable than usual, though she was stern. The lesson pleased Annabel.

"Name the spaces," Sue Holcombe began.

"F, A, C, E."

"The lines."

"Every Good Boy Does Fine."

"Now. Play one of the pieces you've learned. Remember your posture." Sue paced back and forth with her chin in her hand as Annabel played and for a few minutes after the music stopped. Annabel waited, doodling on the rug with the tip of her bow. Sue said, "Attack. We work on attack and release today. Attack: how you begin a note, a phrase, an entire work. Release: how you end it. These things are important, young lady, more than you evidently suppose."

"You're right," Annabel said. "I hadn't . . ."

"Quiet. This exercise may prove beneficial. Play the first phrase, to here," pointing at the music, "over, over, and over. Each time you end the phrase think of the one that ought to follow, even as you refuse it. Continue in this manner until your sense of the transition is well enough developed for you to *release* the first phrase and *attack* the second. And then do so. You understand? Begin." She lit a cigarette and perched on the window seat. Her expression was skeptical.

Annabel played,

> *Au clair de la lune,*
> *Au clair de la lune,*
> *Au clair de la lune* . . . .

She expected to end the exercise arbitrarily and quickly, for fear of Sue's impatience and because it seemed perhaps better to get on to something else. But as she repeated the phrase she forgot those considerations. Indeed she almost forgot Sue Holcombe's presence. She played more slowly and steadily until at last—

Au clair de la lune,
Mon ami Pierrot

—it came. Annabel lifted the bow off the strings.

"Hmm," mused Sue. Annabel waited. Sue said, "You see? Now before your next lesson I want you to do that with each phrase-boundary in the piece. Your intonation has improved. I'm surprised. You must have been woodshedding. But it's far from acceptable so keep that nose to the grindstone. When I was your age I practiced until my fingers bled. Yes, but . . ." Sue Holcombe frowned. "Play the entire piece slowly," she commanded.

Annabel obeyed. Sue Holcombe's brow darkened, her eyes flashed. "Give me that violin!"

Sue drew the bow once across the strings and then she shouted, "What vicious thing have you done to this instrument?"

Too astonished to reply, Annabel could only watch as the woman tapped the violin here and there over its body, shook it, held it above her head and shook it, until out one of the f-holes fluttered the stolen photograph of Carter. Sue held it at a distance, regarding it distastefully. "My, whatever might this happen to be?"

Annabel blushed. "Oh dear, I forgot it was there. You see I thought that would be a good hiding place. It's not damaged, is it?"

"I assume you mean the violin. No, but the tone was altered, naturally." Sue Holcombe peered into Annabel's rosy face. "In my day," she observed, "young ladies kept pictures of their sweethearts in lockets hidden under their clothing."

"But Sue, he's not . . ."

"Never mind. Listen carefully. I shouldn't bother to advise you but I shall. First, I have reason to know that this young man is a scoundrel. Don't ask how I know, I'm not at liberty to say. But you ought to forget him because he's the sort who'll take advantage of you, given the chance. Take my word for it, he's no damn good!

"But, second, I also know that youthful infatuations are seldom affected by good advice. The malady runs its course. Assuming then that you cannot help yourself, you may as well keep the photograph inside the violin. The coloring of the tone seems lost on you. And, who knows, it could make you less insensate to the instrument. But only if you remember it's there!" She dropped the photograph back in.

The lawn was full of rabbits, at least twenty, who scattered when pupil and teacher stepped outside. "Look at them go," laughed Sue and then she said, "Incidentally, Annabel. Please remind your friend Jimbo that he has an appointment with me." Still laughing, she re-entered the cottage.

At the clearing's edge Annabel wondered whether the rabbits would hop out of their burrows if she stood motionless. But they were warier than the crayfish in the millstream had been. Long as she stood, there was no sign of them. "Quite right, too," thought Annabel on her way to the farmhouse. Already it had been a long day.

The rabbits did reconvene in front of the cottage, but they had occasion to seek shelter three more times before the next day. Sue Holcombe came out after her dinner with a pail of garbage for them. Much later one of them fell victim to Babe's foray and was hideously devoured. Finally before dawn old Jane came to deposit a letter on the cottage porch.

CHAPTER FIFTY-FOUR

Side by side in the same bed Priscilla and Jack Geach dreamed before waking. The dreams were dissimilar, as you will see.

Jack dreamed that he and Priscilla were ice-skating in the Olympic Games. Priscilla whirled on the point of her skate. Jack was about to do the same. They wore Spanish costumes and flamenco music sounded from loudspeakers. What? Near Priscilla the ice broke and a polar bear emerged growling and huffing. Priscilla was in danger. Jack snatched up a scarlet cape and flourished it to attract the bear's attention. It sped toward him, somehow using its claws as skates. Jack snapped the cape aside and the bear, unable to stop, slid out of the arena. Thunderous applause. Jack bowed. Then he noticed that Priscilla, halfway across the ice, was bowing too. Ignorant of the danger he had saved her from, she supposed her whirling had evoked the applause!

Jack awoke foggily resentful. He found a pair of scissors in the night table and began to clip his toenails.

Priscilla dreamed that she and a beautiful black woman her age were babysitting. Maids brought toys and food for the child and its parents were sleeping upstairs. Two babysitters seemed superfluous. The same thought had occurred to the black woman. "Let's go for a ride," she suggested. Priscilla nodded eagerly. The woman drove to the other side of the world evidently, for it was daytime when they stopped. Alone on a sunny terrace they sipped cocktails, talked, laughed. An oily waiter asked them to pay. Each had forgotten her purse. The waiter said, "You'll have to go inside then. You can't stay here!" Inside was a sort of tavern. Priscilla and her friend sat in an alcove. From other tables people waved to them. Priscilla wanted to comfort her friend. She said, "I like this place." Then she realized that what she had said was true. Priscilla's friend agreed. She said, "We have a great deal to talk about, don't we."

Priscilla woke half recalling the dream and confusedly regretting that it had ended before its conclusion, as it were.

"Good morning."

"Good morning."

Clear air, clear light entered the large room through moving leaves. Jack and Priscilla were naked. A figured satin comforter lay heaped and billowed against the foot of the bed on the stone floor. Slivers of toenail fell from Jack's cupped hand into a sea shell. He turned to regard his wife. Her thighs were paler than the sheets and her little tuft of hair was like cornsilk. She rubbed her eyes with one hand closed into a fist, a loose and fragile one.

Jack's grumpiness vanished. "Priscilla, listen, I . . ."

"Wait—I'm remembering a dream."

"Okay."

When she finished Priscilla looked up at Jack as from afar. His expectant face, his raised eyebrows made her wonder whether she could ever say a final good-by to him. His penis was growing. Priscilla pointed at it and shook her head no. He nodded yes, the penis kept growing.

"I'm serious, Jack."

"Me too," leaping on her. After a short scuffle he desisted and asked, "What's the matter?"

"Don't make me angry," said Priscilla.

"Angry?"

"Don't rile me."

"Jesus Christ," thought Jack. As he did his morning pushups on the floor beside the bed he recounted his dream. There were tears in Priscilla's eyes.

Jack was dousing his face in the basin when he was struck by an idea that brought him bolt upright, dripping. "The bullring, the bear: Priscilla, my dream was about the stock market!"

CHAPTER FIFTY-FIVE

Suddenly all together Daisy, Jimbo, Thuggy, and the dogs come tumbling out the front of the farmhouse, down the steps, across the grass this sunny morning. Soon a raspberry-colored frisbee floats from axis to axis around a spacious triangle. The dogs follow it leaping into the air. When it sails afield one of them will bring it in his or her mouth to the nearest young person.

Daisy wears an indigo sundress with white rickrack, a tortoise-shell barrette holds her hair in a bun. Jimbo's hair is tied with a rawhide thong. He has found a striped bathing costume from the previous century. He and Daisy are barefoot but Thuggy wears colorful cowboy boots, with shorts and a black leather vest through whose opening his belly shines.

Goose has the frisbee. When Rufus tries to take it she flees. They run into the barn. Thuggy urges Jimbo to retrieve the frisbee. "Unless they've given it to Big Boy. If they have, the game's up. Right?"

Jimbo laughs at the taunting. On all fours he says, "I have a better idea. Leapfrog!" Daisy lays her hands on his back, vaults over, lands in front. Thuggy flies over Jimbo and Daisy, Jimbo over Daisy and Thuggy, faster and faster until all collapse laughing.

Daisy points at the sky with her foot. Jimbo says, "Pretend it's down instead of up and hold onto the grass to keep from falling." Thuggy says, "You're a card, Jimbo." Jimbo rolls onto his stomach beside Daisy and says, "Daisy's a card too. You want to be hit?" Thinking of the leapfrog, Daisy says, "Where's the old red card, where's he hiding. That reminds me, I have to collect a box of dope and stuff right now. We can celebrate with it tonight."

"We'll escort you."

"No thanks. You rowdy boys might spook Gail and Faye. See you later."

The boys watch her skip across the field and into the woods. "Want to throw some softball?"

"Sure," says Jimbo. "I'll get it." In a moment he is back. "Which mitt do you want?"

"That one."

"Good choice," says Jimbo.

"Hey, what's this inside it?"

"A bonbon. Swallow it whole and I'll give you another."

"Far out. What's in yours?"

"Nothing. Now my hand."

Far apart in the open field, lazily, gracefully, the boys throw the softball back and forth. Soon Thuggy's aim falters. Jimbo waits with his arms crossed. Thuggy winds up, swings his arm, kicks out his foot, teeters, and falls sideways onto his shank. Jimbo savors the moment wickedly. How he swaggers in his bathing suit, how his spectacles flash! as he comes over the grass to where Thuggy lies shaken with laughter. Like a drunken panda Thuggy kneels or sits when he tries to stand and he laughs at himself. Jimbo too is amused but he maintains a solumn demeanor as he delivers this admonition:

"You enjoyed mocking me about Big Boy, didn't you. Well, look at you now. You can't even walk. Know why? There was a red in the jelly bean you swallowed. I dislike tricking you, but people have to learn not to make fun of me. So this is your punishment, Thuggy: to act like a fool for several hours."

Thuggy is not abashed. In fact he is charmed and he applauds, now wearing both mitts.

CHAPTER FIFTY-SIX

That afternoon Hester Geach visited old Jane and was disappointed. At lunch little Edith had bragged that on her birthday she was going to receive from her parents "what I always wanted, something you have." Hester didn't know why, but this announcement had made her restless, made her stroll to the boathouse even though it had occurred to her that perhaps for politeness' sake more time ought to have passed since her last visit. When Hester arrived Jane was suffering consequences of having ventured out in the cold and damp to Sue Holcombe's cottage the night before. The pain was so sharp that Jane could barely remember the child, and the proffered bouquet of wildflowers slipped from her hand unnoticed. Hester suggested Fish, Jane declined. Hester insisted, adopting with the best intentions a certain officious tone of her mother's. "Yes, you ought to play. You'll feel much better." Jane had actually shooed Hester out the doorway. "No thank you! another time."

Was this amiable? Poor Hester was downcast. She walked at random until she found herself at the farmhouse. After some hesitation she determined to pay a call there. Her feelings were ambivalent and complex. She wished not to encounter Carter or Jimbo because of the embarrassment each in his way had caused her. On the other hand she would have been pleased to find Thuggy. As for Annabel and Daisy, she neither hoped nor feared to meet them, and it was they she met.

They were in the kitchen preparing frosting for a batch of cupcakes. "They're for Edith's birthday party," Annabel explained. The frosting was white but Daisy divided it into two bowls to be colored as Hester chose. Torn between desires to demonstrate good taste and to wreak vengeance on her sister,

Hester tinted one portion a lovely magenta and the other a muddy green.

Then Hester went gathering herbs with the two girls. In their company the woods seemed unfamiliar and larger, as they gathered leaves, berries, bark, and roots to fill Annabel's gunny sack and Daisy's basket—fireweed, cinquefoil, pipsissewa, lovage, couch grass. It seemed that every plant had its own name.

"What's this, Daisy?"

"Sea wrack."

"This?"

"Queen of the meadow. We want its root as well as the leaves. And look, hyssop, mullein, and, look, shepherd's purse."

"What's this one?"

"I don't know. Pretty, isn't it."

Annabel's gold hoop earrings made Hester imagine the girl had been stolen and reared by Gypsies.

"Daisy?"

"Squaw vine."

Annabel knew a few plants. "A lady's slipper! I've never seen one before. Look, Hester. It's like a little yellow shoe."

Daisy said, "We could use the root, but . . ."

"I'll dig it up," Hester offered.

"No," said Daisy, "no, I think it's really too rare to take. Better leave it."

"What about honeysuckle?" asked Annabel. "That's every where."

"Yes, the leaves. And look." She showed Hester and Annabel how to suck a drop of nectar from the base of each blossom. Hawthorn, vervain and coltsfoot, deer tongue, burdock and tansy, woodruff and sassafras and other treasures were collected, including witch hazel, whose name made Hester ask in astonishment, "Do we want *that?*" "Yes indeed." Yet when Hester was forbidden to touch, because of its deadly poison, a plant with plump berries and delicate purple and yellow flowers, she was told that its name was "belladonna."

During the walk and when they returned and drank a tisane at the farmhouse, Hester was trying to decide which of the two girls she would prefer to be friends with and, more distantly, which she would rather grow up to resemble. She was more sympathetically drawn to Daisy—Annabel didn't seem quite ladylike. But when, as happened from time to time, Hester asked a question that gave both girls pause, she noticed that Daisy would glance at Annabel and that often as not she would wait for Annabel to reply. Hester appreciated the authority, like that of a parent or an older sister, that hereby seemed to accrue to the short-haired girl. Nor in the woods had Annabel seemed ashamed of the disparity between her knowledge of herbs and Daisy's. Having considered and weighed alternatives, Hester arrived at a praiseworthy if awkward solution: "I prefer both."

On the table was an open cookie tin of uncleaned marijuana. "What herb is this?" asked Hester.

After a moment it was Annabel who answered. "You wouldn't be interested in that. It's not for children."

Hester nodded with an air of understanding.

"I wonder why though," mused Daisy. "I mean, what might a stoned child do that could be so terrible?"

Annabel shrugged. "Talk out of turn? But I think it's that a child is supposed to be somehow more affected by it than we are. Like with sex."

Knowing as she looked, intently as she listened, Hester could not imagine what the girls were talking about now.

CHAPTER FIFTY-SEVEN

Along the windward shore a steady sou'easter was lifting whitecaps. Thuggy had left the softball and mitts at the farmhouse and come here for a walk, erroneously supposing that like alcohol the downer Jimbo had tricked him into swallowing could be worked off. This was while Annabel and Daisy were gathering herbs with Hester Geach in the interior of the island.

The tide was rising but so low that the wind brought sharp odors from exposed flats and shoals, cold mud and weed, and thus seemed itself cooler than it was and rather belied the heat of the sun. Thuggy jogged unsteadily in the sand, waving his bare arms and singing, "Give me some time to blow the man down." As he ran he rotated slowly and saw water, land—crying gulls, white butterflies over wild roses, flocks of gulls, butterflies, ocean, island.

When the sand gave way to rocks and pebbles Thuggy slowed. Time passed as he pored over interesting shells or pieces of driftwood. His head swam. "Annabel," he said. There was a clanging. "Anna bell-buoy." Thuggy stood motionless.

Then he did something extraordinary. Well aware of the incongruous figure he cut in his vest, short pants, and pointed boots, he minced and swayed across the pebbles, one hand on his hip, with the coyest flutterings of his eyelids. It was so ridiculous he laughed aloud. Then he shrugged and said, "Sure. Underneath, everybody wants to be a chick, man." He meant to say more but a wave of something like seasickness washed over him. He sighed and then (not surprisingly, considering how long the sun had beaten down on his drugged head) he lost consciousness and fell to the ground.

Here the boy lay. He was being baked by hot stones from beneath and from above by the sun but instead of browning like a loaf of bread he went deathly pale. His eyes rolled, his pulse slowed and faltered. Thuggy's life could easily have ended just there. No one would have chanced upon him nor would anyone have come searching for him until it was too late by hours. Nor, had they wished to, could the gulls have awakened him with their cries.

The advancing sea itself prevented his untimely demise. The spray doused him and startled him out of a dream of white painlessness. "What the fuck's happening?" Thuggy understood that he was in danger. He wasn't yet strong enough to reach shade but he managed to struggle out of his clothing and lurch into the bracing waves. He peed under the water. The mainland lay like a mirage along the horizon. Thuggy was himself again, with good color.

CHAPTER FIFTY-EIGHT

Sluice gates open. The stream detours and the ancient wheel, motionless for decades, begins to turn, creaking and rumbling in the silent afternoon. The force is carried along a wooden axle through granite. In the dusty mill room a large machinery of stone, iron, and wood begins to move.

In her sewing room where she has been embroidering Priscilla is amazed and frightened to hear the noise and to see the wheel move at her window. Jack is in the woods. The children too, supposedly. Priscilla leans out—empty lawn and water cascading from the wheel, which now turns calmly as if it had never rested.

Priscilla hurries downstairs. Dreading it, she unlatches the mill room door and slips inside. At the far end the humble gears and grindstones are working. Nearer, two girls stand in the dimness. One strums a zither as they sing this song:

Braid no mayflowers in your hair
Nor dance with a handsome lover.
Heed not his word—however fair,
Too soon you wander
Sole, sole,
All in the rain.

Light summer vows fly otherwhere
And leave a changèd heaven
Too soon, a cold and darkening air
And lovelorn maidens
Sole, sole,
All in the rain.

"Who are you? Why are you here?" Priscilla asks.

"Oh! You startled us! We're Faye."

"And Gail. You must be Ms. Geach. You're lovely. Isn't she lovely, Gail."

"Very."

Priscilla says, "I don't understand at all."

"We owe you an explanation certainly."

"You see we didn't know you were at home."

"We supposed the house to be empty this afternoon."

"You were so quiet about whatever you were engaged in. Napping perhaps."

"In all innocence we thought we might seize the opportunity to do a chore."

"A small devoir, hardly guessing you would discover us. Ah but we've been caught out, haven't we, Faye."

"Without a chance to scurry away."

The ragged hems of their dresses reach the floor. Faye has a leather scrip, Gail's necklace is of amber. Priscilla asks where they live and they explain that they live in the woods. It seems impossible. Priscilla wonders what they are up to. She says, "You still haven't told me why," gesturing toward the loud millworks.

"What did you imagine? We're milling. Nuts and wild legumes."

"Into a kind of flour. It's done now but you can see the process, the operation."

"We thought, why not use it after all? We meant no harm."

"None."

Priscilla says, "I understand. But . . . but you ought to have asked permission. I would have been glad . . ." she breaks off, interrupted by the girls' laughter.

"Ms. Geach!"

"Ms. Geach, we didn't know you were here! How could we ask permission?"

Priscilla says, "If you ever want to use the mill again, you're welcome to. It's only that . . ."

"You'd appreciate being warned."

"Thank you, Ms. Geach. You're more than kind. If we come again we'll halloo in the doorway. Won't we, Faye."

"Of course. And we won't forget to close the sluices as we leave. Good-by."

"Good-by, Faye. Good-by, Gail."

Priscilla waits in the yellow light and noise until the machinery slowing, slowing, comes to a standstill. She sighs.

In the hallway she hears knocking at the front door. Back already? Priscilla surprises herself. In the instant before she moves to answer the summons a speech forms in her mind. "Forgive my silly stiffness and reluctance. I don't know what comes over me. Come in and talk to me if you can. Have you had lunch? May I visit you someday? You're both very pretty. You aren't sisters, are you?" Knock, knock.

At the door Priscilla finds a single boy who says, "Ms. Geach?"

"Yes?"

"Hi. I'm Jimbo, one of Annabel's housemates. She and Daisy asked me to bring you these cupcakes."

"Oh, the cupcakes. Come in, Jimbo, Why so early?"

"Daisy says they're best two or three days after they're baked and that they'll keep for a week. She thought it would be a good idea to deliver them now so they'd be out of temptation's way. Gosh, what's this? A tambourine?"

"It's some needlework I was doing, I must have dropped it. Thanks. Come into the kitchen, Jimbo, and help me sample these cupcakes. I'm sure they're delicious. Are you a student?"

As Priscilla brews tea Jimbo examines her embroidery. On pearl-gray satin held taut over a metal hoop the design of white, brown, and red has been worked in silk thread. "It's nice. Odd," he observes. "Really nice."

"Thank you. I hope my daughter likes it." She tells the story of Edith's picture. "I hope I'll be able to interpret it somehow before her birthday but I may well not. I thought I could at least honor the terms of the agreement by giving her the picture itself, embroidered on the yoke of a dress."

"I see." Jimbo is staring at the design. "By the way, is there a photograph of Edith I could look at?" Priscilla brings one. Jimbo exclaims, "I thought so, of course!" He looks back at the embroidery. "Listen, Ms. Geach, I know what this is a picture of. Red Mary Jane shoes like her sister's, but brand new." He recounts his having been awakened by Edith's voice and overhearing her wish.

Priscilla is delighted and profoundly grateful, as she makes clear to Jimbo. "Don't mention it," he shrugs, yawning. "So, I'll be on my way."

Priscilla finds him charming quite apart from the good turn he has done her. "Nice eyes," she thinks after he is gone, "nice teeth, too."

Jimbo has been rather charmed by her. It had occurred to him when she left the room to bring the photograph of Edith that it would be a good trick to exchange the salt and sugar in their containers on the table. But he had desisted. "So what?" he thinks.

CHAPTER FIFTY-NINE

In summer here in late afternoon for an hour or so it often seems later than it is. Jane had noticed as much before but today it struck her anew. The sunshine was clear and horizontal. Jane made her way through the wilderness up toward the top of the island. Swish, swish, ragged fronds of every kind of green brushed against her white legs, her smooth black canes.

Gulls alarmed by her coming rose and circled crying loudly. In the upper part of the island their droppings, feathers, fragments of eggshell, broken skeletons of their dead, broken sea shells, bits of rabbit fur, and other remnants of their feeding cover the ground with a thick mat. The young at this time of year are large as adults but still wear a dowdy plumage too feeble for flight. Many of them ran from Jane and stood under a shrub or beside a tree, foolishly supposing she couldn't see them. Rabbits ran faster and disappeared into their burrows with a flash of white.

For several days Jane had enjoyed a merciful freedom from the grievance of rheumatism. She had been able to sleep and to think. But today along each leg aches and twinges warned her of the respite's end.

Jane stood at the tip of the island like the figurehead of a ship surveying the steadily moving slate-colored water. Here the land falls abruptly some thirty feet. Below, narrow pebble beach and stretches of mussel shoal are littered with tidal debris. It was there that long ago Jane had come upon a section of centerboard from the wreck of her husband's vessel. At the bluff's edge stands a jumble of rotting concrete, the ruins of a little bunker or bird-blind that hadn't survived a single winter's storms. From a string bag Jane took the architect's drawings of the farmhouse. She had wrapped them in waxed paper and had sprayed the wrappings with insecticide. She wedged the package deep among hunks of concrete and turned to make her way back down the center of the island.

Daisy had been strolling in pleasant idleness about the woods, thinking she might perhaps encounter Jimbo as he returned from the millhouse, perhaps not, but if she did they might sit together and talk or whatever in a secluded place until night fell and whippoorwills began calling in the beautiful transparency—when what should she notice but white hair in the underbrush off the path. "Jane? Is that you? Are you all right?"

From where she crouched Jane called, "I'm peeing, Daisy." She patted herself with lavender-scented cambric. It wasn't easy to hitch up underdrawers or to manage the canes as she struggled to her feet, but she wanted no help. "Hello, Daisy. What are you up to?" The old woman came out into the path with the girl.

Jane was pleased for Daisy to accompany her to the boathouse. "Let's see now, who all is it you've got this summer? I've met Thuggy and Jimbo."

"Nice boys, aren't they. There's also Annabel. She's Jimbo's cousin but they'd never met before. She's my best friend. And there's Carter who's very handsome and funny. That's all. Do you have anybody?"

"No. Not yet at least. Good weather this year."

"Lovely."

"Yes indeed. So then this is your third summer here, isn't it. You must be happy with the farmhouse."

"I am, Jane."

"Good. Before it came to you, it hurt me for it to stand empty and get run down. It wouldn't have lasted much longer, I don't imagine."

"Jane?"

"Yes, Daisy?"

They bade each other good evening at a fork of the path. When Jane came out of the woods near the boathouse the sun seemed scarcely to have moved or the clear light to have darkened. Jane hooked her string bag over a rusty hook on the doorjamb.

CHAPTER SIXTY

"Dear Charlotte," Jane wrote. "Forgive my not replying sooner. I was under the weather. I'm mended now and looking forward to seeing you here more than anything. I wonder if we'll recognize one another after all these years." The light held, there was no need for a lantern. The air cooled and each degree of change registered pain in the bones of Jane's legs. She told herself, "Go to bed, Jane." Resignedly she climbed the stairs. Having located an alarm clock in her night table, she lay still.

At the top of the island Sue Holcombe rushed across droppings and feathers. She thrust a greedy hand into the concrete and withdrew the parcel Jane had left there, replacing it with a smaller one. "Ah, ah, ah," she laughed, "the fool, how he'll rue this day! Oh, ah, ah, ah!" Her laughter blew away over the solemn water and vanished. Though she was tempted to open the parcel then and there, she knew the drawings might prove difficult. "Furthermore," she thought, "he might show up any moment and I've no time for chitchat now," brushing crumbs of concrete off her hands and wrists. And she was suddenly hungry, and a rabbit stew was simmering on the stove in the kitchen of her cottage. Sue Holcombe ran. Whenever a fallen log blocked her path she leapt over it without breaking stride. It seemed to her that the woods held still, awed by her passage. She felt indomitable, almost lazy, as if she had wings.

Thuggy had partly recovered from the effects of the barbiturate he had swallowed, but some heedless foolishness remained. He stood in a pleasant glade idly twirling a lariat. He heard Sue Holcombe coming and, though the light was no longer good, when she burst out into the open near him he lassoed her so skillfully that she didn't notice the circle of rope drop around her and couldn't understand why her feet were at once jerked from under her. She might have been injured had she not landed on a bed of moss. "Whoa!" Thuggy called.

The woman and the boy were dazed. For a moment neither stirred. Sue Holcombe felt and saw the rope that bound her knees and stretched to Thuggy's hand. Her mind raced. Very sweetly she said, "There must be some error in your judgment, young man. I don't believe we've met." Meanwhile she picked at the slip knot.

"No way, kid," said Thuggy, tightening the rope from where he stood. He pretended to draw a pistol, spin it, and aim it at Sue's forehead. "About the deed to your ranch . . ."

"An alcoholic," thought Sue, "soused." She said, "I admire your expertise with this rope. I wonder if you might teach me to fling it?"

"Right on."

Freed, Sue Holcombe became the model pupil she had never encountered, the one she had in truth dreaded to encounter—attentive, thoughtful, questioning as Thuggy demonstrated the management of the lariat, and also displaying a polite interest in the teacher himself. "Do you happen to live here on the island?"

"Right, in the farmhouse. Okay, let's give it a try. I'll stand over there and you lasso me. I think you're gonna be able to do it."

"I hope so."

"Beautiful," shouted Thuggy as the rope tightened pinning his elbows to his sides. With apparently friendly tugs Sue Holcombe drew him to a large oak and then she ran many times around, playing out rope as she went until a thick coil held the boy against the tree. She attached the free end with a strong sailor's knot on the side of the trunk opposite the captive.

She stood in front of him. He grinned. "Lout," she said, and spat in his face. As she dashed away she cried, "A penny for your thoughts."

Sue Holcombe hadn't gone far when she realized that in her excitement she had forgotten her parcel which she assumed must have flown out of her hands when she had been lassoed. Berating herself, she charged back to retrieve it. Now it was so dark she could scarcely see but her sense of direction was excellent. In the glade she did find the parcel easily where it lay on the moss. With it clutched under her arm she marched over to the oak intending to heap more scorn on Thuggy. Poor Sue was unnerved to discover no trace of boy or rope at the kindly old tree. She half expected to be assaulted. But she suffered no further mishap hastening back to her cottage. She locked doors and windows, pulled down window shades, and loaded her shotgun. She served herself a generous portion of stew and a dry martini. She lit a cigarette and began to study the drawings.

Thuggy meanwhile came down the beach toward the farmhouse, whistling, stepping in and out of his whirling lasso, and believing Sue Holcombe had had second thoughts and returned to free him. For soon after her disappearance the knot behind the tree had been untied. When he had uncoiled the rope he had found no one to thank, but he supposed that his benefactor was the small woman. "She's far out, whoever she is," he said.

CHAPTER SIXTY-ONE

"Shock is 'a state of collapse caused by acute peripheral circulatory failure. It may occur in such conditions as severe trauma, major surgery, massive hemorrhage, dehydration, overwhelming infections, and drug toxicity.' "

"More lanterns?"

"And, uh, the simplest form is syncope, fainting. Sudden drop in blood pressure, cerebral anoxia, loss of consciousness. More severe forms fatal—irreversible. Permanent, you might say."

"Mmm. I was thinking I'd like a haircut. Somebody?"

"But listen, what's the function of shock? Its *raison d'être*."

"Doesn't really say."

"I think your hair's fine."

"I still want it cut though. Could you hand me the sugar?"

"Gonna be cold. It's already cold."

"Funny."

"What's the book?"

"A medical manual."

"So Daisy, what treats did you get from Faye and Gail? What kind of party are we going to have?"

"Look." Daisy slips the lid off a shoe box and parts and spreads open points of white tissue paper. In the comfortable parlor the young people sip an herbal infusion from the fine china teacups. The dogs are here too. Near the door stands a tall bouquet of orange day lilies Carter has gathered. On each stalk one blossom is closing and one bud is preparing to bloom tomorrow. The lanterns shed gold light.

"Look." The shoe box is filled with prettily labeled pouches and boxes, bottles and jars of marijuana, hashish, amphetamine tablets and spansules, windowpane LSD, various antidepressants, DMT, white and brown cocaine, mescaline as well as peyote buttons, psylocybin. "Gosh." "Bravo."

A cricket chirps under the fronds of a fern. Smiling, Jimbo scans a page of a fashion magazine on which is printed a desperate description of a ball in a foreign city. Annabel reads over his shoulder. Carter and Thuggy arrange paper, kindling and logs in the fireplace. Daisy tamps marijuana into the bowl of a long-stemmed pipe and supplies a hookah with hashish. Annabel uses a razor blade to chop and rechop a morsel of cocaine into powder. Jimbo wonders whether Carter and Thuggy need more paper. The herbal tea is delicious. There is much discussion of how, in what orders and combinations, and by whom the drugs will be taken. Windows are lowered against the chilly sea wind. The fire crackles.

There is a dance of lovely small movements about the room—a shoulder, an ankle, a fingertip along the edge of a saucer, glances. There are occasional movements on the dogs' faces. Any expression assumed by one of the five human faces is always changing to another. The air is warm but near the windows it is cold. Rufus sighs.

"So, then. Everybody gets off on something fast—DMT, coke, speed. That way nobody's left behind, nobody starts on the wrong foot."

"Slower stuff is up to each one. The treats stay on the table and when you feel like anything you take it."

"Seems eminently perfect."

"Annabel can have her haircut first thing, that way she'll be sure to get it."

"And it won't be too outlandish or freaky."

"I'm sort of nervous."

"So what else is new. Elated?"

"Yes."

"Yes."

"Certainly."

"Thrilled. More than thrilled."

The grandfather clock in the hallway chimes the quarter hour. When scissors close on a handful of Annabel's hair the severance of each strand is felt as part of a shushing graininess. Half an inch of striated brown turns blonde as it falls off the cold blade like stardust. Thuggy brings applesauce and wine from the kitchen. The birch logs are burning excellently. When a bitter wet slice of peyote touches the tongue the mouth fills with saliva and the whole body protests what the mind notes quite without disgust. Gelatin rectangles carry an LSD of rare cleanliness. Annabel's haircut pleases her. It pleases everyone. Distant and vinegary, the grandfather clock is chiming.

"How do you feel?"

"Wow, I mean . . . I mean, spaced."

"There's so much to think about!"

"It's all there if you just know how to think about it."

"Let's try."

The barometer is falling. From the center of the room the windows are black mirrors but nearer, in the embrasure of the curtains, one sees through—the cold night, the porch, the dark meadow and woods, the sky, some white fog coming in from shore.

CHAPTER SIXTY-TWO

How strongly the drugs are affecting these young people! Never before in the farmhouse parlor such buzzing, rush, clenched teeth. The fire may warm the skin, it may not. Spine pringles, edgy cheer. How large eyesockets feel now! If an assassin entered the room he would find only five ordinary-sized young victims, no additional nimbus to be killed afterward.

Thuggy is trying to read to himself before reading aloud a new section of his story. But as he reads and rereads the first sentence ("Disdainfully sniffing Mme. Encore's pussy and Lelouch's cock, the dog yawned"), Thuggy is struck by how difficult the written word even in one's own language grows when one is stoned on almost any drug. Speech heard or performed is shady enough, with multiple entendres every which way (Thuggy thinks), but the written word turns out to be simply impossible!, stuffing the paper into his pocket. On the other hand the loud music that comes out of the two speakers is more accessible, admirable, and (seemingly) understandable because of the drugs.

Without moving his head Thuggy sees Annabel and Jimbo without either's knowledge. When he closes his eyes he can still see them and they become human musical instruments which he plays to create parts of the sound he hears. Annabel's head serves as a violin—her chin under Thuggy's, her mouth agape to expose vocal cords he draws a bow across. Jimbo's lower jaw widens into a keyboard under Thuggy's fingers. When he applies pursed lips to Annabel's cunt and blows, out her opened mouth soars the clear song of a trumpet. Language is tame by comparison (he thinks).

"What's everybody thinking?" Annabel asks.

Carter is thinking that inasmuch as Indian and perhaps Oriental holy men control their pulses and body temperatures and breath, and since children can wiggle their ears, and seeing as how he read or heard somewhere that it was possible to dilate or contract the pupils of the eyes voluntarily, it might be possible for a man to make his penis stand or lie down at will. A pair of secret words—they'd have to be secret—spoken in the mind might work like the bells that make dogs salivate. Carter imagines exhibiting the talent for friends. He sits on a stool, naked. "Make it stand up, Carter." It stands. "Now make it lie down." It does so. Applause. "I'll have to do some experimenting," Carter thinks, "soon, as soon as possible. Tomorrow."

Annabel moves a switch from PLAY to RECORD. The music halts.

Jimbo says, "I was thinking about Ms. Geach. I met her this afternoon when I delivered the cupcakes."

"Yes, but what were you thinking about her?"

"That's the question. What you were thinking, not who you may have been thinking about."

Jimbo smiles slightly. "I don't think I was thinking anything. I was more like feeling something about her, or recalling her in a certain way."

"What way?"

"Avuncular, nostalgic. Also the way you might look at a work of art. A small painting that's not bad even though you don't know the artist's name, and you know he's not well known."

"You mean you were thinking about her in a sort of sentimental aesthetic way."

"With economic overtones."

"Yes," Jimbo says.

Thuggy says, "I was thinking about how being stoned affects listening to music and reading oppositely. Music's like every other art except literature: dope improves it. But dope ruins reading. I was thinking maybe the difference was important. But I couldn't decide whether it counted for or against literature."

"Beautiful."

"Hmm."

Carter's light blue-gray eyes lose focus so that the braided rug doubles, ellipses intersecting, colors washing through each other. The boy feels overcome with admiration, gratitude, and affection for the hands that made the rug slowly a long time ago and also, similarly somehow, for Daisy whom he cannot see without moving his head. Without moving his head Carter says, "I don't know if I should say what I was thinking. But I will." He presents his idea of voluntary control over the rigor of the penis. Everyone listens as he describes his imagined demonstration. Gravity and thoughtfulness appear in Carter's voice. "I hope nobody's . . . You're not, are you, Daisy—shocked?" The word breaks or seems to break the air along zigzag fault lines letting in a wonderful chill. Everyone's hair stands on end.

Daisy says, "I was thinking how perfectly beautiful we all are, how perfectly different from each other in the most beautiful ways, so much that I was thinking anybody at all would have to want to be us exactly as we are here tonight. And then that made me think how scarily transient everything is, so that I was nearly wishing we weren't maybe so beautiful after all—nearly, but not quite."

Why is Daisy's voice urgently reassuring as she tells this lie? Why does she lie? At the moment of Annabel's question she was in fact thinking about food. She was imagining beefsteaks with thyme and tomatoes roasting in the fireplace. A Szechuan hot and sour soup for dinner tomorrow. Herring in sour cream and apple and onion sauce. *Marrons glacés*. "But Annabel, what were you thinking? Besides the question of what was on everybody else's mind."

"I was wondering if anybody'd ask." Annabel moistens her lower lip with the tip of her tongue. She notices Carter's jawline, his throat and, apparent through his tee shirt, shoulder muscle, clavicle, nipple. She sighs and says, "I was thinking about those," nodding toward the row of pictures above the sofa. "I was wishing I knew a million things about them. Like things about Bronzino, about those children, about their clothes What happened to them when they grew up. I mean why exactly were those pictures painted? Where are they now, who owns them, who owned them since they were painted, what'll happen to them in the future, how long will they last, how many reproductions of them are there, who looks at them, what do different kinds of people say about them, what do they think about them, how many times a year does each of them get thought about, I was asking myself. They look shy. When they grew up did they sometimes look at the pictures and think 'That's what I looked like when I was a child'? I wonder whether Bronzino ever saw the paintings after they were done and if he did I wonder what he thought of them."

Everyone seems bemused. Annabel pushes the tape recorder switch to REWIND. "Wish, wish, wish, wish," it whispers Click. Click, ". . . a sort of sentimental aesthetic way."

"With economic overtones."

"Yes," click.

The voices sound quiet but huge. Nor are they familiar. They are identifiable without being recognizable as it were. The same is true of what they say.

The same is true of the room with its fire and dogs and of the young people's bodies, each other's and one's own. "Like something you've heard about but never saw till now," observe Thuggy. "Did I say that aloud or only think it?" he wonders The flames are clear and lovely. They have a bright squeakiness everything does. A chill may crawl up one side of the body and that the side facing the fire. Naùsea can be resisted only so long before one must hurry out onto the porch and vomit over the railing through thickening fog into the grass, and then one feel much better, rejoining friends inside. One wonders what migh have been said in one's absence. It seems best to stay together Carter sneezes.

Jimbo tears the cover of a magazine into strips, tears the strips into small rectangles, deals out the rectangles as playing cards The young people sit in a circle on the rug. Jimbo places one o his bits of paper in the center. Everyone knows it is Daisy's turn for she is at Jimbo's left. The rectangle Jimbo has discarded has letters on it and its colors are black, pink, green, and flesh. Without speaking Daisy selects one of her bits of paper and lays it on Jimbo's. The game continues in silence. Do rules keep changing or is it that they are never entirely understood? There is occasional laughter.

CHAPTER SIXTY-THREE

"Give the doggies some?"

"Why not?"

"They've never . . . but I'm sure . . ."

"Acid?"

"And catnip for any kitties loitering about."

"Goosey, Rufus, you're going to come with us. A trip, doggies!"

"Gosh, I love them. They're so, touch them, so warm."

"And patient."

"They're clearly the most beautiful dogs in the world."

"The most stoned, I think, too. Look."

"Rufus?"

The dog's head jerks. He is beginning to feel the drug and can't guess what he ought to do. He blinks solemnly. He manages to fit his large frame under a bent-wood rocking chair no one is sitting in. He is uncontrollably sad. Goose doesn't notice, she has her own reactions to contend with. Her black fur lifts as though she is about to fight and yet she sees no enemies in the room. Goose stares at flames that move in the fireplace. The heat feels cold on her nipples.

Jimbo has unintentionally ended the game played with bits of the cover of a magazine. Thinking of Daisy and of Annabel, at his turn he has pretended that since no play is open to him he can only shrug good-naturedly, untie his red bandanna, and toss it into the circle as a forfeit, surprising himself as much as anyone else.

Annabel laughs. "We're in no condition. And I'm a coward. I say we should cheat: all undress without further ado. It's easier." Carter's relaxation pleases her. "How do I look with my new haircut?" she wonders.

"Do we want some music?"

"Good heavens no!"

"Unless somebody feels like humming."

"I . . ."

Heaps of garments fall into empty drawers of a wooden filing cabinet in the corner near the day lilies. The young people admire each other's bodies. Everyone laughs to see revealed between Thuggy's pubic hair and his navel a heart enclosing the word "Annabel" drawn on the skin in blue ink. Annabel laughs, though some dismay mingles with her pleasure.

Annabel enjoys the naked boys. She enjoys seeing Daisy naked, Daisy blushing, Daisy's blue eyes appealing to her for sanction. Most of all she enjoys the nakedness of her own fine long torso, her grace and strength which seem to her to echo Carter's.

"Look at Thuggy's arms," Carter is whispering to Daisy, but everyone hears, "imagine getting hugged. Look at his belly." Thuggy's belly is round and firm as a melon. Carter shakes his head in amazement. He looks at Daisy's white belly.

"Somebody could fuck to put the rest of us at ease."

Everything in the room seems beautifully placed with respect to everything else, a wineglass on the mantelpiece as inevitable and permanent as the vast sofa. The harmony of colors seems miraculous.

"I might have known," says Jimbo, "the time to think about clothes is when you're naked. If my tongue works I want to tell three of the things I've thought in the last . . . what? minute?"

"Do."

Jimbo says, "Somebody time me, as a matter of interest."

"Everybody wants to listen."

"Okay, so jot down the time now and then again when I stop. We can subtract."

"Good idea."

"Okay, so . . . uh, the first thing was about fashions. The second thing is this: isn't the idea of appropriate attire uncanny? I don't mean snowshoes for snow, I mean 'party shoes' for a party. It's loony somehow. It's, I don't know, it's like eating newspaper for breakfast. Or if you're going to do that sort of thing, why not go all the way?"

"?"

Jimbo says, "The principle seems to be 'suit yourself to the occasion.' Make your clothes show you know where you are and what's happening. So, if you're going to a party, why not have the word 'Party' embroidered on what you're wearing. And since it's not just any party you might wear the address and the date and the time. Then anybody could look at you and say, 'Right, he knows what's up.'

"The third thing," Jimbo continues, "is like the other side of the coin. I was thinking about Halloween and how good it is to see children in costumes and to see they have no idea how wonderful it is because they take it as seriously as everything else. I was thinking the quality of adult life would improve if (not only on Halloween, but always) children dressed as Gypsies, skeletons, and so forth."

"Devils."

"Doctors."

"Witches, ballerinas, pirates."

"Heaven."

The waterpipe gurgles. Jimbo hands the nozzle to Annabel. Thuggy lays another birch log across the andirons. Footsteps on the porch stair, on the porch. Knock, knock at the door. Wearing Carter's tee shirt and Thuggy's shorts, Daisy hastens to receive the visitor. The others peek into the hallway.

The dark shape Daisy sees against the fog nods and, when she opens the door, enters and says, "This is the farmhouse, isn't it? Then you must be the owner. Your name is Daisy I believe, unless I'm mistaken. I'm Jack Geach. Your friend Annabel is an employee of mine. She's a fine girl and I have the greatest respect for her."

"Your lips are blue, Mr. Geach," Daisy says. "Come in. We have a fire. We were . . ."

"Good, that sounds very nice," exclaims Jack. "You're right, Daisy: it's cold out there. I find it very invigorating and zest-producing, very. I did lose my way tonight though. You know, I've never seen such thick fog. It's literally pea soup. I saw your lights and I thought . . . Oh, have I . . . ?" Jack recognizes marijuana in the air. He recognizes Annabel on the windowseat leafing through a magazine, wearing bluejeans below the waist and nothing above. Jack recognizes the two boys he met in the woods—Thuggy in his leather vest and Carter naked in the firelight. Jimbo whom Jack has never yet seen is fully clothed. He sits like an Indian on the sofa and his spectacles flash as he breathes. "What time is it?" he asks. The question sends a chill through poor Jack and makes tears well in his eyes so that he must tilt his wristwatch to read it.

"It's late," Jack says, "I really should go home now and catch a few winks. You see, the next three days—tomorrow and the next two—are extremely crucial with regard to an extremely important, risky, and far-reaching series of financial transactions under the direction of yours truly. I owe it to myself to be in tiptop condition because the slightest absence of alertness could easily cost hundreds of thousands. Sounds intimidating, doesn't it. I'm sure it would be for you fellows. But I can safely say I remain calm in the very mouth of danger. I, and I even . . . Mmm, what would you think if you dreamed about a bear."

Daisy shrugs and says, "It depends. A bare what?"

"A bear in a bull ring!" Jack exclaims. "You see?, no dice! That's the point, isn't it." He laughs indulgently. "I'll let myself out. Good-by now." He whispers, "Not bad!" in Thuggy's ear, nodding toward Annabel. In the doorway he waves and says, "Bye."

Everyone regrets Jack's departure. Has he taken the power of speech with him? No one is eager to meet anyone else's glance.

"Wait a minute. Did he say something about small craft warnings?"

"That's your imagination talking. I think what he said was something about, about a bull?"

Jimbo believes he hears a rippling of his friends' voices saying "Hmm," and "Oh yes." He believes he feels an attention turning toward him.

CHAPTER SIXTY-FOUR

"After all," thinks Annabel, "nobody knows what I'm thinking. In fact nobody could possibly know." Across the room where a fern droops over the edge of a basket suspended from the ceiling, Daisy turns on a radio which at this hour provides only scratchy whines and whisperings, and they sound rather more beautiful than any music. Her chin on her knee, Daisy laces up a tennis shoe. Thuggy can watch her shamelessly so long as her gaze rests on Jimbo, who stares foolishly at a lantern. The smears of dark gold are Annabel's hair on the floor.

Carter basks in the glow from the fireplace. In the long silky hair on his head, his eyebrows and lashes, the damp hair under his arm, in his rich pubic hair and the hair along his legs and forearms are many kinds of gold. His skin is smoothest brown. He lies on his side. His eyes look half open. Down across the juncture of pelvis and thigh hangs scrotum weighted with testes and cylindrical penis terminating in the miniature helmet of the glans. "Pretty as a picture," thinks Annabel. "Watch it, kid. Before you know it you'll have wet pants!"

"Gosh," thinks Annabel as the fire trembles and breaks, "all these people. Who are they anyway? My friends? But why? And to what extent and how much." Annabel thinks of the arbitrariness of the length of any human life and the thought angers her. Her mind is fretful as an angry child's, her body at ease. She lies on her side on the sofa with her head on a pillow, lovely breasts held in the crook of an arm, feet dangling.

"Well, here goes. I love you, kid," Annabel says to herself in her mind. She stands and stretches as in her morning calisthenics. Almost unbearable excitement is causing her to yawn. Kneeling beside Carter, she lays her hand on his neck. When she speaks her voice is low and clear. She says, "Carter, I wonder if you and I could make love. If we could fuck, you know. I wonder if we could do it tonight." Everyone hears.

CHAPTER SIXTY-FIVE

Old Jane's alarm clock when it rang so startled her that she shouted "Whoop" and sat bolt upright in bed. Since she hadn't had occasion to use the clock in more than a decade, in the moment before she collected her wits she was frightened by the unfamiliar noise. "My!"

At every window she saw cottony fog. It had dampened her string bag and made her porch slippery. It absorbed and diffused light from her lantern rendering it worse than useless. Jane extinguished it, hung it on a branch, and continued on her way. She held a shawl around her shoulders. She hadn't troubled to coil her braid for this excursion—it lay on the maroon wool.

It was cold. There was no wind. Uniform dense fog like a cloud bank lay on the water and on the island muffling sound and light. Tops of trees, continuations of paths grew immaterial as they vanished into it. Well as Jane knew what this shining fog through which she returned to the top of the island presaged, she did not hurry. Jane could not hurry.

At the ragged cairn where Jane leaned down through the floating water droplets she frowned. Before her hand touched the parcel Sue Holcombe had left there she guessed what it contained.

The fog had made navigation difficult for Denny Jackson, Eddie Moon, Kayo Callahan, Jerry Jones, Herbie Parker, and Fred Kershaw, six rough boys who had set out from the mainland in a motorboat, up to no good. When the dark mass of the island loomed ahead they had stopped the engine and raised the propeller to let their momentum carry them ashore. Jane heard the heavy shush of their prow sliding onto the sand. She peered over the edge of the precipice.

"Get out of the boat, Kershaw, you stupid cunt."

"Kiss my ass, Kayo."

"Come on you turds, let's move this blamed motherfucker."

"Da-dang she's huh-heavy!"

The fog was too thick for Jane to be able to see the boys but she could identify some of them by what they said. They were astonished to hear her call out of the mist above them, "Fred Kershaw! Herbie Parker! And whoever your friends are! You boys take yourselves back home. You're trespassing and besides there's a blow brewing that'll knock that boat to smithereens if it's beached here."

The boys stood silent until Jerry Jones shouted, "Aw go fuck yourself, you old battleax," and Eddie Moon chimed in with, "Yeah, and you can kiss my motherfuckin' dick, too!" Emboldened by his comrades' taunts, Denny Jackson scooped up some pebbles and hurled them in what he took to be Jane's direction.

"For heaven's sakes," cried Jane in exasperation. "You should be ashamed of yourselves! *I'm* ashamed of you."

"Buzz off," Herbie Parker jeered.

"*We're* ashamed of *you*, shiteater," added Jerry Jones.

Jane could hardly believe her ears. A hunk of concrete balanced near the cliff edge seemed irresistibly to attract the end of her cane and then to leap down through the mist. Thunk. Terrified, Jane retreated down the center of the island. It was only in her own kitchen that she remembered the package she had found and fished it out of the pocket of her dress to examine it. Inside the brown paper was a note and the missing bottle of Lethe Water. It felt heavy in Jane's hand. Her wool shawl lay over a chair.

CHAPTER SIXTY-SIX

". . . if we could do it tonight." In the complete hush Annabel's words echo in every mind. Carter like an accomplished performer on a stage holds the silence boldly longer and longer before he replies, "Far out," flashing his wonderful smile. When his and Annabel's glances separate and fall as though shyly, the moment ends.

The moment ends but to Annabel's, to everyone's surprise its tension continues as if Carter has not replied. Worse, a thousand new questions swarm in through the opening his reply makes. Annabel looks at the glossy yellow fire. It seems to her that she has been cheated, rooked, played for a sucker but she cannot understand how. She feels sullen and dangerous. Others are more panic-stricken. "I see what you're up to," thinks Jimbo.

Carter wonders why Annabel isn't saying anything. With a

mixture of pride and alarm he imagines himself a world-famous hitchhiker or vagabond. He imagines himself caged, his beauty on display high in the air over seas of faces. Very dextrously he imagines the yellow light thrown out of the fireplace onto the undersides of Annabel's breasts and chin is pollen. If it were daytime he could lie on the warm sand in sunlight. His thoughts are open-textured and lacy. What puzzles him is that much as he admires Annabel he now feels little or no inclination toward any one of a dozen sexual gambits with her. Rather the tugs and sparklings that all unbeknownst to him have stiffened his handsome cock are occasioned mostly by Daisy's sweet heaviness and by Thuggy's—by the assent they both seem to embody or both embody. "Right, but still I wouldn't . . ." he thinks (". . . mind getting something on with Annabel," he means to continue). Goose snuggles against Carter's naked torso. Jimbo thinks, "But wait. I thought we . . . (. . . were going to talk to each other)."

"I'm at the end of some kind of rope, I don't . . . (. . . know about the rest of you)," Annabel seems to say. Her elbow apparently causes an iridescent green violet carnival glass milk pitcher to leap from the mantelpiece onto the hearth, which looks spongy but is stone. Luckily the receptacle lands behind the firescreen. None of the blades or needles it separates into fly at the young people, however many shower through the pumpkin-colored flames, however the sound sprinkles every eardrum, however the gray night flattens at every window. "I'm ready for a vacation," Thuggy thinks. "Take some uppers," suggests Jimbo. "Want some supper?" asks Daisy. Annabel apologizes for having broken the pitcher. "Is it valuable?" she wonders. Daisy shrugs as if to say, "I've no idea and besides it couldn't matter less." No one is able to say what calls to what, what cheers what. "Are we all . . . (. . . friends)?" Jimbo wonders. Laughter breaks out.

It hardly seems possible to Annabel that seducing or at least guaranteeing the seduction of Carter has been so easy. Can it have been? Can what she remembers actually have happened? Why yes. There near her feet Carter lies like . . . like something lovely on the rug, one and four fifths meters, eighty-five kilograms. Perhaps Annabel ought unobtrusively to doff her bluejeans and lower herself onto his stalwart penis. "Would that seem . . . (. . . odd)?" The broken glass resembles candy. From moment to moment the other young people seem unfamiliar to Annabel at the same time that she, she reflects, seems to seem quite familiar to them. "Familiarity breeds contempt," she says to herself, "and why can't I stop . . . (. . . thinking)?"

"My friends," says Jimbo in such a way that if the phrase doesn't inspire confidence it elicits a cynical curling of the lips. Jimbo wonders how—by what precise gradations—friendships are normally formed or for that matter how any friendship comes to be. "What part does talking—conversation—play?" he would like to know. "Anyway isn't conversation weird? Somebody says something and then somebody else does: A, B, A, B. And if you should tiptoe up and ask B what he'll say next he'd say, 'I dunno, it depends on what A says.' Strictly weird. Why aren't we conversing now, by the way? And incidentally what if Annabel puts it to me the way she did to Carter? I'm articulating," Jimbo thinks and he opens his eyes wide. What could be sillier?

"Are you okay?"

"Fine, thanks."

Gales of laughter.

Poor Daisy would enjoy being asleep now and so evade sensations of crumpling and joylessness which are, she reminds herself, merely symptoms of a level of fatigue that occasionally upends or tilts up through the brightness, nothing graver. She wonders whether everyone is pleased. She hopes so, she fears not. "Am I at all loathsome or bedraggled?" she wonders, "because people sometimes are at this point." The idea of beginning conversation with one of the other young people occurs to her but she dismisses it as naïve. She spreads glistening strawberry jam on a biscuit, a little ruefully.

What could be sillier than Thuggy's pouting? Awash in a mild dejection he prefers not to raise his eyes to Annabel's glorious torso. It seems to him that Carter is unreasonably lucky, having done nothing—no name or heart on Carter's belly—to deserve Annabel's favor. Thuggy looks down at his own feet whose dirtiness makes him pity them and think, "It's okay Lefty,

Righty. Don't worry. You look nice to me anyway," though the ankles, he must admit, do seem needlessly thick. "Something's wrong," he blurts out.

"No," entreating.

"Yes," insistently.

The yellow of the fire reminds Daisy of pencils and schoolbuses and of fire hydrants. Carter's eyes are closed.

"Nothing's wrong. We're tripping, that's all. Nothing's wrong."

"I thought we were going to talk," remarks Jimbo. Darkness seems to zip about the room like wildfire.

"The ends of my fingers feel cold."

CHAPTER SIXTY-SEVEN

"Did somebody say something about food?" Thuggy inquires.

"Food?"

"You know."

After a moment Jimbo asks, "When he says 'food,' can't we assume he means what he says?"

"Food might be lovely."

"Yes, I think it might be perfectly . . . edible."

"Except there just fucking isn't any," observes Carter.

"Yes there is, too," Annabel says.

"It's in the kitchen, that's all," adds Daisy.

Because, as everyone now realizes, the rest of the house is dark, the young people filing under the high lintel into the hallway all hold candles aloft. Lanterns would provide more light but the possibility that one might be dropped and the kerosene spill and burn precludes their being used in this expedition. Rufus follows but Goose stands with her head turned to one side and seems on the verge of tears. She doesn't understand that she could perfectly well come along too and she feels abandoned.

Hallway, dining room. The young people bring their light and long shadows range about. They glimpse one another's reflections in the pier glass they pass. The adventure is childish and yet they seem to feel themselves aging and to feel delicate networks sink into the skins of their smooth faces. Everyone knows that at any moment the loveliness might change. Empty chairs around the dining table are sinister. It occurs to no one to light any of the lamps on the walls or suspended from the ceiling.

In the kitchen the young people stand close together. The clear darkness is surrounded with band upon band of small-paned windows against which the luminous fog can be seen to lie.

"What's to eat?"

"Pemmican?"

"Just the ticket for an exploring trip."

"It's, it's in the cupboard the calendar and tide tables are on the door of. I hope it's not too salty."

"Yum, yum, I can't wait to . . . Oops, oops!"

The candles descend in a ring. "Look, it's . . ."

"Was."

"A bottle of tomato ketchup."

Squatting like Indians the young people regard the heavy puddle with its clean cusps of glass, losing themselves in it as in a landscape for a moment.

"Wow, imagine if that had happened . . . (. . . half an hour ago it could have been fairly awesomely nasty)."

"Kinda hairy even now." All retreat. Shudders are genuine.

"I want to explain one thing," says Thuggy. "Even when I try to relax and even when in some sense I do, I really don't."

"I *know*," says Daisy incredulously.

Carter nods. "Still, considering how nervous it is, it's damn smooth."

"Right," says Annabel.

Jimbo is thinking. "It's cold in here."

All agree. Oddments of food and drink are gathered. Now slowly, but not so slowly as it seems to them, the young people proceed back through the dining room, across the hallway and into the living room. Rufus is with them. Goose wags her tail.

Daisy has entered the parlor first. Something prompts her to dust a leaf of a rubber plant. She does it with the hem of her sleeve, solicitously and absent-mindedly. Carter, who arrives next in the doorway (himself very beautiful), is so charmed by the beauty with which Daisy performs this service that he pads across the rug to her side and bestows a kiss on her cheek. Annabel, next in the doorway, sees and smiles. She realizes she is not in the least inclined to make love with Carter tonight. "Tomorrow night when I'm not so stoned, yes—I don't dislike him!"

Rufus and Thuggy shuffle into the parlor together and now Jimbo hastens in and shouts, "What's happened to this room? It's simpler!"

"Simple?" growls Thuggy, "Simple isn't the word."

"Anything else either, kid," says Annabel.

"Drained?"

"We need sleep. We've been awake forever."

Jimbo claps his hands. "Enough fiddle-faddle. We should do something. We should all . . ."

"Get married," says Carter.

"Is that a proposal?"

"Is a five-party marriage two and a half times as good or bad as a two-party one?"

"Seriously though."

"Flesh of my flesh of my flesh, of my flesh of my flesh."

"May I introduce my wife, my other wife, and my two husbands?"

"Obviously we'll do it, right?"

"Of course. Not just now though. For one thing, we're not dressed for it. Some of us aren't dressed at all."

"But what are we going to do *now?*" Jimbo asks piteously. Brightening, he answers, "Everybody writes a suggestion for something we can do. They're dropped into a hat. Everybody draws one and reads it aloud. That way everybody hears every suggestion but we don't know who suggested what. Then we cast secret ballots to decide which of the things to do."

"Sounds feasible. Why didn't we think of it before?"

"We'll need some paper though and some like pencils."

"Pencils here."

"And here are some slips of paper. No, wait."

"?"

"They aren't blank."

"They seem to be a group of questions we wrote . . . earlier."

"Read 'em aloud."

Delighted and intrigued, all gather on the warm hearth before the yellow and red fire. The birch logs sing. "Listen. They all seem to have the form, 'What is an X?' This one for instance. 'What is a tracheotomy?' What do others say instead of 'tracheotomy'?"

" 'War crime.' "

" '*Lumpenproletariat.*' "

" 'Glory hole.' "

The young people continue in this fashion reading a word or phrase and then tossing the paper it was written on into the fire. Happier now, Goose stretches.

CHAPTER SIXTY-EIGHT

Moonlight and silky fog enter the farmhouse attic through windows under the eaves. Some fog twines down a ladder into the smaller of the two rooms at the front of the house on the third floor. On this floor seven rooms give onto a latitudinal hallway under the gambrel roof. None is in use now. Cobwebs curtain dormer windows and tiny fireplaces, dust and lint carpet the bare wood floors and drape a rocking chair and a wardrobe abandoned here. From the middle of the hallway to the middle of the front wall of the house the stairwell bisects the front half of the house. Some pale light falls down along the stairs, the balusters a furred knuckle may strum, the table and chair on the landing. Step by step, Babe descends the stairs, his toenails clicking. Look: his whiskers are full of blood.

He peers over the banister, down the second flight of stairs to the main hallway, where lantern light and voices fall out into the darkness from the parlor. "Rrrr, rrrr." If the dogs were not so stoned they would already be bristling at his rankness. The odor is not lost on them, but it seems merely a new factor in the pervasive oddity. Babe's own perceptions are not so deranged. Through his gory muzzle he can smell dogs, cats, and young people.

Babe detects these odors not only directly from below—saliva pours from beneath his black tongue and out the cruel mouth—

but also here in the form of cooling spoor-trails. Three go right and then separate.

One, Carter's, goes again to the right into a large bedroom. From the doorway Babe sees open closet, full-length mirror, wardrobe, two windows that look on the meadow before the house (but now show only fog), bar-bells, a chair, a wide bed, a window that looks out the side of the house, a fireplace, a wicker basket of magazines. Another trail leads past this doorway into Annabel's smaller room. Drop leaf table with violin case and sea shell, fireplace, window looking out the side of the house toward the barn, table with basin and ewer, heap of clothes, window looking out the back of the house toward the beach, closet door, unmade bed. Returning along the hallway Babe passes two doors on his right, the first giving onto the linen closet (on the shelves of which fresh bedclothes and towels lie folded) and the second onto the smallest of the bedrooms, into which leads the most delectable of the spoor-trails, Daisy's. Babe will not enter Daisy's bedroom now.

Heavy shoulder against white wainscoting, Babe follows the wall and turns right where an ell leads back to a small peaked door behind which a narrow spiral stair connects the two lower floors of the house. "Hrrrh . . ." Perhaps Babe will descend. But first there are two more spoor-trails to be followed in the main hallway to his right as he stands glowering in the entrance to the ell. He follows them and when they diverge he follows first that leading into Thuggy's bedroom, where he sees a bureau, photographs of naked women, frisbees, footballs, basketballs, baseballs and softballs, and mitts piled in the corner, a window looking toward the beach, another toward the woodshed at the side of the house, a fireplace, a comfortable bed, a desk, a closet door. The last trail, Jimbo's, leads through a doorway across the hallway. Babe sees a closet door, fireplace, window looking over the side of the house, marble-topped chest of drawers, table and chair, stack of records and guitar case in the corner, two windows that look on the meadow before the house (but now, like all the other windows they show only fog), night table, brass bed.

Directly below is the parlor. Laughter and conversation filter through the floorboards at which Babe glares. The blood on his rusty mane is clotting.

CHAPTER SIXTY-NINE

Thuggy offers Annabel a stick of chewing gum.

Daisy claps her hands. "We should have a scavenger hunt." The fire burns merrily.

"Scavenger? You mean . . . ?" All wince.

"A game, silly. You know, like you look for a crabapple."

"A blue stone, a horseshoe."

There are footsteps on the porch, a banging at the door. "Gosh," Daisy thinks, "that must be . . . or, rather, who could that possibly be, at this hour?"

Annabel covers her breasts. "Good heavens, look at us!"

"What do you mean?" Carter and Jimbo ask together.

"Not dressed!" Annabel explains, slipping her cowgirl shirt on. "Daisy, don't answer the door till the boys are dressed. Think of our reputations."

Whom should they find at the door but Priscilla Geach distraught, her pallor ghostly. "I saw the lights." Behind her, the fog. The young people are astonished. "Come in," Daisy urges.

"Come in, Ms. Geach." It is Annabel, flushed and disheveled and with a not especially becoming new coiffure. "Hi, Ms. Geach." And the boy Jimbo thanks to whom she discovered what Edith wants for her birthday. And two other boys and the other girl who would be Daisy the owner of the property. They all seem unkempt. But where is Jack? Priscilla has circled every house on the island and found light only here. "Is Jack—Mr. Geach—here? You see I expected him home hours ago." Each of the young people is struck by Priscilla's loveliness and by her vulnerability.

"He *was* here. But that was several hours ago," says Carter.

Priscilla frowns and sighs. "Oh dear. When I saw your lights I was sure he'd be here. Otherwise I wouldn't have disturbed you. I'm anxious." She is also enfeebled and fatigued by the long search for her husband. Tears spill down her cheeks. She dabs at them with her coat sleeve. "I'm sorry, I know I'm being naughty. Annabel? Could you—and any of your friends who want to—possibly sleep at the millhouse tonight? The children shouldn't be left alone so long. I won't be able to rest until I find Jack. He's probably fallen asleep somewhere, of course. He hasn't been able to sleep as much as he should recently because of his work." More tears spill, Priscilla frowns more.

"I have an idea," says Jimbo. "Why don't *you* go back to the millhouse, Ms. Geach, and rest if you can. Meanwhile we five will go over this hunk of land with a fine-toothed comb."

"Flush out your man in no time," adds Thuggy.

Tap, tap, tap—Priscilla taps three times with a lacquered nail against a tooth. She wishes there were some way she could accept the help without incurring a debt of gratitude to the young people. Yet after all (she now thinks) her merely having heard the offer, whether or not she accept . . . "I can't thank you enough," she says. "Could you really?"

"It'll be loads of fun," Daisy insists.

When Priscilla has departed the inhabitants of the farmhouse stare at each other as in disbelief. Daisy produces an old map of the island on which search sectors are marked and assigned, one to each. Amphetamine tablets are gobbled to guarantee wakefulness. Sweaters, coats, and scarves are donned. Spirits are rising.

"Button up, it's cold out there."

"Take flashlights?"

"Useless in that fog."

"Dogs? Sure, look, they want to help. Don't you, doggy babies?"

"The cats? But where have all the kitties gone?"

"No one knows."

They troop outside and, separating, set out into the foggy dark without so much as a moment's discussion of such matters as where to reassemble, how the discovery of Mr. Geach might be announced to fellow searchers.

CHAPTER SEVENTY

After her late supper Sue Holcombe lit a cigarette and lapsed into a glassy-eyed staring at the linoleum on her kitchen floor, noting its colors of brick and yellow earth absently as she followed separate trains of thought about what might be done with the large sum that would accrue should she choose to sell the entire island—assuming she possessed it—on the open market.

Sue Holcombe had seen advertisements in newspapers for luxurious sable coats.

"Wool is more economical. However the respect a fur garment rouses might prove useful. But by and large such respect is beneath my contempt." Sue Holcombe thought of revisiting birthplaces and graves of the great musicians. She had not traveled in Europe since she was a student. She crumpled a paper napkin and tossed it into a grocery bag waste basket. "Europe must be full of tourists nowadays, though. And even supposing nothing has changed, why go back? My memory is excellent. Merely traveling is a waste of time. That amount of money should be employed, however."

Her gaze wandered across the linoleum past the foot of one leg of the table, over the well cover. Once the well was outside the cottage and the water must have been potable. Later the kitchen was built over it and still later the water grew brackish. Sue Holcombe used the well as a refrigerator. At the moment butter, bacon, and a leg of lamb wrapped and attached to a fiberglass wellrope floated under the black surface. Sue yawned, wrinkling her nose. She stubbed out her cigarette.

Near the scallop shell ashtray lay the old architect's plans. "I shan't sell. I might let rooms now and then. Miss Daisy might want to rent a room in the house that once was hers. For a week or two one summer, if she could afford it." Sue Holcombe smiled dragonishly.

Smoking another cigarette she decided that since she wasn't sleepy she ought to use the time and her exultation—it seemed a suitable mood—to rehearse her latest composition, "The German Shepherd." Upstairs in her bedroom she checked her appearance. Yes, yes, except for her hair. She corrected it with a comb. And she would need other shoes. The alligator pumps.

The music room was chilly. Sue Holcombe lighted the Franklin stove and then as the air warmed she stood before the music stand studying "The German Shepherd." Perusing one very disagreeable, even aggressive, passage, the violinist smiled wolfishly, showing all her small teeth. In its way the composition seemed to her to add to the glory of the race. She removed her fine instrument from its case, tuned it, tightened the bow, applied rosin, assumed an appropriate stance, and began. In the ceiling of the room lived a spider whose musical taste seemed excellent. Now as always when Sue Holcombe played he descended on a line of web and hung in the air to listen. She had never seen him come down for Annabel's playing. The music was loud and soft, weak and strong. When it ended there was a brief silence.

Then from outside came a raucous burst of applause, whistles, and cheers. The spider ran back up to the ceiling. Sue Holcombe could not have been more surprised. She laid her violin in its case and closed the case. Then she rushed to the window, flung it open, and leaned out. Below in the foggy night she saw the six faces of Fred Kershaw, Herbie Parker, Jerry Jones, Kayo Callahan, Eddie Moon, and Denny Jackson ranged in a semicircle in the light from her parlor window. How could the rabbit holes not have prevented their approach?

In a moment Sue Holcombe was downstairs, outside, shotgun in hand and cocked. "I hereby inform you that you are trespassing and that you shall find yourselves nicely peppered with birdshot if you loiter here a minute more. Nothing about you amuses or pleases me. Your applause is a travesty of admiration. I shall fire one warning shot over your heads."

The boys' laughter was uncertain. Denny Jackson was picking up a length of fallen tree branch. Sue Holcombe fired. By the time the boys had registered the flash and zing and the acridness she had reloaded the gun with a cartridge taken from the pocket of her dress. Denny threw the piece of wood. It sailed over Sue's head. A windowpane shattered with a noise resembling those cymbal crashes that, comprising the principal accompaniment to "The German Shepherd," Sue had recently been hearing in her imagination as she played. The boys fled. Sue Holcombe pursued, determined to do them harm. Here ran the boys and when they paused to "drop trow" or "shoot moons" they hoped she saw. Here ran the musician wishing she could see well enough to draw a bead on them. Between streamed curtains of the wonderful fog.

CHAPTER SEVENTY-ONE

Perhaps through the silver mistiness black night showed more now. Jack Geach's mustard-colored pullover had dampened. Plunging along he wished he were at home with a nice pot of tea, piping hot under a quilted cozy. He could almost taste it, lapsang souchong, but no imagined perfume could quell this air's wet tree bark, humus, and overpowering ocean fishiness. One lock of the man's crimped grizzled hair bobbed against his brow as he strode. He inhaled mist, blew out a cloudier breath. Not finding his way, he hurried along busily as he could and didn't much mind what he glimpsed: here in paper cells a group of wasps slept, there stood wild irises. Jack's nose was itching. The ground sloped dangerously in places. Jack was uncomfortable but he consoled himself with the reflection that his future biographer could use tonight to illustrate the almost childlike pleasure Geach took in the mere process of living, of meeting and overcoming the most trivial obstacles "with a penetratingly lucid grasp of the situation in all its manifestations, as does the captain of a great ship." The dark fog seemed phosphorescent at the edges, absorbing moonlight like a sponge and endlessly refracting it. "Thrip-shhh . . ." Jack heard the curled flipflop sound of shallow waves, a becalmed sea.

How Jack thought as he walked! "To be a millionaire before thirty-six is no small achievement, ha, ha. On the other hand though, goddamit, I wish there weren't already so many other millionaires. In certain counties in this country you can find hundreds and hundreds upon hundreds, a dime a dozen. True, there are many more without a single millionaire to their credit—without a single decent living, in fact. But somehow that's no comfort. Supposing Priscilla and I and the girls lived in such a place with a million or more dollars and surrounded by poverty on all sides, I'd still know there were millionaires and multimillionaires elsewhere. No amount of adjacent poverty could make me forget that, I don't think. And I wouldn't want to. But let me think. Suppose I've fought my way up tooth and nail with the most creative ruthlessness to the great financial pinnacle of the economic sphere. I'm not just a multimillionaire, not even a billionaire, but a multibillionaire and more. Extensive groveling is being done by billionaires who once looked down their noses at me. Their wives kowtow to Priscilla and their children all want to play with Hester and Edith all the time. I'd be suitably dignified. Yes but what's to prevent somebody else, even somebody less dedicated or inspired than I'm fortunate enough to be, what's to keep somebody like that from coming along and amassing a greater fortune than mine? It might turn out to be easier after I'm dead and gone, for instance. I'd prefer to be sure it would certainly never happen!" Having wandered to the shoreline and beyond, Jack stood on sand dollars in sea water over his ankles. There was a distant foghorn but Jack couldn't determine which direction it came from. He thought, "Merely knowing I'm at the shore won't orient me. I could be anywhere on the shore, facing in any direction." With splashing steps he retreated from the water.

"I don't know, I don't know." Ghostly ripples fanned out from Jack's shaking head. His stomach growled. He fished a salt-water taffy kiss from his shirt pocket, unwrapped it, and popped it into his mouth. Chewing the candy, Jack had a new idea. "Suppose I've become the richest-by-far man in the world. I've enjoyed the accompanying acclaim, glamor, power, gourmet dining, envy, respect, and so forth for several decades. Famous women have tried to change places with Priscilla (I won't betray you though, Priss dear). So then I could use my financial greatness to finance a world-wide Marxist revolution so wealth and power get equalized all over the world. And I guess if world-wide equality ever happened it should be permanent. That would mean nobody could ever get richer than Jack Geach had been." Jack kicked a branch out of his path. "The day might come when people would have more advantages than Jack ever had. But then everybody would have them. It's not the same as being better off than everybody around you. It's not like being on top." Jack shook his head impatiently. "It's not like bossing, not at all."

The man's shoulders sagged, he walked with a heavier gait. "What does it actually mean, a million before thirty-six? There'd still be hundreds of thousands, I'd guess, richer and younger than me. No, a million and thirty-six are arbitrary. The only satisfaction that would be genuinely satisfactory would be to be at least twice as rich as anybody else my age or below. Or above, for good measure, up to, say, ten years older. Well but, even with all my zest and self-motivation, what chance do I have of achieving that? Not much! Goddamit. There's only so much I can do against a stacked deck. Cripes, there are people *born* with a million, and more. So what's the point? Maybe I ought to retire and get it over with." Jack sighed. There were tears in his eyes. He slumped down on a bank of moss. In a moment he was sound alseep. "I'm tired," he breathed.

Look: as he sleeps how charming Jack has become—his jowl flattened against one burly forearm, what peace and innocence surround him. How can this man ever grow thirty-six years old? Flowers scattered over the dark bluish moss stay queerly dry tonight for the thick fog prevents dewfall. Jack is snoring. He rolls onto his back and the small change in his trousers pocket sliding across his thigh clinks. Look: is the fog disturbed by something that glides forward? An ugly mass looms out. The foliage shrinks away. Look!

The grinding teeth, the rotten muskiness and stench, and the fearsome stealth were Babe's. He could hardly believe his eyes when he saw Jack on the moss. Was it a trap baited with the sleeper? Babe advanced cautiously with dreadful sidelong glances. He sniffed of Jack's shoulder, his ear. His rusty mane lay on the man's neck. Jack did not wake even when Babe, growing bolder, lifted an elbow in his mouth and shook it. Poor Jack: it was Babe himself, trembling with vile glee, who lifted him bodily and ran up the center of the island with him tucked under one arm. Jack's eyes opened groggily and he saw trees fly past through the mist as in a dream. He was much too tired to wake. He settled his weight against Babe's flank and accommodated himself to the bouncing. His eyelids fluttered once more when the bouncing stopped. Now in utter darkness Jack lay on wet stone strewn with very nasty refuse in the nethermost recesses of Babe's lair. A toad hopped.

CHAPTER SEVENTY-TWO

Young Mr. Jimbo is finding a second wind thanks to the chilly dark morning. He has directed his flashlight beam and a "Hallo?" down the well-shaft. "Right thoughtless," he has said to himself, "of this Geach to disappear." Jimbo has lost his way and found it without inordinate waste of time. He has considered abandoning his sector to lead his friends on a wild goose chase around the island, each supposed Geach by the one following. It could be done, he opines, but it would entail unconscionable irresponsibility. Whereas now in these wee hours he feels quite trustworthy.

Jimbo thinks of Daisy. "Sometime when I'm lying beside her on a blanket on the sand, what if I kissed the nape of her neck? What if I wrote an I-love-you song and played and sang it to her one evening, a serenade. Or if I suggested going for a walk, just the two of us, one morning. Daisy said yes. We both were shy at first but we began to laugh and mock each other and relax that way. We flirted. After a while we decided to take off our clothes and before we knew it we were fucking."

Cold, darkness, and deep fog environ the boy. He walks with his fingers shoved into the back pockets of his jeans, his chin advanced. He is in the clearing that surrounds the oak the Geach children call "the wishing tree," humming so Jack might hear.

Meanwhile the cluster of rowdy off-islanders has left a track of damage and mischief. They've harmed or frightened birds and small animals, peed on flowers, and thrown stones through windowpanes. They have tied an empty beer can to a cat's tail. No one has encountered them, they strike and run so fast.

Denny Jackson says, "Let's row around and sink all the boats we find moored."

"Not bad enough," says Eddie Moon.

Kayo Callahan says, "Let's set 'em adrift."

"Tuh-tuh-too much tuh-trouble," says Jerry Jones, and Herbie Parker says, "Not bad enough, either."

"Fuck it, men, let's set fire to this whole lousy shiteater of an island," says Fred Kershaw.

"Shhh!" The boys have heard Jimbo's humming. They rush forward and capture, gag, punch, and sock him and tie him to the oak tighter than Sue Holcombe had tied Thuggy there. They insult him with the most uncouth epithets they can summon.

Jimbo is beside himself with rage at the injustice of the gang's treatment of him. Their being his contemporaries aggravates the offense. He grows potentially eloquent but the bandanna in his mouth prevents his voicing anything more than a loud "Unh, unh!" He cannot see his assailants but he knows they see him when flashlight beams are trained on him. The expression on his face is a furious imploring. Behind spectacles his eyes flash.

Now Jimbo is alone and calmer. Barely, barely he can distinguish boughs above darker than the darkness of the air. Dawn approaches. "Mr. Geach is out of luck if he's in my sector," the boy thinks.

CHAPTER SEVENTY-THREE

Jack dreamed a colorful dream about his daughters. Extraordinarily neither he nor Priscilla appeared in it. The little girls were roller skating down bright tree-lined streets, past parked cars of the late 1920s. These streets had been rained on. The trees made a high continuous green above the children.

Jack sighed, gnashing his teeth. "Hi, honey," he said. But whatever had rubbed against his ear wasn't Priscilla, and it scurried away. Jack opened his eyes on extreme darkness.

His first emotion was resentment. His first thought was that he needed to contact his secretary on the mainland. To what end? Jack began to wake up more. He was lying on stone and dirt. Cold, disagreeable. Resentment modulated into something like a dignified contempt for his surroundings. Jack sat up and shook his head to clear it. He was not in his bed in the millhouse. But where? He remembered walking in the woods. For a moment Babe's gory muzzle appeared in the peripheral vision of his mind's eye too fantastic to be so much as noticed. Where was Jack? He assumed an expression of concern and readiness. "Ahem!" Nothing. Jack extended his arms. Nothing. He wasn't dreaming now, either. He became frightened.

Jack Geach retracted his arms.

Who wouldn't be frightened? Jack felt chillier than ever. He hugged himself. Where was . . . Priscilla? Jack's teeth were chattering.

He was not blind. He could see the luminous face of his wrist-watch—twelve numbers in a circle, minute hand, hour hand. But nothing else relieved the amazing dark. When he squinted upward he found no stars, he saw no horizon in any direction. He couldn't see the ground beneath nor his own body. The black air was rancid and cold. Jack ventured a not very loud "Hello?" and heard no response. Then he heard a rustling off to his right. He shuddered.

How could so promising and enterprising a young man find himself in such a plight? Did someone intend . . . to harm him? The quality and degree of this darkness was remarkable, especially to Jack, accustomed as he was to daylight or at night the starry island sky. This severe darkness seemed to work like a vacuum on Jack's vision, as though colors and shapes were being drawn out his pupils and vanishing.

He began to cease to feel panicky now. His nostrils were less affronted by the cave's vile odors. "Of course I might be in a problematical situation," he thought, "but the only thing to do is cope with it. A man doesn't become a self-made millionaire by taking things like this lying down." Jack stood and found his way to the cave's entrance and so out into the woods again.

In the luminous fog the faintly darker shafts are trees. Jack feels heroic and ready to enjoy some well-earned rest. He smiles to think of Babe's den's troublesome inkiness.

"By the way," he thinks, "I really should put Priscilla's good taste to work, so to speak, and plough some of our new income into works of art as glamor investments. We need more servants around the house, too. It increases credibility if nothing else and we can write off what they steal and eat as business losses. Dignified servants who know how to serve with dignity. A chef who speaks fluent French. A respectful one, I can afford it."

CHAPTER SEVENTY-FOUR

"Huh-who do these puh-pissers think they are anyhow, luh-living out here on this tuh-tuh-turd of a stupid island in the ocean?"

"Think they're too good for regular land, do they? We'll show 'em. Fix 'em good, won't we, boyos?"

"Right, Herbie. Fix their tails fuckin' good."

"We could blow up a shithouse if we had some 'crackers."

"We don't though, so that plan sucks."

"*You* suck, Moon."

"Buzz off, you little weenie."

"*Me* a weenie. Fuckin' hell!"

"Where the fuck are we, you fuckheads?"

"Got *my* ass."

"Fuckin' Kayo don't know shit from Shinola."

"Kiss my motherfuckin' *dick*, Denny."

"Punch his mug, Denny."

"Shuh-shuh-shit. Look, I skint my fuckin nuh-knee and it smarts like hell."

"Listen."

"What?"

"I thought I heard somebody. I thought maybe it was that scrambly old shiteater and her shotgun."

"My *knee* smarts, you fuckers."

"Your knee *sucks*, Jones."

The mainlanders had made their way farther down the island, well past the oak they had bound Jimbo to. They dismantled a wheelbarrow at the millhouse and would have done more damage there had not an angry Sue Holcombe rushed out of the woods toward them, aiming her shotgun as she came. They circled the millhouse and fled along a zigzag course which obliged them to hop the streambed often until they looped down and backward. Sue Holcombe had stopped to catch her breath at a place where the stream flows through the roots of a fallen tree.

Jones had scraped his knee, Parker his elbow, and Moon had torn his flannel shirt. Cresting a dim hill as they fled, all six had lost their footing, skidded and rolled all the way down, dirtying clothes, hands, faces. Kayo Callahan had sprained his wrist.

Now they came out onto an open field. The fog was thinning and lightening. Across the lovely hush waves were audible, also a distant foghorn. There stood the big farmhouse.

The bad boys entered the barn sneezing and pushing. Hens at their roosts awoke with a start and flapped dusty wings and cried "Alarm! Indignation!" They weren't accustomed to intrusions at this hour. They certainly weren't accustomed to having their own eggs thrown at them where they crouched, hiding yet fluffing out feathers so that should they be noticed they might seem larger and less vulnerable—blinking foolishly, wondering whether another corner might be safer, whether to risk a dash thither, and all the while hardly daring even to dodge the flying eggs.

The boys would have met a different reception had they treated the bull so. As it happened they weren't aware of his presence and he only vaguely of theirs when they passed the stall where he stood half awake, half dozing. Through, out the other end of the barn, along the back of the house to the stoop the boys came and here it was that, setting foot onto the wooden steps, they had a dreadful surprise.

They were reminding themselves of how they had raided the farmhouse the summer before and inciting each other to make the present visit especially destructive. Quiet, dark, and pale, the vast fogbank lay over the island and over the water. "Rrrrh . . ." Abruptly Babe came slavering hideously from under the porch and bit off the toe of Herbie Parker's electrician's boot, leaving the boy's toes wriggling in open air. The boys couldn't believe their eyes. Cold sweat poured off their brows and they trembled so that each sounded like Jones, exclaiming, "Whuh-whuh-what?" and "Huh-huh-help!" Meanwhile Babe masticated the bit of shoe, growling and leering up at them. He was about to jump onto the porch.

The six flew over the opposite railing, out to the sand, and up the shore all the way up to their boat under the promontory at the upper end, never once pausing to look back over their shoulders, not even as they set the outboard motor in motion. They were gone over the waves into the night, into the fog and would never return, not this summer nor any other. Their absence wasn't regretted by the islanders.

CHAPTER SEVENTY-FIVE

Upstairs in the smallest bedroom, Daisy's, Babe shambled in the gloom, his growl-breathing a purr, his shamble monstrous. He stared, wondered, drooled. When he picked up this or that delicate thing, when he hooked a scarf on thick nails he could taste Daisy's sweet flesh, almost he could. Hunger. Dawn was approaching too. Babe decided he would soon return to his lair and eat Jack Geach or part of Jack.

Daisy's curtains and the skirt and canopy of her bed were organdy figured with a design of small chaste flowers. On the bed atop a heap of bolsters, comforters, and pillows lay a china doll older than the farmhouse whom Daisy called Lucy though she had had many other names. Lucy's clothes and slick hard skin had grayed but she remained complete and pretty. When Babe understood that she was not and had never been alive, he was so incensed that he almost destroyed her. Babe let a handkerchief edged with violet crocheting drop over Lucy.

The window gave onto dense morning fog, interesting Babe no more than the Beardsley drawings taped to the wall. He examined Daisy's easy chair, whose function he could not quite fathom however he might sniff or paw. Underneath the seat cushion lay coins and hairpins and what? . . . a charm bracelet, gold chain with miniature gold objects attached.

What puzzled Babe most was Daisy's journal. Everything else, the chair for instance, seemed half familiar but the journal was uncanny and even alarming. Beside it on the sewing table were a snowy quill pen, an inkwell, a box of French water colors and camel's hair brushes, some petit point, and the reindeer sweater in progress. Babe pushed these articles off onto the floor.

In the closet freshly laundered clothes hung above a hamper of soiled clothes. "Hrrrh, hrrrh." The monster touched nightdresses, daydresses, underclothes. Dim light was creeping in a window. Around, above, below, every room of the house was silent.

Atop Daisy's bureau these things lay and stood on doilies: jewelry including a coral heart on a ribbon, a bottle of aspirin tablets, a bottle of rosewater Daisy had distilled from wild island roses, a smoked-glass beaker of bonbons, candles, spilled wax, a vase of blue strawflowers. Babe sniffed the bonbons. Food? Yes. Eat? No—he was strictly carnivorous. Above the bureau hung a mirror in which Babe could see himself reflected more precisely than ever in water. He glared into his own baleful yellow eyes. He wanted to kill and eat everyone on the island before the sun rose but he knew it was impossible.

He padded through the woods. Urine was dribbling down his legs.

CHAPTER SEVENTY-SIX

In the middle of Priscilla Geach's sleep she dreams she is strolling at dusk with her daughters in an old resort complex of cafés, bistros, and shops on interconnected quays built over the water of an inland sea. Most inhabitants have returned for dinner. A young student plays an accordion. Priscilla thinks, "In a place like this one could live forever without regret." Boats are at anchor. Something frightening is about to happen. Priscilla tries to shrug it off. She sits on a bench and tosses breadcrumbs from her lap to the pigeons. But where are the daughters? Down there a wind blows both girls off the edge of a wharf headfirst into the water. All that remains is four feet wiggling above the dark surface. "What kind of a place is this?" Priscilla wonders, horror-struck. She manages to call for help.

The dogs Goose and Rufus race along the dock and save the wet but undamaged children, whom they present to Priscilla where she sits. Overwhelming gratefulness causes the lovely woman to caress herself and finally to masturbate as she sleeps alone in the wide bed. She is dreaming again.

In reality Goose and Rufus, stoned tonight, hardly have such command of situations as in Priscilla's dream. Disoriented and unable to locate any of the young people, they are on their own in a world of fog where fireflies make dim globes of light that vanish.

Goose trembles from the tip of her tail to the end of her wet nose. A voice seems to be calling her. She wrinkles her brow, listening. She doesn't understand that what she hears is a foghorn. The sound continues to trouble her at intervals through the night. She lies beside Rufus on a mossy patch of ground she doesn't recognize (though she has crossed it many times). She growls at a shooting pain in her left rear paw. The air smells odd. "Goo-oose . . ." In the distance, but where? Goose ignores Rufus's soft imploring barks, puppyish barks. She licks her paw.

Rufus sniffs a shrub here and there thrusting his muzzle into the foliage. It doesn't smell like a plant to him. He bites it. The leaves in his mouth are not quite like leaves. They are not quite like anything else either. Rufus coughs them out. He lifts his leg and pees on the shrub. He sniffs it again. Yes, but . . . He cannot imagine who will feed him now that Daisy doesn't appear with a dish of scraps from the table mixed with crunchy bits of dogfood.

Goose tries to mount Rufus, something she hasn't done in years. Rufus is surprised but patient. The dogs play and run through the woods, teeth bared and ears laid back. Click, click, snapping at phantasms in the air. Rufus lifts a paw as though to shake hands and lays it over Goose's shoulders. Tails wag. The love the dogs feel for each other stands like a landmark in the luminous strange horizontal world. Nightbirds whistle and cry. There is no wind.

Rufus and Goose encountered Thuggy before dawn. He laughed and cuffed their heads. They were overjoyed. He wanted to take a new kind of walk with them, one in which they determined the route and pace. It was a good idea but not practicable. When they ran ahead and he loped after, it was clear that they weren't really leading since they believed the direction to be of his choosing. It showed in the fact that, while they made detours and excursions without affecting the prevailing course, whenever Thuggy turned aside so did the overall direction of the group. The world was falling into place, Goose and Rufus were coming down and couldn't do other than follow the presumed human lead as they had done all their lives. Near wild roses and honeysuckle Thuggy wondered whether the scent of flowers pleased dogs as much as him. He wondered whether Rufus and Goose had encountered the missing Geach during the night. They hadn't. They had met no one, although they had heard the exclamations and thudding feet of the rowdy off-islanders in flight up the beach, and without knowing it they had once been within ten yards of the sheltered spot where Faye and Gail slept peacefully.

CHAPTER SEVENTY-SEVEN

The violent storm portended by the night's low air pressure, heavy fog, and stillness failed to materialize. Dawn brought a freshening nor'easter, gulls crying in a blue sky over high trees and houses and the various bedraggled islanders, two of whom—Sue Holcombe and Jack Geach—conversed briefly before making for their respective beds. Jack lay in a young beach plum thicket when Sue Holcombe came upon him. She nudged him with her boot.

"Mr. Geach? Mr. Geach!"

"Why, why . . . Miss Holcombe?"

Both smiled.

Jack rubbed his face. "Where is this place? Where have you, I mean, I beg your pardon but do you know by chance what day this is?"

"Thursday, June thirtieth. Why were you sleeping here? Been on a binge?"

"Miss Holcombe! Please, certainly not. Please."

"Well?"

"What time is it, by the way?"

"Five thirty-seven according to your wristwatch."

"Thank you, Miss Holcombe. I believe that will be all for . . . or, I mean . . . ?"

"Marital difficulties I imagine. Your spouse refused to allow you inside the house last night."

"If you'd met Priscilla as I suggested, you'd know how wrong and perfectly laughable your suggestion is. Priscilla and I are a model couple, in a sense, inasmuch as there has never been a day's or even a tiny moment's recession in the deeply profound love we feel so very strongly for one another. Oh, we have our silly quarrels, sure."

"Stop talking. I'm trying to think."

Jack smiled. Being addressed thus was a rarity, almost a luxury for him. The violinist regarded him askance. She wondered if his chums called him "Tycoon." She smiled.

"Incidentally," she said, "your daughter's birthday is tomorrow."

"Yes I, I believe that is the case."

"It *is* the case."

"Mmm. But what am I doing here? I don't sleepwalk. Priscilla does sometimes but I've never been known to. I guess there's always a first time though. Except that it's just that it doesn't really seem like me somehow. Know what I mean?"

"Perhaps you talk in your sleep from time to time."

Jack had been thinking. "What was it again that you wanted in return for your information about Edith's birthday present? I don't recall. Miss Holcombe?"

"I was thinking, excuse me. Yes. What I ask of you Mr. Geach is that you accompany me Sunday afternoon to a certain place here on the island. It should take about an hour. I want you to act as witness of my performance of a certain duty. Merely that. That should suffice nicely. You see? I ask almost nothing. How can you refuse?"

Jack yawned. "A businessman worthy of the name knows he can refuse anything, Miss Holcombe."

"Good-by then."

"Wait! Wait, Miss Holcombe. Sit down and let's talk turkey."

"Well, but not for long mind you. I probably shouldn't have suggested a trade in the first place. I should simply have asked for your help and known any gentleman would comply."

"Mmm."

"The life of a musician. Sometimes we feel so helpless and lonely we forget how eager people are to be helpful. Unquestionably I should have asked for your assistance directly."

"Gee, I honestly wish you had. I'd have agreed and then I'm sure you would just as freely have told me what Edith wants for her birthday. Especially since that favor would have cost you almost nothing—a few seconds of your time and the effort of saying a word or two, let's say, and really nothing else as far as I can see. Maybe I've failed to notice something?"

"Maybe not."

"Hmm."

"Hmm."

An opening, a kind of window in the foliage gave onto a strip of sand and a section of the blue ocean which a tiny white sailboat was crossing.

"Pleasant morning."

"Sure is! It's the kind of morning that makes a man glad to be alive, regardless of his financial status. By the way, Miss Holcombe, isn't that a shotgun?"

"I'll use it on you if you don't help me."

"Ha, ha. No but seriously, have you been hunting this morning?"

"No, I was shooting water rats."

"I wish I could understand what I'm doing here at this hour this way."

"Mr. Geach."

"Yes?"

"Mr. Geach, what your daughter wants for her birthday is . . ."

"Wait! Did you say today was the thirtieth?"

"I did."

"That means Edith's birthday is tomorrow, Miss Holcombe!"

"As I was saying, what young Edith hopes to receive from you and your wife as a birthday present is a pair of red patent-leather Mary Jane shoes like her sister's. New ones. Not hand-me-downs. There, I've told you."

"How do you know? Edith told you?"

"Hmph! Never mind how I know this or any other of the many many things you'd be astonished to discover I know. I won't tell. But you can be quite sure my information about the child's wishes is accurate."

"You don't suppose she might prefer a dollhouse?"

"Absolutely not."

"No. Well, then. We'll have to go over to the mainland today, I guess, to pick the shoes up. How's the tide, Miss Holcombe? Do you happen to know?"

"High around eight this morning."

"Perfect. Well, Miss Holcombe, I've enjoyed our little chat but I'm afraid I must cut it short. There's barely time for me to get back to the millhouse and shave and change clothes and locate a checkbook and explain the errand to Priscilla. Good-by for now. Take care of yourself. I hope you're advancing rapidly in the music world these days."

"Mr. Geach."

"Yes?"

"Aren't you going to thank me for the information about the shoes?"

"I certainly am. Thanks sincerely. And I want to reward you by telling you I'll be glad to serve as witness or whatever it was you had in mind. When was it?"

"The afternoon of the fourth. Can we meet here at two?"

"Fine."

"Good. That path leads to your house. I go this way."

"Thanks again. Bye-bye for now, Miss Holcombe."

"Good-by, Mr. Geach. Remember our appointment."

CHAPTER SEVENTY-EIGHT

It is Father's Day in Jimbo's dream. The air is mild and clear. What will he give his father later in the day? his father who after a picnic lunch naps on a blanket under the willow. Jimbo has no cash, there are no gift shops in the vicinity. What might please the old gentleman? A demonstration of aerial acrobatics, Jimbo decides. He dons wings. He takes a running start across the grass and flaps aloft. Flying isn't so difficult as he had expected but it is tiring, especially for the arms.

"Plus the guy'll die before he wakes up," thinks Jimbo, himself waking now. Ropes hold his arms at his sides. He remembers the roughnecks. He feels so weary and cramped and stiff and so wants to be free that tears of vexation start. About the glade titmice and other birds greet the morning.

Now Daisy appears singing the old air "Greensleeves" and discovers her friend Jimbo. When she releases him he slumps to the ground. "What happened? Jimbo, did Mr. Geach . . . ? No, don't try to move yet. Goodness, how long have you been tied there? It was those boys, wasn't it? I knew it, I knew it. Oh, they make me furious!"

Jimbo sighs, asks Daisy to tie his shoelace for him. Strength is returning to his aching body the more quickly for Daisy's ministrations. They gaze into one another's weary eyes fondly for minutes at a time, letting thoughts wander so freely they may lose track of what is being said or heard as they recount recent events—Jimbo his capture, bondage, sleep, and dreaming, Daisy how uneventful her patrol of her sector of the island was until she glimpsed the six marauders as they fled up the shore and, recognizing them and supposing they might be responsible for Jack Geach's disappearance, determined to pursue them along a parallel course up the interior and so arrived here. "You didn't find Mr. Geach though?"

"No. You?"

"Me neither."

"I wonder where he is."

"In his own house under his own bed, tripping or something. Pretending he's not himself but this timid vacuum cleaner salesman who's fallen in love with Ms. Geach."

"Oooh I'll bet you're right."

"Just a hunch. Daisy?"

"Yes?"

"Can I ask you something?"

"You can. But you know I won't answer if it's about Big Boy."

"Why not?"

"Oh dear, Jimbo. I can't, it's not fair. Maybe I will though."

"Daisy?"

"Yes?" She kisses him lightly on the cheek. "Yes, Jimbo?"

"What's the difference . . . between . . ." Jimbo and Daisy are nodding off to sleep when Annabel and Carter appear arm in arm laughing easily. They join the others and relate their adventures. They too have encountered the off-islanders. Carter, assaulted by them, has routed and chased them into Annabel's territory where, hearing her coming toward them and fearing an ambush, the gang has stampeded off the path through a stand of poison ivy, "as they'll begin to realize tomorrow." But neither Annabel nor Carter can provide the slightest clue to Mr. Geach's whereabouts.

"Oh dear," says Daisy.

Annabel nods. "Oh dear is right."

"Hey listen," exclaims Carter, "could that be him now?"

Everyone sighs. It is only Thuggy and the dogs. But the disappointment turns to relief when Thuggy says he has seen the Geach family including Jack at the island dock, apparently about to embark for the mainland and all seemingly in good health and spirits.

"But where was he all night?"

"Who knows."

"Who cares. Everything's cool. Everything's solid."

At last all the stories have been told and Jimbo is ready to walk. The young people troop back to the farmhouse singing, Thuggy blowing his harmonica, the dogs circling and barking happily.

CHAPTER SEVENTY-NINE

In the large shady rooms of the farmhouse they converse more and postpone the moment when they will all fall asleep. Here now they are free and graceful and at rest. Much harm had been possible and little or none has occurred through the changes and tensions of a day and a long night. They have not injured each other or anyone else and, although the situation is not so rare (for them at least) as might be supposed, still it is noteworthy and seems especially so now. They do not presume that all possible stresses among them have been resolved (though some have) or that no new difficulties will arise tomorrow or the next day. No, what they know is that just now there are no difficulties to be faced and they need only sleep. They are at peace and they are beautiful. The smiles and glances given from one to another down the stairwell, through doorways, are direct and unconstrained. Each feels and shows admiration and respect and love for each. In the hallway or on the landing where light filters through a curtain onto a chair, onto the floor, they stand and sit in groups and talk quietly, each hearing each. They stand one with an arm on another's shoulder, a foot on a rung of another's tilted chair. It is true that they have not accomplished what they had hoped to accomplish quite, through all the recent activity and effort expended. Yet they feel as if the credit is almost theirs, the credit for things having worked out well as they have done, miraculously well if recent hours were as perilous as they have seemed. But can it really be? Can they really have woven their way through and by so many disasters and catastrophes, skirting every one? Can so much harm have been in the offing? Yes, but never mind. The grandfather clock chimes nine times. The faithful dogs are already sleeping.

CHAPTER EIGHTY

There are two landings on the island, one on either side. The older is at the boathouse in the island's only harbor. Traditionally it has been a private facility used by the owner of the boathouse. Roughly opposite, facing toward the mainland is the newer "island dock" built, maintained, and used collectively by the entire island population.

The problem of changing tide level has been dealt with in different ways at the two places. At the boathouse vessels are attached by lines with suitable slack to one of the iron rings set into the stone steps. The slack allows the vessel to rise and fall with the tide, a stern anchor holds it off the stone and the steps provide access at whatever tide. The island dock is more conventional. Built of wood, it consists of three parts. A narrow walkway runs atop pilings out from the land some ten feet above highest moon tides. At the end is a hinged incline, a long flat rectangle crossed with raised strips which provide safe footing. This leads from the catwalk down to the floating platform where boats dock. As the platform rises and falls on the tide the angle of the incline changes. This dock provides more convenient landing than the stone stair at the boathouse but in the worst storms, the highest seas, the platform breaks away, carrying with it any boats foolhardily left attached there. It has happened three times since the dock was raised and each time island residents have done the rebuilding together, co-operating in the face of emergency even when it has meant setting aside lifelong antipathies.

Gulls can rest on the island dock and still keep an eye on water deep enough for fish large enough to warrant a dive. Many of them were here when the Geach family arrived. Warned by Hester's and Edith's cries they rose and circled over the running children, the strolling adults, and a motor launch cutting in toward the dock. Today the weather would be splendid.

Priscilla leaned on Jack's arm. When she had returned after her circuit of the island in search of him she had found her daughters safely asleep. Strain and fatigue had left her irrational. She had sighed, "Here all along, can you imagine!" meaning that since the children were in the house so must be the husband. Whereupon she had fallen across her bed and slept, to be awakened hours later by Jack with scones and *café au lait*, kisses and projects. "Priscilla, I know what Edith wants for her birthday. She wants some of those Mary Jane shoes." "But Jack, I knew that already!" "No, how?" "Jack, where were you last night?" "Last night? I . . . Drink your coffee, dear. I've already radioed for the boat." Breakfasting, waking the girls, descending to the dock, they had pieced together what they could of the night's confusing events. There was much they could make no sense of, much that simply did not fit, many loose ends. The Geaches stood arm in arm on the high walkway and watched their daughters race about the platform below over coils of rope, anchors, and sail boxes, and they felt a strange exhilaration and chill. One girl wore pink, one green. The weathered platform was gray-white and painfully clean as though some Dutch housewife had spent a lifetime scrubbing and rinsing it. The cold ocean was deep. Seaweed made a dark olive tangle.

Priscilla and Jack glanced at each other. It was the kind of questioning checking signal exchanged by two members of a group when a third unwittingly touches on a matter of vital interest to them—a sudden wordless sign of intelligence and complicity. A handsome couple, they smiled quickly. Jack wore canvas shoes, white duck trousers, a soft gray alpaca sweater under his navy nylon windbreaker, and a canvas sailor's hat. Priscilla wore sandals, a simple dress of flowered cotton challis, and large sunglasses. Her handbag was of braided straw, with a hinged wooden lid. She kissed Jack lightly on the cheek. The launch swerved in smoothly. The children leaped and screamed. The parents descended.

Besides finding Edith's shoes the Geaches had other errands on the mainland. Priscilla intended to visit a hairdresser and the public library. Jack had arranged to meet one of his secretaries at an ice-cream parlor to affix his signature to various documents and to give instructions too delicate to risk radioing. As they were embarking another errand was given them. Around an outcrop of shale came old Jane in her rowboat. Edith grimaced, Hester squirmed with pleasure. Jane had brought lollipops for them and she had a brief message she wanted the elder Geaches to convey to a telegraph office.

CHAPTER EIGHTY-ONE

Jane rowed away from the island dock. She had postponed replying to her friend Charlotte until it had been necessary to telegraph the message, a warm expression of pleasure at the idea of Charlotte's imminent arrival, signed with Jane's schoolgirl nickname Muff. Jane clucked and shook her head. Some of her girlfriends had called her Muffin instead. Charlotte's nickname had been Owl. "Gracious sakes," Jane said. Her oarlocks rattled. It was a fine morning, the waves were only high enough to make rowing interesting. She maneuvered the boat among rocks and shoals as she had done for decades and decades. So long as she could count on her skill and strength and her by now perfect familiarity with the shoreline she didn't much mind being old.

This morning Jane had awakened extremely refreshed and confident after a night of deep sleep induced by a dose of the recovered Lethe Water. Her legs hadn't ached, either. No part of her ached. And numerous mild chronic pains, to which over the years she had grown accustomed and then oblivious, had ceased. Her legs were still slow, she couldn't run or dance certainly. Indeed what her body did today seemed quite like what it always did. But how it felt! She was light as air and perhaps she could indeed dance—yes, certainly she could and would, here in her drifting boat for all the island to see, except that it would be indecorous for a woman her age, a widow.

Charlotte had been the flighty frivolous member of their set and famous for her absent-mindedness. She left lace gloves or a parasol near the kiosk in the park after a concert, ran back to retrieve them, and laughed to find them gone, even though such luxuries had cost her a week's work in the shoe factory. In winter she lost mittens in the snow beside the pond. She had been the prettiest and merriest and yet as they married one by one it had seemed that Charlotte would be a spinster all her life, until to everyone's astonishment she had married a fabulously rich man in a distant city. Then everyone began to decide that Charlotte was not in the least frivolous, had never been, had always been shrewd, shrewder than shrewd, crafty in fact and even somewhat grasping. Jane had known better. "Feathered her nest right well, though." And sometimes through the years Jane had wondered whether she, Jane, had not proved more woefully frivolous than Charlotte had ever been thought to be. One card John had mailed from China arrived in time for the birthday after that it was meant for.

Jane arrived at her dock. She made the boat fast and stepped out onto the stone, dragging her canes. She bent, loosed the rope, and ascended the steps, leading the boat as one leads an animal on a leash, playing out rope as she went. She made the boat fast again. The guest room would have to be dusted, food prepared. Nothing fancy though. If Charlotte wanted *haute cuisine* she was coming to the wrong place. Let her fly to Paris instead. Jane gave a satisfied chuckle. Chowder, stuffed quahogs, a cobbler. But would Charlotte have photographs from the old days? Would the two of them have anything to say to each other? Would they cry? Would Charlotte offer her money? What was that black thing in the path?

It was a blacksnake basking in the morning sun, absorbing energy. A neighbor to be grateful for since it ate vermin. Still . . . Jane watched it uncoil and move off through the grass. The large old woman's way was clear.

How long did Charlotte intend to stay? Might she and Jane hit it off so well they would decide to live together indefinitely? Had Charlotte's husband been as handsome as John had been? As cheerful?

CHAPTER EIGHTY-TWO

Thuggy wakes with a hard-on. Through open windows he hears birds and waves: sloooooshka-kuk-sss . . . Treek-treek, treek. Pyjamas? He has none. Bathing trunks. His mouth is dry. He creeps out his doorway along the polished corridor into Annabel's room where she lies sleeping. He creeps into the bed beside her.

Everything he notices in the room pleases him. Tables, rug, heap of clothes, patchwork quilt, sunlight, breeze. On one table are a paperback detective novel written by an Englishwoman with some letters tucked in it, a book about massage, the violin case, a leaf, an aerosol can of dry shampoo. On the other table half a bacon-lettuce-and-tomato sandwich on a paper napkin, a newspaper more than five years old (Annabel had found it in her kindling box), a candlestick, a brooch. Thuggy enjoys seeing these things but he can hardly take his eyes off Annabel. She is naked except for a green rubber band on her wrist. She is finishing a dream. Thuggy slips off his bathing suit. He hasn't touched Annabel.

Annabel begins to wake up. She shifts and stretches, laying her arm across Thuggy's face. He kisses her elbow before it moves away. She opens her eyes. "Oh, hi," she says. She hears waves and birds through the open windows. Waking more, she understands that the situation is extraordinary. They are in her bedroom in her bed. She starts to laugh. "What are you up to, Thuggy?" He smiles as pleasantly as he can.

Annabel tries to remember. The hunt for Jack Geach, then all together back here, right. He must have crept in while she was asleep. "Apparently I neglected to lock my door," she says. He edges closer like a puppy. He strokes her ankle with his toe. At first she thinks she won't co-operate.

The bed creaks when they begin to move. They hold still for a moment, looking at each other in a way that means, "Suppose the others hear." They listen. No sound of anyone stirring in the house. Thuggy makes the tiniest most tentative movement. Annabel doesn't object. They recommence fucking.

They fuck and fuck, they love it. A dizzying orgasm is going to start at Annabel's clitoris, it is starting and happening. It seems to create a body that flowers from her clitoris to her toes and fingers, to her ears. Thuggy's nipples brush hers. She lies limp and now he is coming too. He has a momentary vision of a child's painting: night, a lightning bolt striking a white frame house.

They lie quite still. Annabel thinks, "If anybody moves . . ." Thuggy licks his thumb and smooths her mussed eyebrows, and as his shrunk penis slips out of her Annabel comes again very quickly with wonderful weak violence.

They doze back to back and touching at buttocks and heels.

Later at the window they see wrens playing on a bough, the clean barnyard. The beach is white, the sea blue, the clouds white. Thuggy sees that the name in the heart has been transferred from his belly to Annabel's, reversed in the process. Later the reversal will be undone when Annabel stands before her mirror.

CHAPTER EIGHTY-THREE

At first there was no answer when Annabel knocked at Sue Holcombe's cottage. She was on time for once too—three o'clock sharp. Odd, the girl thought. She scanned the clearing, shading her eyes. She had nearly turned her ankle in one of the concealed rabbit holes. She thought, "This quiet deserted-looking yard is full of rabbits. The holes are openings of a maze of interconnected burrows and tunnels. The bunnies are down there now twitching their noses in the dark, sitting alone or beside a spouse or maybe paying a visit to a neighbor." Annabel wondered how deep into the earth the metropolis extended. Did moles, chipmunks, or other burrowing creatures make surreptitious use of the system? Or did they have their own threaded through and among but not opening onto the larger arteries of the rabbit warren. The inhabitants of each network were aware of the others. At certain places the chipmunks had heard something large and soft with large soft feet moving in the earth nearby. The rabbits had sometimes listened to light feet running in the earth. But if one encountered another on the surface above there was not an inkling that this peculiar creature peering through the grass was responsible for sounds one often heard at home. Annabel frowned. It must be like a sponge down there, so how come it doesn't cave in?

"Come in, come in. Stop gawking," said Sue Holcombe. She wore flannel pyjamas, a man's black-leather bedroom slippers, and a man's maroon silk dressing gown. It was after three o'clock in the afternoon. "Listen, Sue," Annabel said, "if it's inconvenient, I mean if I'm interrupting anything I'll come back later."

"Rubbish." Annabel was wearing sandals, nondescript shorts, a rugby jersy with black and white stripes. "Wash the dishes and clean the lamp chimneys. And don't nod at your work or you'll regret it. If you break anything I'll charge you double."

Annabel smiled.

"I'm dressed this way," Sue Holcombe went on, "because I was sleeping. Musicians lead irregular lives."

Several days' worth of dishes were soaking in cold gray water. Annabel drained it. While fresh water heated she gathered soiled dishes from other rooms. Soon all the cutlery and dishes, pots and pans were bright as new and warm, piled in the rack beside the sink, the sink drained and the orange ring of grease, suds, and tobacco washed away. Then Annabel cleaned the lamp chimneys. Kerosene, the fuel, also served to dissolve sticky deposits on the chimneys.

Sue Holcombe changed into her lime-green shirtwaist dress and her black oxfords, scrubbed her face and brushed her hair. She stood at the top of the stairs a moment to listen—wasn't the girl slacking?—and then descended briskly. Annabel was replacing the last chimney. She looked large and pretty in Sue Holcombe's cottage with its knobby brittle furnishings.

Before the lesson they drank tea in the parlor, trading accounts of the mischief-makers from the mainland. Sue Holcombe intended to press charges. "They should be locked up but since they're minors I may only be able to get at them through their parents."

"What . . . what bailiwick or jurisdiction is this island under? Which police have authority?"

"The question is in dispute and no one bothers to resolve it.

Usually it's immaterial. But it should be settled for the sake of just such vermin as those six."

"Why do you suppose they do it, Sue? Why are they trouble-makers?"

"Why is the sky blue?"

In the music room the teacher's mien grew stern. She paced about trailing ribbons of cigarette smoke, muttering to herself. Annabel was impressed. Sue halted. "Now, Miss. I want you to play the piece you've memorized. Play it as correctly, expressively, and intelligently as you can. When you have done, lift the bow smoothly without any scratching, lower it and the violin to your sides, and stand still. Don't fidget, don't speak. Keep your eyes lowered until I break the silence. This will give us both a chance to judge your performance. You understand? Begin when ready."

In a few moments Annabel began to play.

> Lavender's blue, dilly dilly,
> Lavender's green . . .

There was a tightness in the air and once as she played, when she glanced her teacher's way, it seemed to Annabel that the woman was startled. She ended the song—

> I told myself, dilly dilly,
> I told me so.

—as instructed. The silence was long. During it Annabel tried to judge her performance, but it had vanished from her conscious memory.

"I see," said Sue. "Very interesting. Probably you suppose you're the only one he's ever kissed. Silly girl."

"She's berserk," Annabel thought. She prepared to use the bow as an épée if need be. "Sue? I beg your pardon."

"Last night I imagine. Recently anyway. Behind the kitchen door, in the bushes, wherever. You've allowed him to smooch you. What do you expect? It shows in your phrasing and tempi, your tone coloring, the mistakes you make. It *shows*."

Annabel smiled in spite of herself, remembering Thuggy.

"If I had time and cared," Sue Holcombe went on, "I could

tell you everything I heard. Where he put his reckless lips against yours, when and so forth. It comes through, my dear, even in so coarse a medium as your performance. Hidden perhaps but there, and as audible as his picture."

Annabel laughed. Again she had forgotten the picture of Carter in the violin. What to say? Sue seemed enormously pleased and triumphant, with her raised eyebrows and pursed mouth. Why dim this radiance? For that matter, what difference did it make that she mistook the smoocher's identity? Annabel said nothing.

Sue Holcombe said, "You've ignored my warning about him—I wash my hands of the matter. As far as your music is concerned, don't flatter yourself. Change is not necessarily improvement. It's only change. Have you anything to say? Good, we must move along. Play the piece backward now."

Annabel made a valiant attempt but beyond a few notes it was impossible.

"Mozart could have done it when he was half your age," observed Sue.

Annabel shrugged.

"Don't be insolent," barked the musician.

"Oh dear," thought Annabel.

"Never mind," sighed Sue Holcombe. "Let me explain the notion of key. Pay attention." She played "Lavender's Blue" in various keys and quizzed Annabel about how the transpositions affected the song. Some of the girl's answers surprised her, others she brushed aside as worthless or worse. Annabel couldn't guess what criteria might distinguish so sharply among her replies.

Then came the oddest part of the lesson. Annabel had to play "Lavender's Blue" not stationary as before but running in a circle around the empty music stand Sue positioned "as a reference point." It wasn't arduous for the strong girl but she found Sue Holcombe's laughter unnerving. "It made me feel as if you were mocking me," she explained, "as if you'd made up the exercise to amuse yourself at my expense."

Sue Holcombe stifled a laugh. "Maybe I did! So? If you're a serious student you'll learn regardless of what I do. Now for some sight reading. Try this first." It was "The German Shepherd." Annabel had struggled through two measures when it was whisked off the stand and replaced by "Brahms' Lullaby." This was intrinsically easier and the melody familiar. Nevertheless it too was abruptly removed and replaced by "Tannenbaum," which in turn gave way to "Frère Jacques." When that disappeared as Annabel completed the first *"Dormez-vous?"* there was no replacement.

Sue Holcombe seemed preoccupied. "Put away your instrument," she said. She lit a cigarette, let the extinguished match fall to the floor. Annabel closed the violin case, picked up the match, and dropped it into an ashtray.

"I can't imagine why," began Sue, "but I rather like you. Therefore I shall tell you something even though it's not in my interest to do so. Unfortunately, Annabel, there's not the slightest chance in the world of your becoming a competent violinist. Absolutely no chance."

Poor Annabel! She was taken aback and somewhat shamed by this news. She bit her lip.

"We may as well have one more lesson to clinch it," Sue continued. "But more would be a waste of your time. You might consider taking up a different instrument. Snare drum for instance—rhythm's the least defective component of your music. Or perhaps you should try another art. Does drawing appeal to you? I've often thought drawing and music aren't so different as people make them out to be. This, after all," (holding up a sheet of "The German Shepherd") "may be taken to be a drawing. An unusual one, but a drawing nonetheless."

Annabel smiled feebly.

"Think it over," said Sue. "Come back on Sunday, same time. Good-by for now. Please give my regards to your friend Daisy. My warmest regards."

Alone, Sue Holcombe strolled through the cottage with a sort of bittersweet proprietariness. She had passed many pleasant and productive hours here and there was a coziness the farmhouse would lack.

CHAPTER EIGHTY-FOUR

"Hi, Jimbo."

"Hi, Annabel. How was the lesson?"

"So-so. On your way to the well?"

"It's not my turn but I felt like it."

"See you."

The girl goes that way swinging her violin case. The boy goes this way swinging his yellow plastic bucket, barefoot on the grass. His path parallels one of the stone fences that once bounded pastures and are now mostly lost in the woods that have grown up around them. On the map the young people used last night in their search for Jack Geach the fences appear as broken lines. Jimbo removes his portion of the map from his shirt pocket. Yes, this fence, exactly so. Jimbo frowns. Padding along the path he turns his mind to boundaries and maps.

"Maps are magnificent. I think mapping has to be one of the most beautiful ideas the human race has ever had, and that's why it bothers me to find wrongheadedness and arbitrariness mixed into the idea.

"Like up and down. It's arbitrary and absurd that north should always be up and south down. Probably pernicious too. Because we learn to think of up as plus and down as minus, so it must carry over. The southern hemisphere with all its inhabitants is on the deficit side of the equator. Mindless shit and a bummer of course, but everybody must tend to think that way because of maps. Or actually it's not the maps themselves but rather the words and numbers printed on them that condition people to think of one orientation as right side up and the other as upside down.

"It even carries over into photographs. There's reason to print a photo of a tree with leaves at the top and roots at the bottom. But why print a photo of the earth with Africa at the bottom and Europe at the top?

"I guess there's some natural reason for letting the axial points of the map or globe go through Antarctica and the North Pole. The planet's own axis is oriented that way. Plus it lets features you might want to note on a map be simple. Like climatic features—the equator can be perpendicular to the axis. But simplicity's all that's gained and a map with any other axis would be quite as accurate. Every place could have its own globe with itself where the North Pole is now. Nobody lives at the North Pole anyway: why should it have the favored position?

"Also if you wanted to keep things simple you could let the axis go through the poles but be horizontal. South Pole right, North Pole left, or vice versa. Incidentally, the connotations left and right carry because of how our hands operate must color how we think of east and west. But this is arbitrary too. If south were up east would be left instead of right.

"Colors on maps do similar things. I love them, who doesn't. Transparent enough for names of rivers and towns to show through but still intense and brightish except near boundaries where they darken and grow opaque, as if digging in and asserting their identities against adjacent colors. If I were a painter I'd paint nothing but maplike pictures for a while. Who wouldn't. Maps could make you happy just by how they're colored.

"Still there are problems. A country or whatever isn't simply colored, but colored a specific color like yellow or green, with its own peculiar significances and connotations, some culture-specific maybe and some (like green's) almost universal. The pretense of course is that the colors get assigned randomly, that they aren't to be interpreted, that they have nothing to do with how the cartographers think about the parts of the map they cover. If map readers believed that to be the case and read the map so, no hassle. But cartographers make such a reading next to impossible. Because one color on the map isn't at all arbitrary but rather is clearly representational or verisimilar: blue, the wonderful special map-ocean blue. It corresponds so directly to what it marks—what it marks *is* that color, in a sense—that we must be led unconsciously to suppose that somehow Yugoslavia really is actually piss-colored.

"Map color's interesting also because it gives cartographers something to do with what otherwise would be empty space. No matter how many dots, squiggles, numbers, letters, and other signs and symbols they include, it remains true that most of the map space is occupied by none of these things and would be empty except for color. It's all the pretty colored emptiness that enables the dots and squiggles to situate themselves with respect to one another.

"Politically a map where orange thickens and builds up against a black line against which violet does the same from the other side, politically such a map is clearly bad news. On a better one colors would fade into each other and rearrange shapes freely. There might even be land colored blue.

"Right. But suppose you're trying to find out where the fuck you are. Then you want boundaries between colors precise. In fact the colors might not be any help and the boundary lines might be more useful than anything they surround. I mean imagine you're lost on a street corner in Paris. You see street signs but you could spend an hour trying to locate any one of these street names on the map. But you also notice you're at the juncture of three *arrondissements*. Your problem is solved. You see the map as a comparatively simple network of borders instead of as a baffling jumble of streets.

"So what else. Isn't there an unsolved problem about how few colors would suffice for any possible map? Anyway, it'd be nice to know how many kinds of things besides the obvious ones could count as maps without one's having to bend or stretch the concept unduly. A sheet of music for instance maybe. What?"

Jimbo stops short. He is at the well and there thumbtacked to the scaffold is an envelope addressed to him in an old-fashioned script with spiky flourishes. Inside is the following message:

> Dear Jimbo:
> You shall ride the bull. Look in the hollow tree to your left.

The message is unsigned. In the tree Jimbo finds a matchbox whose contents, when he understands their function, make him shout with amazement.

The water doesn't seem heavy on the way back to the farmhouse. When Jimbo pauses it is to pick clover blossoms.

CHAPTER EIGHTY-FIVE

Annabel has swum in the cold ocean this morning. She has lain on the sand to warm and dry. Now she is in her room deciding what to wear. Her bathing suit hangs out the window, her bathing cap lies on the floor. She sits on her bed brushing sand and salt crystals off her skin. There aren't many costumes to choose among. Cut-off corduroy shorts are within reach, she dons them. "If I were a boy I wouldn't need anything more," she thinks. She pulls on a tee shirt spotted with paint and glances in the mirror. Her haircut still surprises her. She doesn't dislike it but she thinks it may look a little absurd.

Outside she comes upon Thuggy and Carter playing chess in the grass under an elm.

"Hi, kid."

"Hi, Annabel."

"Hi." Annabel pretends to study the board.

In the spacious tree singing birds flutter from branch to branch. Annabel wonders whether Thuggy has told Carter about fucking with her. Carter smiles lazily and Thuggy's eyes twinkle but these clues could point either way. Annabel is blushing. "He's told, told Jimbo too. Boys can't wait to boast. Yes but Thuggy's too much of a gentleman. Oh, it couldn't matter less." Annabel stands with her hands in the pockets of her shorts. "Whose move?" she asks.

"What we're trying to figure."

"We got stoned and lost track. Plus the men keep blowing over."

"Wanna toke, kid?" asks Thuggy.

"No thanks. I have to work on the back steps and also get in some fiddling. I'm a busy girl."

"Right on," Thuggy calls after her.

"Annabel sure does look good," Carter observes.

In fact both boys are perfectly cognizant of the state of their game and either could reproduce it from opening to present array. They continue playing. "You okay, man?" "You?" Each notices his opponent's errors and his own as the game progresses. They are relaxed and friendly. The air is fresh under the tree.

Tomorrow Annabel and Daisy are to paint the stoop and short stairs leading from the back door down toward the beach. Today Annabel must strip the wood and cover it with a primer coat. Seams and blisters give way under the blade of the scraper and throw out dust, sequins, tiny splinters. The girl works steadily. Of the young people, only Thuggy has more patience and stamina, and none enjoys manual labor more. Her skin is rosy brown, her creased lips pale. A wood-eating bumblebee dazed by the vibrations squeezes up between two boards and flies in wobbly loops toward the ocean.

Pushing sandpaper in circles over the wood, Annabel creates what amounts to a relief map of the surface. From any lowest area covered by last year's dark green one can traverse bands of colors from successively earlier summers marking successively higher levels and so reach a plateau or island of bared wood. The pattern must now disappear. Next summer it will reappear altered by today's and tomorrow's painting. So it changes summer after summer. Lows grow as they rise with each deposit and in time the system would stabilize in level uniformity were the wood not always subject to dents, bucklings, and other accidents that reintroduce the layered sequence in new places over the years.

Annabel stirs the gray paint, dips in a brush, and begins. Jimbo at the kitchen window sees her and comes to help. "How's the violin going?"

"I think the musical ability all drifted to your side of the family. I have trouble just keeping in tune. Did it take you long?"

Jimbo shrugs. "With guitar the frets do it for you. You don't think about it."

Annabel marvels. "*No.* Of course, though."

"Listen, compared to violin guitar's a cinch. If you want, I'll show you how the guitar works sometime. With the foundation you already have you should be able to pick it up quick. I'm not an experienced teacher like Sue Holcombe . . ." They smile. "Violin's a real bitch."

"You're telling me." They work in silence and then Annabel says, "It's funny, our not meeting until this summer. And yet it never struck me as peculiar before. I must have heard you mentioned but I suppose not enough to make me very curious."

"Me too. But it's kind of nice to discover a full-grown cousin this way."

Annabel nods. "It's like a gift. Free."

"Annabel, do you know why Sue Holcombe has it in for Daisy?"

"Not really. I think somebody was supposed to leave Sue the farmhouse but left it to Daisy instead. Why not ask Daisy."

"Mmm. If I'd been expecting to get this house I guess I'd resent Daisy's having it. If I were Sue Holcombe, I mean. If I were me I wouldn't. Daisy's okay. In fact she's dynamite. But listen, Annabel, suppose you and I sometime get involved in a family property settlement."

"Not that there's much to settle, far as I know."

"But suppose. I suggest we not be greedy. You can have my share if I'm rich and you poor. And I'd expect you to do the same."

"You can count on me Jimbo. After all . . ."

"By the way—speaking of gifts—you know little Edith Geach's birthday is tomorrow and we've got to figure presents. So I was thinking of making her a book of riddles. Except that the ones I know might be lost on her. Any suggestions?"

Annabel is watching her cousin with interest. After a moment she says, "What's red and white and black all over?"

Jimbo begins, "No, you mean what's black and . . ." Then he smiles.

"Even that's probably more Hester's speed."

Delighted now and imperturbable, Jimbo rallies. "Well, I'll have to think of something good. Because the Fourth of July coming right after must tend to cancel the kid's birthday." Annabel watches. Jimbo continues, "That reminds me, have you heard about the bonfire they build here to celebrate the Fourth?"

Annabel smiles and shakes her head. "Tell me about it, Jimbo."

The steps are covered. Jimbo has left cleaning the brushes to Annabel. When she has done she comes around to the front of the house. Under the elm Carter and Thuggy are still playing chess. They wave. Annabel sits in the porch swing and watches them.

CHAPTER EIGHTY-SIX

Anyone may reach a point of breaking down. No matter how one tries to smile, one can do no more than raise the corners of the lips. Cheerfulness will not come, the prognosis for the immediate future is an aching heart. The spirit feels drab, derelict. One did laugh in the past but that laughter now seems to have been for no good reason, seems to have been pathetic and foolish, unlovely, best forgotten. So little would suffice, too! A few words, an invitation to walk on the beach. Less would suffice, but no relief is in sight. Dismal, dismal—one may as well . . . what? Nothing seems very funny. A lifetime of loneliness does not seem very funny. Tears will fall, give them time, when the heart aches from love.

Clear dusk, the end of a beautiful day. No lamps yet. Her journal open on her lap Daisy sat in her rocking chair in the living room of the farmhouse. The dogs lay nearby. Everything was dark and clear. Outside the meadow, the fence and the woods held still and darkened. Daisy's skirt drooped in long folds to the floor. A white quill lay in her small hand. On the table a pool of ink hung suspended in heavy glass. There was also a wooden bowl holding pieces of fruit, mainly grapefruits. Daisy sighed. She inked the nib of her pen and wrote, "Who can speak for a grapefruit?" She wrote it on a blank page of her journal. She had smoked some dope. The quill scratched against the surface of the paper. When the ink had dried Daisy closed the book and put it and the pen aside. "Come, doggies. Let's take a turn outdoors." They were glad to accompany her but because of her sadness they were subdued and solicitous, careful to listen whenever she spoke. They had been hers since they were puppies. Naturally they were alive to her moods and their spirits followed hers, rising and falling. There was nothing they wouldn't do for her, burly red Rufus and trim Goose with her mournful eyes, black Goose.

After a while Daisy and her dogs left the shore and followed a seldom used path into the woods. The air was quiet here. There was a graveyard with four graves, the headstones all bearing the same family name. One was black and set apart because, as legend had it, the man buried there had been murdered by his hired man. The place was calm, no ghosts lurked about. Farther on one passed foundation stones, all that remained of the island's first house. Tears rolled down the face and wetted the lips. Fireflies drifted among the trees.

Daisy met Faye and Gail where the obscure path joined a more frequented one and they walked with her and her dogs through the woods and halfway across the farmhouse meadow. "Good-by, Daisy." "Good-by Faye, good-by, Gail." "Good-by, Daisy."

There were lights upstairs in Jimbo's and Carter's rooms and downstairs in the parlor. Soon the dining room would be lighted and all would gather for a long slow meal. Daisy came inside, into the parlor. On the table beside the rocking chair were her plume and inkwell and her journal. On the journal lay a bouquet of white clover blossoms.

"Hmm." Daisy spent the next quarter hour drawing a picture of the nosegay on a clean page in her book. She hoped Jimbo had left the flowers for her as a token of his affection.

CHAPTER EIGHTY-SEVEN

Edith Geach's birthday party began at eight o'clock in the millhouse. Ordinarily Edith was in bed by then and so was Hester. There were red and blue balloons, orange and red crepe paper, conical party hats.

Light spilled from every window onto the dark grass and water, guiding the invited. The young people from the farmhouse felt like spies when they saw the windowed house with people sometimes passing the windows. They held hands and circled the building and looked into every room they could before announcing their arrival at the front door. As they circled there were moments when the stone and light and the family inside seemed quite certainly a figment of their imagination. A little later old Jane tugged the bell cord. Jack greeted her, "Yes, yes, glad you could make it." Edith squinted. She would have been happier had the old woman been forbidden to attend.

People were introduced to each other. The children were told to amuse themselves while adults sipped cocktails and chatted. The inhabitants of the farmhouse had smoked some hashish on their way here and old Jane had swallowed two aspirin tablets. Jack and Priscilla had drunk an excellent white burgundy at dinner. Tapes of rock operas at low volume provided a soothing kind of background water for voices to float in.

Annabel and Jane conversed timidly at first, complimenting one another on clothes, agreeing about recent weather. But since they had not met before and would probably not meet again they wanted the encounter to be memorable.

"You work for the Geaches."

"Upstairs maid and babysitter, sort of. I . . . I need money and the work's not so demeaning as it might seem."

"You don't stand on your dignity then, Annabel? Why not—is your family very wealthy?"

"I wish they were! I suppose. No, not wealthy. Yours?"

"Good heavens, child, my family's all dead except for my son-in-law and my granddaughter!"

"Sorry. Sorry, what I meant was . . ."

"Never mind. Tell me, Annabel: what will you be doing in the fall when you leave the island? What are you up to when you're not here? Giving some young man a cold shoulder but not too cold a one? I'd not be surprised."

"As a matter of fact . . . You used to be a schoolteacher didn't you, Jane?"

"Who told you?"

"Daisy. As a matter of fact, Jane, geology is what I'm up to. I may earn my living teaching it. If not, I'll probably make jewelry. There are boys but no special one. I don't know if there ever will be. You were married . . ."

"Annabel, I wish there were time for us to be friends. I wish we were the same age."

"Yours or mine?" Annabel laughed.

In another part of the room Jack Geach was quizzing Jimbo whom he did not quite remember having met two nights before at the farmhouse. "What are you going into? What long- and intermediate-range hurdles have you set yourself? Are you interested in real estate?"

"Interested in real estate?"

"Property. Buildings. Land."

"Some yes, some no. In general yes. But certainly not to buy or sell, Mr. Geach. I hope that's not what you meant. Property can be said to be theft. Places, places are what I like. I like maps of places too. I was wondering today if a place could be a map of . . . of something else."

Jack lighted his pipe. "Ha ha ha. Very funny. Seriously though." Annabel and Jane were listening, Jimbo noticed. The little girls on the sofa between Thuggy and Carter turned pages of a picture book and watched the packages on a low table before them. Daisy had gone to the kitchen with Ms. Geach. Jimbo wondered, "Is this Geach redeemable, educable? And would it be worth the trouble?" He thought not and though he was a guest in the man's house he decided not to reply immediately. He sipped his Mai Tai and eyed Jack. "Is he a smart aleck?" Jack wondered. "What's he up to? Who does he think he is? Does he realize who he's talking to? Or rather, not talking to?"

At this point Jane entered the conversation. "Are you interested in real estate yourself, Mr. Geach?" she asked sweetly, as she had asked equivalent questions millions of times in her long life. Jack nodded thoughtfully in a way that meant, "I understand your query. Just a moment please."

Priscilla and Daisy brought in vanilla ice cream, a fruit punch, and the cupcakes whose frosting Hester had tinted. Then some of the lanterns were extinguished, Priscilla slipped away and returned with a birthday cake. The four lighted candles were pink, the frosting white with pink rosettes. "Oooh." Priscilla set the cake in front of her daughter. Thuggy, Annabel, and Jimbo stood together and played "Happy Birthday" with harmonica, violin, and guitar, and everyone sang. Edith's head swam, she was bathed in a cold sweat. She wished.

Everyone applauded.

Priscilla and Daisy served the cake and ice cream and punch. The woman and the girl felt allied beneath superficial differences of age, marital status, and costume. Priscilla wouldn't pin a bouquet of clover blossoms to the bib of a pair of overalls. Daisy mightn't shake a distillate of lilies of the valley onto her neck. Each enjoyed reading cookbooks and imagining the gradual preparation of sumptuous dishes. Neither saw any alternative to a man's (or boy's) love. "We invited everyone on the island," Priscilla was explaining, "including Miss Holcombe. But we hoped she wouldn't come because the girls dislike her." Daisy nodded. "Don't worry, she certainly won't come. It wouldn't be at all like her."

It was time for Edith to open her presents. Hester had been shuffling a deck of playing cards to lure Jane into a game of Fish. Now she slipped the cards into her dress pocket. She sat with her ankles crossed. Edith seemed to have a great many presents.

Edith was faint, weak, and clumsy. She scratched at the wrapping of the first package, yellow with blue clowns. Her nails slid over the paper without tearing it. Mother made an opening. There was a shoebox-shaped box wrapped in polka-dot paper which Edith would save till last, but in the meantime exhilaration and fright made her suppose shoes might be found in any package, even this that was flat like a book, and indeed under the clown paper was a coloring book, from Daisy. "Aren't you going to thank Daisy?" "Thank you for the nice book. It's what I wanted," Edith said as she flung it aside and attacked another gift.

This lumpish heavy parcel didn't seem promising and Edith suspected a joke when under the tissue paper she found a gray stone the size of a baseball. "Who's it from?" she asked. "Let's see. Oh yes, Annabel." "It's very nice. Thank you," growled Edith. "It's called a geode. Turn it over," said Annabel. The other side was like a bowl of diamonds. Edith stared at Annabel. Where had such a thing come from? She set it down carefully on the coloring book.

The next present did seem a kind of joke but Edith was grateful nonetheless. At first she thought the box was empty. Then she discovered a slip of paper from which her mother read, "W.O.U.: One fishing trip. Happy Birthday from Thuggy, Carter, Jimbo." Then there was a metal teapot from old Jane, turquoise sprigged with flowers. "It's nice," Edith said, "but I'd like it better if it was red. Where's the present from Hester?"

"I'll bring it. I couldn't wrap it," Hester said. She returned with a fishbowl containing water and a beautiful unconcerned goldfish. "Oooh . . ." Edith kissed her sister and then the glass side of the bowl.

"His name is Swimming Sunshine," Hester explained modestly.

There were two more packages, both from Mother and Daddy. The limp one was the dress on whose bodice Priscilla had worked a copy of Edith's drawing. Edith liked the dress though in her excitement she failed to recognize the embroidered design.

The one package remained. White wrapping paper with blue polka dots. Curly blue ribbon. Inside was a shoebox inside which, swathed in layers of tissue paper filling the air with a rare odor of newness, were red patent-leather Mary Janes. Edith's wish had been granted. There on the sofa she looked from face to face in wonderment as her mother helped her on with the shoes. Her wish had come true.

The party ended with Edith rampant, whizzing about the room stamping on everyone's toes. In an instant she would stop, raise her knee high as her face, and then bring shiny vermillion down hard on scuffed black leather or blue canvas, uttering wild shrieks.

CHAPTER EIGHTY-EIGHT

Edith spent the morning with her new coloring book. She selected colors from a wooden box of crayons, some thick, some thin, broken or with the paper peeled back, many blue, many yellow. Sometimes their sweet annoying odor led her to nibble at the one she happened to be using.

She filled the outlines of castles and elephants, airplanes, whales and cows, ice-cream cones. As she worked a sort of miracle occurred. She colored more slowly and as if absently and the color she chose meant less and less. A blue bunny sat on a pink hill. Edith tucked the blue crayon behind her ear and stared at the picture. She touched the bunny's face with her forefinger. The edge of the blue approximated the black outline. Edith's finger moved still touching at the edge of blue around, around the rabbit's head. Her finger climbed one side of a tall blue ear, crept down the opposite side. Similarly for the other ear, the body, the feet, the round blue tail. Slipping and rubbing at the edge Edith's fingertip circumnavigated the rabbit.

Edith smiled.

She took the crayon from behind her ear and drew and filled the outline of a second rabbit, a blue sister rabbit on the hilltop beside her sister whose shape hers approximated.

"Hester, Edith. Come to lunch, girls. Where's Edith?"

After lunch Edith goes fishing with Thuggy, Carter, and Jimbo in Daisy's sailboat. Carter is an expert sailor and Jimbo and Thuggy have had some practice since their ignominious running aground and rescue by Jane, so that the danger is small. Edith is delighted to be surrounded and made much of by three large interesting boys in bathing trunks.

They put out from the common dock with a good wind, sail around the bottom of the island—look, Annabel and Daisy painting the back stoop, and they are waving—into open water. A sea anchor out, sail lowered, lines baited and cast over, they drift. The boys drink beer. Edith tastes it but prefers her orange soda. They catch several fish which flipflop in a pail. The sunshine is hot. Edith screams when a wave splashes cold water on her back. There are delicious peanut-butter-and-jelly sandwiches to eat.

"Is that a tattoo on your leg, Edith?"

"It's a rabbit. I drew it."

"No . . . Your father drew it, didn't he?"

"*I* did! *I* did!"

"Well it's dynamite. I wish I had one, don't you guys?"

"Sure."

"Okay. If you really want them . . ."

"Far out. Look she has a ballpoint pen in her plastic handbag. Far out, Edith. Me first. Here on my shoulder."

"It's kind of hard . . ."

"Sure, with the boat moving."

"It tickles too. Done? Gosh, it's nice. Thanks, Edith."

"I want mine on my wrist. No wait. I'd rather have it on my tit here, like he's sitting on my nipple. Okay?"

"Okay. But don't change your mind again."

"Okay. Hey, it does tickle!"

"This is a good one."

"Wow, it sure is. Thanks."

"Well, where do you want yours, anyway?"

"On my foot, for good luck."

"All right."

"Eeee . . . !"

"Does it tickle?"

"It sure does, Edith!"

"You can bear it though man. Here, bite this bullet."

"I'm almost done."

"Eeee, don't stop!"

"Oooo, look. She's done it again."

"Thanks, Edith. It's beautiful."

"They're all three beautiful."

"Yes they are."

"But Thuggy!" Edith exclaimed. "You already had something drawn. On your tummy, look. It's almost gone. Was it a valentine?"

"Yes, Edith."

"You probably took a bath and washed it off."

"Yes."

She shrugged in a way that meant, "I hope you'll be more careful with your rabbit but I know we all have to take baths, and a ballpoint pen drawing on the skin can't be expected to last forever."

Returning to the dock they stopped to haul a lobster pot. A line went from a buoy down into the dark water all the way to the bottom. The boys pulled it up and on the end was a wooden cage that bumped against the boat. Edith had never seen a lobster before. There were two large ones and a small one. The boys threw the small one overboard. Edith watched him turn somersaults as he fell through the water. When the big lobsters came out of the pot their claws waved and snapped and their tails jerked. Carter inserted wooden pegs into the claws and dropped the lobsters into a bucket. He put new bait in the trap and the boys dropped it back into the water. Edith wondered if the small lobster would re-enter it. At the dock the boys wrapped one of the fish in paper and gave it to Edith to take home. It was still alive.

CHAPTER EIGHTY-NINE

A well of nonpotable water supplies the sink at the farmhouse and the shower and basin in the tiny bathroom. Gas for the water heater is brought from the mainland in seventy-five-pound tanks which must be unloaded at the dock and transported in a wheelbarrow to the house. The chore is so disagreeable the young people limit themselves to one shower a week. Carter is enjoying his now, drenched for a long time under the hot water, filling the room with steam. The chrome rings jingle when he pushes aside the green curtain.

It is late afternoon. Green and violet horizontal light enters through leaves, flowers moving at the narrow window. The room is violet and green and smudgy gold from candles. Carter steps out of the tub. He adjusts the faucet so that a stream dribbles and splatters about the drain and he opens the cold water tap at the basin. He loves the steam and the falling tinkling splashing water.

The full-length mirror on the back of the door is misted over. Water collects into drops that run down clearing bright crinkly channels. Carter lays the flat of his hand on the glass and clears an opening through which he can see himself reflected true but for slight wavinesses.

A line of water goes from his elbow to the towel he stands on. Another line with intervals between droplets goes from the end of his penis to the towel. Others fall from fingertips, earlobes, and chin.

When he was younger at mirrors Carter assumed poses and expressions of fighters, dancers, statues. Now he watches himself like another person unable to make that beautiful one do anything. He hardly smiles, hardly knows whether the brightness of his face is tears or water, and when bluish semen splatters against the wet glass he can hardly believe it. He towels himself and the mirror off, shaves, extinguishes candles, and shuts faucets. He dons fresh faded jeans and a fresh tee shirt. "Think I'll take a nap."

Upstairs Daisy and Annabel stand in the doorway of Annabel's room. Carter talks with them, they drift into the room. Sitting on the bed they pass a pipe of marijuana. After a while Daisy goes down to the kitchen.

Annabel is wearing corduroy shorts and a man's white broadcloth shirt. Carter falls asleep leaning against her. She falls asleep too. Her skin is honey-colored and lightly freckled. They sleep and begin to wake. The afternoon light is fading. As Carter and Annabel wake they discover that they are embracing each other. Perhaps because of the marijuana. They say nothing but smile and gaze into one another's eyes. Soon their clothes are on the floor beside the bed and they are making love very slowly. Arms and legs twine, torsos arch apart, thud. It is sweet and frightful. They seem to be losing their minds. She climaxes and climaxes and he climaxes.

They rest. Annabel sighs. "Gosh, sex is nice."

"Mmm. Annabel?"

"Yes?"

"Do you really think I'm really attractive? Really?"

She laughs.

"Could you fall in love with me?" Carter wants to know.

"Sure. But I won't. But I certainly could."

"In that case I hope I don't fall in love with you," he says.

Downstairs Daisy is preparing dinner. A kettle of seawater for the lobsters heats. She fills another to cook spinach in. The nonpotable tap water is safe if boiled.

CHAPTER NINETY

Hester Geach weathered her sister's birthday fairly well. She reminded herself that in time she would have one of her own and since it would be on the mainland it would be grander and more galling than Edith's. And Hester had honestly enjoyed choosing, naming, and giving Swimming Sunshine. She had blushed with pride and love to see how much her sister liked the goldfish.

Yet the strain of the party took its toll and the next day Hester moped. Why hadn't Jane been more solicitous? she wondered. Didn't Jane know what being a friend meant? And Daisy and Annabel: she might never have gathered wild herbs or tinted frosting with them, for all the attention they had paid her last night. Surely real friends wouldn't be so fickle. "I don't even have a goldfish to be my friend," thought Hester, wrinkling her nose. To top it off, the boys from the farmhouse had taken Edith fishing. If Daisy were a real friend, would she have given her boat to such a use? The millhouse was a bore this afternoon. In his office Daddy sat with hands clasped behind his head, daydreaming. Mother in her sewing room sat turning a lock of hair around her forefinger. Hester would have set off firecrackers, Roman candles to wake them, had it been possible. They weren't even working! It was a beautiful day. Hester decided to stroll over to the dock. Maybe Edith and the boys would be back from fishing. They might be friendly. Edith might have fallen into the ocean.

There was a boat at the dock but it wasn't Daisy's, it wasn't even a sailboat. It was a motorboat with a windshield and a roof and a steering wheel like a car. The driver with his very brown skin looked like an Indian. A small woman stepped out onto the dock. She had an old pretty face and she seemed lost. She smiled and blinked. When she saw Hester she exclaimed, "Oh!" Hester laughed.

"Hello," said the woman. "Do you live here?"

"Of course. My name is Hester."

"I'm happy to know you, Hester. My name is Charlotte."

"I'm happy to know you."

"Hester, perhaps you can help me. Do you by chance know an older lady named Jane?"

"Yes."

"Oh good, Hester. I wonder, could you direct me to her house? I see several paths leading into the forest there and I fear I'd lose my way if I simply chose one at random."

Hester laughed. "You don't go that way. You should go around to the other side. That's where Jane lives."

The man in the boat said, "I think there *is* another landing on the seaward shore, Mrs. Conti. I believe there's a house too."

The pretty charming lady invited Hester to ride to Jane's house with her and the man. There was a white chihuahua called Pearl who sat in Charlotte's lap and licked Hester's hand when she petted it. The man sat in the front to steer the boat. Charlotte and Hester and Pearl were in the back.

"I'm Jane's friend. Are you?" Hester asked.

"Yes I am, though we've not been together in a long time. Since before you were born, I should imagine. Exactly how old are you, Hester?"

"Five."

"My! Why that's splendid. I'd never have guessed."

"How old are you?"

"Much older. Tell me, Hester, do you live on the island all the time?"

"Oh no. This is our vacation. My daddy is taking a vacation and working at the same time. He wants to make a million dollars before the summer gets over. He thinks and writes things when he's working. Sometimes he walks places."

"I see. Well. And do you intend to make a million dollars too, when you grow up?"

"Yes."

"How interesting! And do you propose to do it like your father, by thinking and writing and walking?"

"No, by . . . by *playing*."

"A lovely idea. My, Hester, I believe you're the most interesting young lady I've met in a very long time."

"Thank you."

"Don't mention it, my dear."

"Here we are," the man said over his shoulder. He stopped the engine and the boat glided into the darkening cove, high stone and pines on either side. The man tied up next to Jane's dory. Hester and Charlotte with Pearl in her arms mounted the steps and the man followed with the luggage. Near the top Charlotte said, "You'll be my friend too I hope, Hester. And here, I want you to have this amethyst bracelet," slipping it doubled onto Hester's wrist. "It suits your coloring better than mine."

"Thank you," Hester whispered. She saw Jane advancing across the grass.

CHAPTER NINETY-ONE

Voluble and silent by turns and often shy as schoolgirls with fluttering hearts, Jane and Charlotte each wished they could find some way to dissolve into helpless laughter. They fascinated, frightened, and annoyed each other not a little as the evening wore on. The boatman had returned to the mainland. Hester Geach had greeted Jane briefly, thanked Charlotte again for the bracelet, and departed. The old friends were alone together. Very delightful, very endearing they were. At dusk they were in the kitchen preparing their dinner. Each at odd moments—stirring porridge with a wooden spoon, left hand resting in her apron pocket—would steal a glance at the other. Earlier the chihuahua Pearl had rashly chased Jane's cats. Some had fled the barker but others had stood their ground and spat and swiped at Pearl's nose with extended claws. Afterward Pearl stayed near Charlotte. Under a chair she danced in circles and watched the big gliding calicos by the stove. Jane and Charlotte inquired about girlhood friends, discovering whether admiration, contempt, or pity was in order, or whether the case remained mysterious. Jane noticed that Charlotte noticed the radish rosettes, the molded butter, the sherry. Jane filled the beautiful (and dear, she knew) cut-glass bowl, the bowl Charlotte had presented her, with sweet peas and set it on the table for a centerpiece. How many people were on the island? How many years was it since Charlotte and Jane last met—on the mainland wasn't it, for lunch, in a city to the south? The sweet peas were adorable, weren't they, with their tendrils dripping over the brilliant glass. One felt like crying.

Blancmange, coffee, and a cordial. Lanterns. A stiff cold wind had risen but a fire warmed the boathouse parlor. Just now neither Jane nor Charlotte much wanted to ask, "Do you remember the time when . . ." These questions could come later if indeed they needed to come. Sipping coffee from enameled demitasses, on the sofa, in the wing chair they stole glances at each other. Could one's own face possibly have aged so? Jane's attire was serviceable and inexpensive, Charlotte's expensive and serviceable. Clink, clink, the china cups in china saucers. Pearl was sleeping. "She's a ridiculous creature, isn't she, Jane." Jane yawned. Her canes lay across her lap. A few drops of rain blew against the window. "All we'll get tonight though, I expect."

There was nothing to say yet, but the wariness was gradually abating. Charlotte had gone up to bed with the silly dog under her arm. Jane moved a chair nearer the hearth. Tomorrow the two of them could tour the . . . Jane dozed and snored.

CHAPTER NINETY-TWO

At the farmhouse all are sleeping. Jimbo wakes and dresses, feels his chin, and decides he will not bother shaving this morning. Halfway down the stairs he is struck by the partial recollection of a half-dream or imagining he had as he woke. All he remembers is having tipped his hat. To whom, where, in what spirit, he can't say, nor can he remember what sort of hat it was, but he is intrigued because he has never in his life worn a tippable hat. The dream hat was a green fedora and it was his father who received the debonaire greeting. Jimbo nearly surmises as much before he shrugs the matter off.

Downstairs in the study he gives a pat and a spin to a yellowed globe map of the world as he passes it. The globe is mounted in a wooden stand on the rim of which the boy sees a flat compartmented box, the sort fishermen keep flies and lures in. Jimbo knows the box is Daisy's and that she would be pleased to give him one of the amphetamine capsules he finds in it and that therefore he may freely take one now and inform her of it later. He decides to take one and not inform her later. In the kitchen he swallows it with orange juice.

Jimbo drinks coffee and casts an appraising eye about. Whose turn was it last night to wash the dishes that lie soiled on counters and tables and in the sink? whose turn to sweep? The enameled pot Daisy dyed tee shirts in yesterday hasn't been washed either. "First," thinks Jimbo, "let me turn my attention to something less mundane. Let's see."

He fills a pail with warm water and adds vinegar. He removes his spectacles, dips them in, and dries them with newspaper, and then drops in a sponge and begins to wash the many windows. The task proves larger than expected—more than twice as large for, as the boy soon realizes, windows should be cleaned outside as well as in. Nevertheless, buoyed up by frequent tallies of his progress and thoughts of how surprised everyone will be, he works efficiently. He sponges with vinegar water, dries with wadded newspaper. The glass shines and squeaks. When the work is done Jimbo stands in the center to admire. The sun has risen and the kitchen is full of transparent light.

Jimbo now undertakes more mundane chores. He washes pots and pans and heterogeneous dishes, vases and cutlery, including things he hasn't noticed before, such as a fork from the S.S. *Queen Mary* and an earthenware goblet made by Daisy. He drains the sink and scours it and for good measure polishes the chrome spigot and faucet handles. He replaces the napkins with fresh ones in the wooden rings and sweeps the floor. Raised dust makes him sneeze. There is a safety pin, a shard of glass with dried ketchup on it, sand.

Jimbo decides to prepare a special treat for everyone's breakfast. He consults a cookbook and quickly selects a recipe for banana nut bread. Although he has never baked anything in his life, he understands and follows the directions and soon the loaves are in the oven. The mixing bowl and other utensils are washed and dried and put away in cupboards and drawers along with the other dishes which have dried by now. Someone is coming downstairs.

Carter wanders into the kitchen and the sight of beaming Jimbo makes him smile. "Right."

"Hi, Carter. Good morning."

"So I . . . What's cooking?"

"A surprise for breakfast. It should be ready in about twelve minutes."

"Smells good. Where's Daisy?"

"Isn't she upstairs asleep?"

"Wait, you mean *you're* cooking?"

Buttered slices of the baked and cooled but still warm bread more than fulfill the promise of its odor. Carter wakes up a little. He stretches, pushes the fingers of both hands through his beautiful hair. "Breakfast is my favorite meal."

"Mine too," says Jimbo. "Although I must say, when I'm having dinner or lunch I don't really wish it were breakfast instead."

"Me neither."

"Although once or twice I've had ham and eggs for supper. And once I . . ." A faraway look comes into Jimbo's eyes.

"Once I had supper for breakfast." Jimbo pauses and then he continues. "It was far out, Carter, you can't imagine. I'd just arrived at this fairly big city. It was, no, I can't remember the name. Anyway it was a couple of years ago. Early fall. I was wiped out because I'd hitched all day. Good rides when I got them but there'd been long waits and I'd done a lot of walking. You know, you figure you may as well and it might be bad luck to stop completely."

"Plus maybe drivers'd be more inclined to favor a dude who's getting a sweat on. Bettering his own lot, showing initiative."

"Them that has, gets. It does seem to work that way."

"Walking can keep you from getting bored too. Were you stoned?"

"I don't think so. Anyway I'd been left in the middle of this city around ten, walked around some to check the layout, and by midnight I'd decided I should find a place to crash. It was chilly and windy and I didn't have the right clothing. I hadn't eaten much either. I went up to a cheapie-looking hotel on a side street and asked for their cheapest room, but it turned out I didn't have nearly enough bread."

"Why not just rip them off?"

"They wanted cash in advance because I didn't have luggage. Discrimination like that is grossly unfair, by the way. I always resent it and especially that night."

Carter nods. "Fuckheads."

"They were obdurate. They had several rooms empty and I

tried to point out that they weren't going to fill them all that night anyway. And I offered to make up the difference cleaning or whatever. No dice.

"It was the same story at the next places I tried so I started looking in alleys and back streets for cheaper places, a real flophouse if need be. But hotels were fewer and harder to find there and every one I found was closed tight.

"I thought maybe the problem was the particular section of the city I was in so I'd walk till things looked different and then check out prices. But it was the same, closed or too high. Somewhere in that city there had to be an open cheap-enough place but I kept on not finding it. I may well even have seen it, because by then I was so tired that sometimes I'd see a place that looked possible but it would be on the other side of the river or up a steep hill and I'd know I couldn't walk that far unless it was a sure thing."

"Listen, Jimbo. What you should have done is find a park or something. Didn't you have a sleeping bag?"

"I did. But I was kind of scared of doing that."

"Junkies?"

"Plus the fuzz kept like cruising me. There were rats around too, and I didn't know what they might do if they found me asleep outside. But my legs were falling off and I was starting to realize I wouldn't be able to stay awake much longer. And by that time there weren't any cafés or bars open where I could have warmed up and eaten. And it was cold.

"I had some coke I'd intended to sell the next day. I decided I had to do it right then to keep awake.

"Whatever was in it was dynamite. I don't think I've ever felt so good. I kept walking and everything looked completely beautiful. Streetlights, big monuments, bridges over the river, old streets with cobblestones. I couldn't believe how fucking lucky I was to be there, I couldn't believe it.

"Before dawn I wound up in the food market. They were bringing in fruit and vegetables, fish, millions of kinds of fish, meat and everything for the whole city for that day and setting it out in booths and stalls, and people were already there buying, retailers and restaurateurs and so forth. It was beautiful, especially after I'd been getting off on the emptiness of the streets. I sat on a bench and took out my guitar and started playing.

"So the patron of this little restaurant came out and asked if I was hungry—he'd give me a meal if I'd play inside. I played an hour and a half, straight classical, for the workers who were coming in for their supper. They liked it. They didn't stop talking to listen, but it was clear they appreciated it.

"Then the guy gave me the meal. It was my breakfast—it was dawn and I'd done so much coke I was going to be up all day. But it was supper for the workers."

"What was it? I mean . . ."

"Soup. Incredible soup and wine and bread. It was amazingly good. Like, the guy wanted me to stay on and play every day and I was tempted—not so much by the money, though it wasn't bad, but by that soup. But I'd decided some time before not to settle down anywhere in the immediate future. It was a matter of principle."

"Right," says Carter. "But listen, Jimbo. Why didn't you make that soup this morning in place of this bread?"

"I would have if I'd known how."

The banana nut bread has perfumed the whole farmhouse including Annabel's bedroom, where it awakens her and leads her down to the kitchen.

"Does this place look beautiful," she says. "Even the windows, no less."

"I did it," says Jimbo. "I baked this, too. Want some?"

CHAPTER NINETY-THREE

At two-thirty on the afternoon of Sunday, July third, a peculiar sight presented itself to Annabel. At an inlet on the lee shore she sat sunning herself on one of a jumble of boulders. An interstice in the rock gave onto the beach below where she had watched a crab dance and hold up his one large claw and one tiny one. On the sand lay empty papery carapaces of immature horseshoe crabs and a frill of seaweed. Also a large perfect scallop shell, very beautiful with bands of brown and pink ivory. Annabel decided to add it to her chest of seaside treasures.

The young people at the farmhouse had speculated about discovering buried treasure on the island, pirate booty or perhaps wampum. Everyone had agreed with Annabel that the island must be riddled with loot. This morning upon waking she had hatched the plan for her present project. She would bury the box of pretty things from the shore somewhere near the center of the island. Someday someone might chance upon it, years from now maybe. Or it might never be found.

Annabel was on the point of stepping down to pick the shell up when she saw hands appear from behind the rock on either side of it, a right hand from the right, a left from the left. The hands approached the shell and grasped it at the same instant. An exploratory wiggle was followed by rapid tugs back and forth. Then two surprised faces came out of the rocks and peered at each other. One was Sue Holcombe's and the other belonged to Charlotte Conti, whom Annabel had not seen before. The shell fell to the sand. Charlotte's jaw dropped, she looked over the tops of her sunglasses. "Miss Holcombe!"

Annabel coughed tactfully. When the women had noted her presence they returned their attention to each other. Charlotte removed her sunglasses. "Oh yes," said Sue Holcombe, "you're the aunt, isn't it?, of that rapscallion Conti. I remember you tried to influence my assessment of her. You wanted her to pass music appreciation. I recall your effrontery."

"She was very young."

"Human garbage."

"She's happily married now. Tell me, Miss Holcombe, what brings you here? Isn't this a funny coincidence!"

Charlotte had been picnicking nearby. She had left her hamper of champagne and peaches and come in search of souvenirs of her visit to the island. Sue Holcombe was beachcombing too, gathering a stock of gifts, mostly bivalve ashtrays, for next Christmas and other occasions that called for them. So it was that they had happened to lay hand simultaneously on the scallop shell that now lay forgotten at their feet until Annabel collected it for her treasure trove. Annabel and Sue Holcombe bade Charlotte good afternoon and went to Sue's cottage for their last violin lesson. It took place upstairs in the music room as always.

"I want you to play a single note, an open string. Which do you prefer?"

"The A, I think."

"Because it's your initial?"

". . . and because it's not wire or wire-wrapped. It's pure gut and it frays."

"Hmm. Well, play the open A then. As you play I want you to express the fact that you'll never play the violin again, at least not this particular instrument. Express the fact that you've studied for a month here with me. And as you play remember who your audience is. We play differently for different kinds. In this case your teacher is your audience. Remember that and express your consciousness of it in your playing."

"I can't express all that!"

"Perhaps not, perhaps not. Mmm, only . . . Well, then play the open A *without* expressing all that. Do you suppose you could?" Annabel shifted from foot to foot. Sue Holcombe cackled.

"In fact," said Sue, "I'd like you to play the open A without expressing or manifesting or giving away anything. Not even the fact that you know it's a violin you're playing. Or that there is such a thing as music. Or that you have heard my instructions. Do you understand? I want you to play and not play at the same time. And mind your stance, you're already growing simian. Now begin."

Annabel didn't budge. "Goddamit Sue, I can't."

"Don't then. It really doesn't matter."

Annabel sighed, brightening.

"It hardly matters at all," said Sue Holcombe.

Annabel laid the instrument in its green plush. The case was shaped like the violin but streamlined. If a sandstone violin were left on a beach it would come to have such a smoothed shape. Annabel closed the lid and snapped it shut for the last time. Probably Sue was right, she was incapable of becoming a good violinist. Still, no one could deny that she had learned something about the instrument in a short time. She might give it a second try in a few years, regardless of Sue's advice. Or she might follow Jimbo's suggestion and take up the guitar.

One thing Annabel didn't think about was the photograph

of Carter. Nevertheless it was inside the encased violin. Sue Holcombe knew it was there and after Annabel's departure she would extract it and hide it elsewhere, resolved to disclaim all knowledge of it should she be questioned.

They took tea. Annabel offered to continue working for Sue without recompense. She made the offer from sheer friendliness and because house cleaning gave her entry here, a privilege she valued above the time and energy she spent. But Sue Holcombe with a distant look said she expected soon not to need a charwoman, at least not for the cottage. Then they talked of this and that.

Out of the blue Annabel asked, "Are you a virgin, Sue?"

"I am wedded to my art. Nothing else signifies. But do you mean haven't I ever literally, physically, been . . . ? I don't recall. Oh dear. Now see what you've done with your impertinence?" Tears on the weathered cheeks.

"Forgive me." Annabel wondered how and why it was that she felt strong affection and further a kind of protectiveness toward the little woman. Sue's age showed in every way and yet Annabel thought, "If I ever have a child I'll probably take it the way I take her—absolutely seriously."

Whatever other reasons there may have been for Sue Holcombe's sudden tears, she knew they were partly prompted by the wish that there were some way to exempt Annabel from the harm she intended shortly to do the farmhouse dwellers.

CHAPTER NINETY-FOUR

Annabel is at her violin lesson, the other young people are away on various errands, all but Carter, who has melted and ignited hashish oil in the homemade bhang he is smoking under the wild cherry tree beside the farmhouse. Carter is stoned. When he swings in the tire swing the bottoms of his trousers flap around his ankles. The barn hasn't been painted in a long time. Chickens, dogs, and cats ignore each other. The sky is bluer than blue, saturated baby blue. Above one gable a metal rooster idly about-faces. Dear Carter. The grass is perfectly green.

The woods are fresh and cool and in each tree a bird sings. Stoned Carter may lose his way in familiar paths or laugh at anything. He is euphoric. He is the most beautiful boy in the world, anyone would love him. In each streambed musical water runs.

Carter would like to meet Faye and Gail in the woods today. As he walks he begins to think maybe they weren't altogether real. It seemed improbable, their living outdoors with no roof over their heads. Though supposedly the hash oil he had smoked came from them . . . The dogs explore underbrush among ferns and wildflowers, moderately alert. Things interest and please Carter. This grove of dead trees covered with ivy, the salt tang. Yonder someone seems to be whistling "Ora Lee."

There is flowerlike lichen on a mossy stump. Carter kneels to examine it, barefoot, his trousers flimsy, his tee shirt clean. The lichen makes a gray doily on dark green velvet.

Sunshine came along with thee
And swallows in the air . . .

The boy's eyes shine. He and the dogs advance. Yes?

Down here Gail and Faye kiss each other on temple and neck and let hands fall on a thigh, down breasts and belly, wearing apple green, fawn, persimmon, and emerald, breathing slowly as pretty girls ever breathed, eyes half closed. Carter shakes his head. He is about to back away. But when Goose and Rufus bound down the incline wagging their tails and prance around the girls, Carter follows. "Hi."

"Hi."

"Hi, Carter."

"Carter doesn't have shoes on either."

On the grass near the girls and the boy and the dogs is a bird's nest with transparent red and green dice in it.

"How is Carter this afternoon?"

"Happy. Stoned, I think. My palms are sweating a little."

Ideas tumble through Carter's mind.

"The last time he was talking about . . ."

". . . fame, the ravishing boy."

Carter smiles. Faye's garnet earring hangs against her neck. Gail looks at the grass. Carter's penis is growing.

"I believe so."

He nods.

"Many achieve fame only after their deaths."

"Indeed many achieve it because of their deaths. But Carter doesn't want that sort."

"I hope not!"

He shakes his head.

"Fame after death . . ."

". . . fluctuates. It may increase, it may not. It may decrease."

"Fuck it," says Carter. "I don't give a shit about after I'm dead."

"No . . ."

"No, Carter wants it while he's alive as now."

"One could estimate his chances if one knew how much was available."

"And how many of his contemporaries had hearts set on it."

"Quite. The number of his rivals would affect his chances."

"Assuming the available quantity is finite. As it seems."

"Scarce even. It wouldn't be feasible for everyone to be famous."

"Never. Suppose you wanted to list the twenty best-dressed. Why, you'd have to consider everyone in the world! No . . ."

"No."

Carter says "Best-dressed . . ." He imagines himself and the two girls as three of the twenty.

"But the available quantity may change, mayn't it? Be indeterminate, so that . . ."

"I suppose so," she sighs, "so that we can't estimate Carter's chances in good conscience."

"Possibly not."

Carter moves closer. A part of his body touches each girl. He can see much of their bodies and shapes of clothed parts show through the clothing. He hears what they say very well. The good quiet dogs hear too. Carter shrugs.

"Yes, but suppose he did become famous. Very famous. Completely famous. All . . ."

". . . all fame was his. Imagine, Carter. Imagine your picture on the cover of every magazine published in the world."

"On every page of every magazine. Similarly for newspapers major and minor."

"And where now the categories are World and Local News, Business or Finance, Sports, Fashion . . ."

". . . Amusements, Weather, and so forth, instead there would be sections like Carter's Recent Moods, Accidents Happening to Carter, What Carter Says."

"Special installments like 'Carter's Shoulders: Their Solemn Grace.' "

" 'Carter's Famous Hair: White Gold or Wheat?' Every television program would be about you, every movie. No one would talk about anything but you."

"Whatever they were doing—building houses, enjoying sexual relations, attending one of your movies—no one would think about anything but you."

"All pets would be named Carter." She leans down to pat Rufus's head. "All automobiles and eventually all people, all places."

"This island would be called Carter."

"All books would be about you and university students would learn only about you. On the radio all songs would be sung by you."

"I can't sing," says Carter.

"Then what you do instead would supersede singing and come to be called singing."

"The president of every country, every large corporation, the mayor of every great city of the world would be you."

"No one would be able to imagine anyone but you. Your face would be on all money, everyone would wear his or her hair more or less the way you wear yours."

Carter tucks his hair behind his ears. "Far out," he says. The pretty girls are going. Carter says, "I only want a reasonable amount of fame." Faye and Gail depart in gales of laughter.

CHAPTER NINETY-FIVE

Carter thinks about what Faye and Gail have said as he sleeps through the night and in the morning as he relieves himself and shaves with cold water. The house seems empty but returning to his room he hears chuckling from Thuggy's room and goes to the doorway. Plump nude Thuggy sits in the center of the room writing.

"Where is everybody?"

"Swimming," says Thuggy. He flips his pencil like a knife so that it lands in place with other pencils in a topless beer can.

"Far out." The two boys who recently have made love with the same girl regard each other. "I think I'll go too. What's that you're writing?"

"The end of my dirty story."

Carter steps into the room. "Can I see?"

Thuggy hesitates. "Later, man. It needs to cool off."

"Right. You coming swimming?"

"Maybe later."

Meanwhile in the millhouse Jack Geach is coming to his senses out of a profound sleep. Priscilla sleeps beside him. Jack recalls making love with her the night before when the moon streamed in the window and she was silent and agile. There had been oral-genital contact. Remembering, Jack is inclined to recommence. But he is deterred by the peacefulness of his wife's sleep and also by what now occurs to him. This morning, already maybe, his long shrewd design must be climaxing. "A measly million is hardly worth thinking about by today's standards," thinks Jack. "It just has to have accrued to me. If not I guess it'll be my own fault for setting my sights so low. 'A million?' " he imagines his future biographer writing, " 'A mere million? Fiddlesticks.' " Jack is greenish and weak in the knees when he reaches his office.

His desk calendar reminds him of an appointment with Miss Holcombe later in the day. He considers ignoring it and then, setting his jaw, reconsiders. " 'Even in the thick of the turbulent sea of high finance and indeed in the very eye of the hurricane, young Geach had a genuine plethora of managerial and economic insight to spare. To cite one example. On the day of his famous first awesome leap into the perilous big-monetary arena he nevertheless lowered himself in passing to assist an admittedly pathetic older female musician whose total assets simply sank far beneath his notice. We can only gasp with respect to this feat, and of course we can also be ashamed because our little lives loom so small in comparison with that of Geach himself. He stands as a perfectly unattainable example to us all in this dizzy world of ups and downs. Another of the many noble feathers in his cap, and a truly thrilling, if sad, lesson to us all.' " Jack inhales.

As his ship-to-shore radio set warms he realizes he has overslept, for out the window on the grass he can see his daughters playing. One of his secretaries responds immediately. "Mr. Geach? Is that you? I didn't catch that, sir."

Jack's hand trembles so that he has dropped the microphone. He mutters and whispers, "It's got to work, it's got to work, let it work." Into the microphone his voice is brisk and assured. "This is he. Over."

"Yes indeed, chief. On this front the returns are first-rate. We do show a holding action at zone eleven of track delta. But otherwise it's a sweep. Let me be the first to congratulate you, sir."

"Thank you, Dot. Over and . . . out."

Jack grins feebly. He is a millionaire.

Someone is knocking at the front door. Newsmen already? Bested rivals come to bite dust in grudging tribute? Jack hurries down. It is Thuggy.

"Oh. Hello," says Jack. "Hello, hello. Come in, come in, let me fix you a drink, how about a Scotch, my best, the best there is, I won't tell you how much it costs, you probably wouldn't believe me. Gee what a beautiful day, it's more than good to be alive on a day like today. I just became a millionaire at my age. Isn't it wonderful? I just found out. I'm deeply gratified, it's a very great honor—astounding in all modesty, and gratifying to the *n*th degree."

"Far out," says Thuggy.

"Thank you, thank you." Jack swirls his amber Scotch.

Thuggy swirls his Scotch. "Whatcha gonna do with it?"

Jack smiles munificently.

"Listen," says Thuggy, "you should throw a monstrous blast with it. You must have some salted away for rainy days, so you can blow this. Think of the broads, man. Think of the fuckin' hooch!"

Jack strolls about the room. "I could if I wanted to. I can do anything I want with it."

"I was wondering," muses Thuggy. "No, well . . ."

"Yes? What were you wondering, my boy?"

"A million wouldn't swing a party for everybody in the world, I guess. Wouldn't even buy the music, huh."

"I may though," says Jack, "have a little celebration for my underlings on the mainland. That's a good idea."

"A knockout. Which reminds me. I came to tell you about an island celebration. Today's the Fourth of July so tonight there's this bonfire on the point below the farmhouse. You're supposed to bring shit to eat and drink plus whatever you have you want to burn. It's an island tradition."

"Sounds very gleeful," says Jack.

"Right on. Well, so . . ." As Thuggy stands, swaying slightly because of the alcohol, the conclusion of his story falls from his hip pocket.

"What is it, a love letter to Annabel? Or maybe to her friend."

"I don't think so. It's more like . . ." Thuggy explains.

Jack is giddy. "Read it to me. Have another drink if you want one to wet your whistle with."

Thuggy's smooth cheeks dimple like a child's. He reads.

> More than one crowned head of Europe turned when the shapely Ms. Drake sidled into the opulent gambling hall with her athletic husband. Her gown had been custom-designed to look like a nightie. Her naked jugs jiggling under the silk brought every rod droolingly erect, including the sage tool of an aged philosopher whose protégé had brought him to sneer at the idle pastimes of the glamorous. Nor was Drake's own unit a backslider, as many stacked heiresses and cover girls were quick to observe from the corners of their smoky eyes.
>
> Luck smiled across the green baize at the insinuatingly

vigorous American couple. Luck leered so fondly that by the end of the evening when the suave proprietor signed a check for them with a dash of Gallic *sang-froid* he found himself inscribing more zeroes than ever before. In full view of the envious crush the Drakes sauntered away into the Mediterranean night, French kissing and thumbing their noses, hopping into their automobile and speeding back to their villa. Ms. Drake climbed the stairs feistily wet from twat to instep, and her broad-shouldered slim-buttocked spouse remained below.

Ms. Drake danced out of her gown and skipped onto the terrace where she plumped down on a *chaise longue* and began to knead her astounding *mons* without a word. In the shadows panted Lelouch, unbuttoning his fly and thus freeing his thin though alert organ. "Vizout dout she ees hot, to trot!" he intoned. In the twinkling of an eye they were busily humping.

Thuggy chuckles. Jack smiles and nods, sips Scotch.

Other events transpired on the lower terrace. Daughter Betsy was sleeping under the Riviera sky clad puckishly in no more than her first pair of high-heeled shoes. When Harry, Mr. Drake, leaned down to kiss her good night he was overcome with sexiness. Before either father or daughter knew what was occurring they found themselves balling. When Betsy squealed with delight Mr. Drake merely let forth a groan that racked his hairy body and ground himself into her cooing flesh, nibbling her titties. Little did they suspect that the sly Mme. Encore had crouched nearby in the elegant manorial shrubbery to diddle with the fiery canine peter of the mastiff Rufus. It was an eventful *soirée* for all.

Be that as it may, the following morning their elation was tempered with heartache when it developed that young Ernie was dead. The naughty child had thumbed a ride to Marseille where, amid the notorious seaminess of the waterfront, after having been the recipient of countless blow jobs, he had agreed to transport a king's ransom in proscribed cannabis from one dive to another, and had been murdered for his pains. The funeral was a melancholy affair. "We'll miss your little pecker," blubbered his sibling. Mme. Encore and Lelouch were also present.

A few weeks later and it was time for the more than decimated family to wend their way back to America. As they descended the palatial stair the Frenchwoman made as if to wave *au revoir*. Instead, however, she executed a pass which hypnotized the vacationers as briskly as on the day of their arrival. With that she implanted in their thoughts a clever posthypnotic suggestion to insure their return. Whereupon she applied musky kisses to the astonished mouths of Mr. and Ms. Drake and to the tender puss-puss of their daughter.

Little dreaming what she had done, they set off, leaving their stateside addresses and extending to her and her valet a warm invitation to visit them there.

Jack hardly knows what sort of comment might be in order. He nods thoughtfully.

"Give you a boner?" Thuggy asks.

" 'Boner'?"

"A hard-on."

"Well . . ."

"It's okay man. I have eyes."

"Seriously though, it's not bad. For that kind of thing."

"I keep wondering if I left something out," says Thuggy. "Anyway thanks for the liquor. See you down on the point after sundown."

Halfway across the lawn the boy kneels to talk with Jack's daughters in the strong sunlight. The scene is memorable. Jack sighs. He realizes he has somehow decided not to buy this island after all, not to develop it into a resort for prominent businessmen.

CHAPTER NINETY-SIX

At breakfast, through the morning, and at lunch merry references to Big Boy fell thick and fast about Jimbo. Able to forgo neither the pleasure of feigning discomfiture in order to make his imminent triumph more surprising, nor yet the pleasure of baffling his friends with a confident serenity, Jimbo alternated between the two roles and, because he sometimes lost track of which he was playing to whom, or needed to play both simultaneously, he involved himself in many amusing contradictions. By two o'clock the others were napping or reading and Jimbo was ready to make his move. His costume for the occasion was cowboy boots, overalls over a plaid flannel shirt, and a white crash helmet. A bugle hung on gold braid from his shoulder. He winked and slipped out of his room.

A hen scratching in loose straw turned her head to look up when he entered the barn. Other roosting ones stared and blinked. Big Boy was huge, black as coal, his red eyes murderous. He lowered his head and shook it.

"Hi," said Jimbo. "Let me ride you, okay? Look, I brought you a treat. It's from Sue Holcombe actually. It was her idea and you should hold her responsible for any loss of face you suffer. Although I think you'll come through this with all brutishness intact. Here." Jimbo let two sugar cubes fall into his palm from the matchbox he had found in the hollow tree near the well. "You should be able to stomach it." Jimbo extended his hand into the stall. "I must say I feel silly not having thought of it myself, after that rap I laid on you. It was right there in front of my eyes and I certainly should have seen it."

Big Boy stepped forward and licked the cubes off Jimbo's hand. "Snake eyes," said Jimbo. The bull backed away. Jimbo sat on the wall. He unfastened the helmet to scratch his head and then replaced it. Flies buzzed in lazy spirals. "Feel anything?"

A while later the other young people in the farmhouse were roused and summoned by a bright bugling. Daisy, Annabel, Carter, and Thuggy came out onto the porch and stood in a kind of wonderment in the fresh air. There in the sunny barnyard Big Boy shuffled slowly around and around in a circle. Atop him sat Jimbo.

CHAPTER NINETY-SEVEN

No breeze stirred the heavy leaves in the beach-plum thicket. The leathery fruit hung still. There were midges and sand fleas. Sand seeped into one's shoes, a mild irritant. Jack and Priscilla threaded their way. Priscilla thought it the oddest of escapades on the oddest of days. Jack was more subdued than any other millionaire she remembered encountering. "People make jelly from these beach plums. They're supposed to be a good source of vitamin C," she said. Jack nodded and petted the foliage. He was smoking a corncob pipe. From behind, his naked sunburned calves had the shape of valentines. He was very solid. It seemed to him that he and Priscilla were like explorers carving out a niche for themselves in the history of the world. "Kew, kew," cried the gulls.

Sue Holcombe awaited them. From a strap buckled around her head a transparent green bill projected to filter and cool the glare that fell over her small face. She wore seersucker. "Kew."

The three followed the beach to the point where already there stood a high jumble of wadded paper, broken chairs, and driftwood for the bonfire. Exclamations and laughter came from the direction of the barn. "They're drinking champagne in the barnyard. The one named Jimbo is enjoying a moment of glory. Now Jack, Priscilla, follow me. I believe, yes," consulting the architect's drawings, "yes, there's a spiral stair here at the back. We'll use that. Don't dawdle."

Priscilla bridled. "Trespassing?" The women regarded each other with distaste. Jack had hoped they would become friends.

"Never mind," said Sue. "I only need you for witnesses. Anyhow you'll soon see we're not trespassers by any stretch of the imagination." Inside, she lit a cigarette.

They came out on the second floor. Sue Holcombe in advance marched down the spacious corridor with a flashlight whose beam she played over pieces of furniture and architectural details, muttering to herself. The Geaches followed.

Beyond the door of the linen closet Sue Holcombe approached the wall. "Hold the light. Direct it here." Jack obeyed. Sue Holcombe inspected the molding. She smiled. She was possessed with a familiar exaltation, that of the moment before music begins, before the bow falls to the strings. The wood gleamed through the dust. Sue Holcombe could hear Jack's and Priscilla's breathing. She could hear the size and age of the house. She moved the molding and a portion of the wall opened away.

"A secret passage?"

"A secret room," said Sue Holcombe.

The air inside was thin, dry, and old, and voices echoed. The floor was bare. The moving light revealed that the room was small but high ceilinged. There were no windows. The walls were covered with a pale gray, blue, and dim green scenic wallpaper showing wooded hills and streams where women and men in costumes of the European eighteenth century strolled arm in arm or reclined under a tree with fans and lutes. The room was empty except for a three-legged applewood table on which rested a wide low chest bound in tooled leather with brass fittings.

Sue Holcombe's teeth were chattering. She wrung her hands. "Vindicated! How they'll squirm, whine, and sob their fruitless tears. Yes indeed. Winter is coming for five grasshoppers! Open the box please, Jack. Ha, ha, ha. The wretches."

The box proved a sea captain's desk with compartments for wax, quills, a bottle of sand, and an inkwell. The hinged writing surface lifted. Underneath Jack found a roll of parchment. Priscilla came forward to hold the flashlight as Jack slipped off the ribbon and unrolled the parchment. Strange script, strange orthography, and unfamiliar words made Jack frown. "It's some sort of document. It appears . . . it appears to be a will."

"You're damned tooting it's a will," said Sue. "Read it aloud, young man."

"I will," said Jack. He and Priscilla gave each other a downhearted glance. Jack took a long breath and began to read. Through the preamble Sue Holcombe gloated but in the body of the will her expression darkened. "You've made a mistake. Re-read that sentence." Sue's face fell. "Once more please. I can't . . . I don't understand." The sentence persisted unchanged through a third reading.

"That doesn't change anything!" Sue Holcombe said in a loud voice. "That verifies Daisy's claim! I've never been so insulted!" She ran away from the room down the hallway, down the spiral stair, out the back door, up the beach, and through the woods to her cottage, where she threw herself on the braided rug in her parlor. She lay there for a long time. Sunlight inched over the floor, across her and the furniture, and up the wall. Sue Holcombe traversed stage after stage of humiliation, resentment, anger, vengefulness, disgust, self-pity, and furious joy. At last she picked herself up and lit a cigarette. "Those pikers," she muttered. Dusk was falling. Sue Holcombe stood at a window puffing her cigarette.

Across her lawn rabbits were beginning to hop out of their burrows. She watched them. Slowly and insensibly at first and then accelerating, a remarkable idea dawned on her. Her ignominious defeat could be used gloriously. Played as an expression of what she had felt and suffered, the first movement of the concerto she was to perform on the mainland in the fall would become something excellent and unheard of.

CHAPTER NINETY-EIGHT

Late afternoon. In her room Daisy sits with legs slung over the arm of an easy chair to let freshly painted pink toenails dry. Tonight the bonfire, and already it has been an eventful day. To everyone's surprise Jimbo has actually ridden Big Boy. Then the Geaches have appeared with their story of the secret room. Everyone has admired it. Furthermore Priscilla Geach has said that the scenic wallpaper is incredibly valuable. It had been made in France and was famous. Priscilla had seen a photograph of what was presumed the only surviving sample, a small scrap. And Priscilla estimated that this wall paper alone (in excellent condition, having escaped effects of dampness and habitation, and having been completely protected from light) was worth more money than the farmhouse itself, perhaps more than the whole island. The whole island. Daisy smiles. For although she can imagine selling the farmhouse, and the owner of the millhouse (a chronic invalid on the mainland) might also sell, neither old Jane nor Sue Holcombe would sell her property for any sum that would ever be offered. "And if they wouldn't, why should I? So the island must be more priceless than the wallpaper. It I probably should sell. In a museum it could be preserved better. Except it's awfully pretty in that little room."

Daisy's toes are dry. She steps out into the hallway intending to visit Jimbo in his room. She sees him come out his doorway at the far end of the corridor. He sees her too. He, as it happens, has decided to visit her. There's nothing for it, each thinks, but to smile and nod and walk forward, with an air interpretable as unconcerned, in case the other should be headed downstairs, and slowly, to let the other reach the stairwell first. They reach the stairwell together.

"Hi."

"Hi."

"You . . ."

"I . . ."

They look every which way. They smile when their eyes meet. Annabel, Carter, and Thuggy are distantly audible downstairs. The grandfather clock chimes. The pause cannot last forever.

"I was coming to your room," Jimbo confesses in a rush.

"I was going to drop in on you!"

They beam.

Jimbo fishes a penny out of his pocket. "Heads yours, tails mine." The coin spins off the boy's thumbnail, up and down, is caught, lies on the back of his hand. "Look. We visit you another time."

Dusk is falling. Jimbo lights a candle. "Want some marzipan?"

"Yes, thank you. Mmm, yum. May I have another?"

"Take all you want—I'm not terribly fond of it. See what I was reading? On the night table?"

"Oh—poems. Chinese ones."

"Look at this one." He sits beside her on the bed.

"Mmm, mmm, mmm. Yes, it's nice."

"It's excellent, isn't it?"

"Yes it is."

Elbows, knees touch. Jimbo bends to peruse a footnote. The book lies open on Daisy's lap. She smooths the lank hair over the back of his neck. He squeezes his eyes shut and gives her a quick kiss on her upper arm. She closes her eyes. The candle flame flickers. Hearts are pounding.

"Daisy? Jimbo?" Annabel's voice up the stairwell. In a moment they hear her move back toward the kitchen. "Outside I guess, or asleep. They'll know we're at the point. Off we go, off we go then, mateys."

Eyes venture to open. As Jimbo kisses Daisy's shoulder she kisses his head. Each unbuttoning the other's clothing is surprised to feel a hand at her or his own buttons. "This is silly," says Daisy. Jimbo agrees. The back door slams. Naked on the bed, Daisy and Jimbo cannot take their eyes off each other. His hand is on her buttocks, her lips graze his nipples. Each wants things to happen as slowly as possible. In fact things happen quickly. Fucking, hair meshing agreeably. Jimbo's penis feels huge in Daisy's sweet vagina. They roll over, over again, faces too close to be seen clearly. How dizzy they are, how worthwhile everything seems! Flushed and intent, Daisy is more lovable than she has ever been, and so is Jimbo.

They lie side by side under a sheet. Both have grown shy.

"Daisy?"

"Yes?"

"Daisy—thank you very much."

"Thank *you*, Jimbo. Very much."

Should one laugh? Why not. With a shift in the wind the curtains flutter.

"Jimbo?"

"Yes?"

"They must be starting the bonfire . . ."

"Gosh, I completely forgot."

"May I use your candle? I think I'll go back to my room for a second."

"Sure. Daisy?"

"Yes?"

"Before I came here to the island, none of you really rode Big Boy, did you?"

"Gracious! What an idea!"

Jimbo dons his wire-rimmed spectacles to glimpse Daisy's naked body from behind as she leaves, her clothes in one hand and in the other a candle to light her way.

CHAPTER NINETY-NINE

The setting sun left billowing fiery clouds on the western horizon. From the east darkness approached over the water. Thuggy, Annabel and Carter were completing the structure for the bonfire when the Geach family appeared. Edith wore her birthday shoes, having prevailed over her mother by hysterical insistence and tantrums. She brought the hand-me-downs they had replaced to burn. Hester's contribution, odd jigsaw puzzle pieces, was more reasonable. The children marveled at the height of the pyre. "It won't rain, will it?" Priscilla found an opening for her paper bag filled with the day's combustible kitchen refuse—coffee grounds, a milk carton, rinds, paper plates, and napkins. Jack puffed his corncob pipe as he strode about to inspect the laying of the fire from every angle: he was, after all, the only man present. Annabel explained that the site was low enough on the beach for the coming tide to drown any embers that might remain. Jack nodded and pushed into the base of the pyre a box of papers that had littered his desk until today. He had concluded that it would be better if there were no records of the maneuvers by which he had made his dream a reality.

Through an opening in the sword grass Daisy and Jimbo came down onto the beach. Jimbo wore the sweater with a design of snowflakes and reindeer knitted for him by Daisy. Almost at the same time Faye and Gail stepped out onto the sand so shyly that Daisy ran to greet them. They strewed bouquets of dried wildflowers and grasses over the pyre and Daisy scattered colorful remnants of cloth and yarn.

"What did you bring to burn, kid?" Annabel asked Jimbo.

"Nothing. You?"

"Not a thing."

"There was nothing I wanted to dispose of. I considered bringing something anyway but that seemed . . ."

"Uncalled for?"

Picnic baskets and hampers were opened, cookie tins, bottles of wine. Long dark waves washed steadily in. Gulls cried over the water. Rufus and Goose lay side by side and listened.

"Carter! Come here!" Gail and Faye called from the pyre. The breeze was cool but Carter wore only his sky-blue bathing suit.

"Look what we found rolled in these magazines!"

"Someone was going to burn these, Carter."

"I was," he said, smiling at the photographs of himself and at the girls. "They're rejects from a batch Thuggy took and Jimbo developed. You can keep one if you wish."

"I think we should get this started, don't you men?" Jack Geach said to the boys. "Priscilla and I don't like for the girls to stay up very late. And the older ladies wouldn't want us to hold things up on their account, since they may not make it down here anyway. Stand back." Jack struck a match and held it under a crumpled newspaper. Liberally sprinkled with kerosene, the entire structure ignited with a roar and such a blast of heat that everyone sprang back, many with eyebrows singed.

Sue Holcombe saw the flare and the leaping people from a distance as she came round the beach out of the darkness. They struggled to their feet only to retreat again from the astonishing heat. The distance and their antics made them look ridiculous. Sue Holcombe watched as they filed around the perimeter of light and gathered laughing and gesticulating. Then she proceeded over the sand to them.

No one had expected her. There was an awkward hush. Then Carter smiled his most welcoming smile and said, "Hi. Did you see it start? Listen, let me get you a beer or some wine or a whisky sour."

"A sour please."

As Carter skipped away to the cooler Sue Holcombe threw a small parcel smoothly into the crest of the fire. Immediately there was a volley of horribly loud explosions. Edith and Hester shrieked and ran sobbing to Priscilla. The dogs yammered. Jack

Geach glared at everyone. "What in the world was that?" he demanded.

After a moment Sue Holcombe said, "Shotgun cartridges. Without the shot. Blanks."

"Miss Holcombe!" said Jack, glancing at Priscilla. "Shotgun shells, Miss Holcombe? That was a very reckless and thoughtless thing for you to do. It was dangerous!"

Sue Holcombe smiled. "Life is dangerous."

"Well, please don't do it again."

Carter returned with Sue's drink. "Hey Thug," he said, "how about reading us the end of that story of yours."

"Yes Thuggy, read it."

"Yes, yes."

"Do."

Thuggy sighed. "I can't. It's in the fire."

"No!"

"Why?"

Thuggy shrugged. "It was too sad."

The last to arrive at the bonfire were old Jane and her friend Charlotte. Charlotte had gathered some driftwood for the fire. Jane had brought the rusty leather valise that had been new when she and John set out on their honeymoon, the one she had thrown into the ocean only to have it rescued by Jimbo and Thuggy. Now she threw it into the bonfire. Salt crackled and popped as it burned. Jane and Charlotte sat on a rock together telling each other stories, interrupting each other, laughing. Hester Geach sat in Jane's lap. She wore the amethyst bracelet Charlotte had given her. The chihuahua Pearl was sniffed and welcomed by big Rufus and shy black Goose.

Thuggy buried his feet in the sand. When Sue Holcombe ignited her cigarette lighter there was a coronet of sparkles over the flame.

All ate and drank to heart's content. There were firecrackers and also Roman candles to launch puffs of yellow and green and blue flame over the water. There were songs and laughter. The bonfire burned lower, collapsed, subsided. Finally the advancing tide extinguished the embers and floated charred wood and light ash away.

CHAPTER ONE HUNDRED

At the farmhouse, at the cottage deep in the woods, at the millhouse and over at the boathouse, and under a tree in a quiet glade, everyone is sleeping. Around the shoreline of the island from top to bottom on both sides cold dark water moves, smoothly whitening or lapping and lapping. Sand crabs dance on wet sand. The air is mild. At the upper end of the island gulls roost in low shrubbery or on ground matted with forebears' bones and feathers. Lower, winking fireflies drift among sumac and poison ivy. Rabbits hop, nibble a stem here, a leaf there, and hop. Nocturnal birds awake, sing and feed and later sleep. Shaggy Babe is aprowl. In the clearing at the well he masticates a young rabbit whiskers and all. The lower lids of Babe's shining eyes droop away. He snatches a bird out of the air and swallows it. Sometimes near one of the houses he grinds broken teeth in fear and hatred, but most of the night he is in the woods creeping through underbrush or dropping from branch to branch, roaming and foraging until it is time for him to return to his lair. Flowers open and close in the darkness. Sweet odors of earth join those of the wide ocean. And everywhere here the weather is excellent. Red sky at night, sailor's delight, shading to violet toward morning.